To Kyleigh Brynn Knowles,
You are a Blessing to
me always + Forever ♥!
Keep Being You Beautiful
I love You Daughter
Love, Mommy

2022

THE LIGHTCASTERS

UMBRA ✳ TALES

THE LIGHTCASTERS

✳ 1 ✳

JANELLE McCURDY

ALADDIN

NEW YORK   LONDON   TORONTO   SYDNEY   NEW DELHI

ALADDIN

An imprint of Simon & Schuster Children's Publishing Division

1230 Avenue of the Americas, New York, New York 10020

First Aladdin hardcover edition September 2022

Text copyright © 2022 by Janelle McCurdy

Originally published in Great Britain in 2022 by Faber & Faber as *Mia and the Lightcasters*

Jacket illustration copyright © 2022 by Jeffrey Oyem

Map illustration on pages vi–vii copyright © 2022 by Virginia Allyn

Illustrations of textured paper and patterns throughout by iStock

All rights reserved, including the right of reproduction in whole or in part in any form.

ALADDIN and related logo are registered trademarks of Simon & Schuster, Inc.

For information about special discounts for bulk purchases, please contact Simon & Schuster Special Sales at 1-866-506-1949 or business@simonandschuster.com.

The Simon & Schuster Speakers Bureau can bring authors to your live event. For more information or to book an event contact the Simon & Schuster Speakers Bureau at 1-866-248-3049 or visit our website at www.simonspeakers.com.

Book designed by Heather Palisi

The text of this book was set in Adobe Garamond Pro.

Manufactured in the United States of America 0822 FFG

2 4 6 8 10 9 7 5 3 1

CIP data for this book is available from the Library of Congress.

ISBN 9781665901277 (hc)

ISBN 9781665901291 (ebook)

For my amazing mama

THE LIGHTCASTERS

Umbra Tales:
Legends of the Lightcasters
Author: Unknown

Introduction

The stars never lie. They tell stories every day, and once a month they tell the same story: the Legend of the Lightcasters.

The constellation is a prophecy, one that says that the kingdom may one day fall to a man filled with shadows and rage.

For the kingdom to have any chance of survival, the shadow beasts—creatures born in the heart of dark and light—are key. And beside them will be two children with the power to change the world.

A girl wielding a staff takes the lead at the forefront of battle, the boy beside her aiding her fight. The light that shines around them symbolizes the hope they will bring back to our people.

There is no telling when this prophecy will come to fruition, but may my family far in the future take heed and keep this book safe until then. It will contain everything I know of the world that we, the founders, have created.

May the light save us all.

PROLOGUE

THREE YEARS AGO . . .

Today, no matter what, we are going to see a wild umbra.
Under the light of the forever moon, we wove in and out of our starlit city. My shoes clicked against the pavement of the empty streets, and I listened for any sign that we were not alone.

With glowing blue roofs, the houses and shops towered over us like silent watchers, keeping our secret. In the distance the faint buzz of the market-day festival sounded ahead, keeping all the adults in town busy with celebration pastries, donuts, and trinkets to buy from the few cities left in our kingdom.

"Are you sure this is a good idea, Mia? What if we get caught?" Miles whispered, trying to keep up.

Pfft, of course it's a good idea. This was the best plan I'd ever had.

We ducked, the sweet waft of bread filling my nose as we snuck past Mr. Davies's bread stall when he turned his back to check his leftover stock.

The cold breeze tugged at my dark, curly locks as we blended into the shadows where the light of the floating glow bugs and bright streetlights didn't touch. I looked back at Miles with a grin. My heart was beating a thousand times a minute. There was no way I was giving up. *We got this!*

"I know what I'm doing. Trust me."

The stars that dotted the sky sparkled, cheering us on as we dipped past Ms. Dawn's little flower shop, decorated with the prettiest crystal lights and cherry vines. I exhaled with relief, having passed unnoticed, but nerves had my body tingling all over.

The Aquila constellation shone down as we neared the edge of our city, and my excitement bubbled up more and more.

As long as we were back in time for dinner, Nan and Grandad would never know. Mum was in the lab all day, and Dad was out on town patrol. It was perfect.

I smiled, taking off down an alley with Miles close behind. Attached to my back, my baby brother gurgled, babbling to himself, all tucked into the blue star swaddle blanket.

The last thing I'd expected was to be lugging Lucas around on my back, but like clockwork, Nan and Grandad had fallen asleep listening to the news channel on our hologram TV, and Miles and I couldn't just leave my little brother behind. He had to come too.

"Oh, just so you know, I'm going to be the best tamer in the world. I'm gonna have five—no, six—different umbra!" I said.

My pale, dark-haired friend quirked an eyebrow, slowing down to a stop. "Yeah, right. *I'm* gonna be the best. You're too short to be the number one tamer. You have to be *this* tall."

He stretched his arm way above me and grinned. I stuck my tongue out, but zipped it back in before he could pinch it. The meanie.

"You're such a liar. You don't even know anything about the umbra." Ever since I could read, I'd devoured every book, hologram report, and research paper I could find about umbra in the library and my mum's lab. These creatures had helped us when the Darkness came and took over our city. They fought beside us against the reapers, and we survived. They're the best.

"I know they're made of shadowy stuff." Miles shrugged. "And they look like a mix of different animals with awesome gold eyes. What else is there to know?"

I flicked his cheek and he hissed, rubbing it.

"They're so much more than that, you clown," I said, looking left and right down the alley. "Some have teeth so sharp they can bite through anything, even bones, and some have talons that can tear you apart in one second flat."

His eyes widened. I raised my hands like claws, ready to say more, but he stuck his fingers in his ears, spun around, and shouted, "Lalala, I can't hear you, you're just trying to scare me."

I held back my laughter. Mum's and Dad's umbra would never hurt us, and I was sure that wild ones wouldn't either. They were the smartest, kindest, and strongest creatures in the kingdom. Not once had I read anything about them actually being dangerous to people—only to the Reaper King's minions, the reapers. But Miles didn't have to know that.

He was still singing out loud with his eyes shut and fingers in his ears when I flicked him again, earning another hiss.

"Shh, come on. We can't be late to the gate," I said. He peeked through one eye, grinned, and we were off again.

We raced down the alley and slowed to a stop, having reached our destination. A big smile spread across my face. A humongous gateway, taller than any house in the city, stood ahead. It was what separated us from the Nightmare Plains—the wild abandoned fields of forests, swamps, and a bottomless sea—that had taken the lives of many. Home to all the wild umbra.

My heart thumped heavily with each breath. We were so close now.

"You don't think we're gonna see any reapers outside the walls, do you?" Miles asked.

"I doubt it."

It was true that reapers were the real dangers outside the walls, but an actual reaper hadn't been seen since Mum and Dad made the city livable again years ago with the other tamers. We had all heard the stories of what happened when the dark first took over our city, Nubis, and before that the lost city of Astaroth, before Miles and I were born. First came the black smoke, so thick that it burned your eyes. Then came the reapers. Bony creatures, clad in cloaks, with teeth like sharks and eyes like bats, who bowed to the Reaper King, bringer of darkness and nightmares, and taker of souls. No one knew—or knows, even now—how the Reaper King's dark powers slipped into our world, making the Nightmare Plains a death sentence for everyone but the tamers, whose umbra protect them.

Mum, Dad, and the others were confident the reapers wouldn't try to breach the walls of our city again; if they were going to, then they would have already. Plus, we had tamers who guarded the gate and patrolled the area just in case, but never say never, I guess.

It was said that if the reapers ever took over all six cities, time itself would end. The king would be released from the

Spirit Plain and rise once again—and one look at him would cause you to have nightmares forever. He was truly the worst.

"Okay," Miles said as we neared the gate, bringing my thoughts back to our mission. "But if we do see a reaper, we're running."

"Deal."

Just as we planned, it was the hour of switching guards, a slim two-minute window where they would be more focused on changing positions than their immediate surroundings. The perfect time to sneak past.

I silently watched the men and women dressed in blue uniforms up ahead as they collected their things and walked away from the gate. That was our chance.

I tiptoed forward, checking on Lucas before approaching the small wooden pallet that leaned against the wall, farther down from the giant gate. Just where we had left it.

Beside me, Miles took a deep breath, and we bumped fists.

"Ready?" he asked with a small smile. I nodded and took off first.

I leaped over the first barrier, ducking and weaving through signs and stop posts as sounds of the replacement guards' stomping feet got louder. I tripped as the concrete gave way to mud but recovered my footing just in time, keeping Lucas secured on my back and staying out of sight. Almost there. My chest heaved as the footsteps echoed closer, and I crawled under the final barrier. The cold mud squelched against my knees as I clawed the dirt, and my palm slapped the wall. *Made it!*

Right behind me, Miles came through huffing and puffing as I slid the pallet aside, revealing a small gap under the wall. We'd spent weeks digging and keeping it hidden during the annual repairs, when the tamers were making sure the moon crystals embedded in the walls were still functioning well. Sometimes, though, pesky four-eared rabbits and horned beavers would try and dig tunnels, so the tamers always double-checked to make sure there weren't any holes or cracks. But Miles and I had found one, made it bigger, *and* kept it hidden. Ha!

All our secret planning had come to this. We were gonna do it. We were going to see a wild umbra! Miles went under first, and after he called through to tell me it was safe, I unwrapped Lucas from my back and passed him through. Once Miles had him, I took a deep breath and crawled through the hole myself. Freedom!

I'd only ever seen glimpses of the Nightmare Plains from inside the walls of the city, but being *in* it was completely different.

Tall grass stretched out as far as we could see, a darker violet color than what grew within the walls. It was wild and untamed, and reached all the way up to our knees in some places. No doubt filled with creepy-crawlies and who knows what, but we trudged through anyway. Nothing was going to stop me. Once Lucas was secured on my back again, Miles and I slowly walked into the plains, away from the city.

The trees were bare, some with only a few stray silver leaves that shook violently in the wind. Their branches jutted up and down like hooks or crooked fingers, like faceless scarecrows that watched our every move, and I shivered. "Creepy" wasn't a strong enough word. But we'd come this far, and I wasn't going back. Not until I saw a wild umbra.

The moonlight glistened, making my hands glow golden brown, and Lucas's dark, tight curls shone brightly.

"All right, Tanaka, this seems like a good spot," I said, coming to a stop. "We don't want to scare them off."

Miles made a face at being called by his surname. I grinned, inspecting the area ahead. If we were too loud, the umbra would run away. The purple bunches of grass reached only to our ankles here, and the sweet, flowery smell of the rosy-dill plants with teardrop petals comforted me. Mum's favorite flower. Nan's too.

Something rustled ahead by one of the trees, and I squinted my eyes. My pulse raced.

Little horns poked out from the bushes, and I gasped. A small three-horned goat popped his head up, looking at me with its beady blue eyes before it scampered off, and my shoulders slumped. It was just a normal animal, not a being made of shadows and stars. Disappointment washed over me. Silly goat.

Miles sighed.

"It's okay, Miles, I'm sure the next one will be—" I turned my head and froze.

Behind the sparse silver trees, a creature was standing, still and quiet. Its fur shimmered like a million black diamonds, but its wolfish appearance sent a shiver down my spine, even though its floppy ears were rabbitlike. Spikes spread around its neck like a collar. Lucas whimpered against my back, but despite all that, I found myself stepping forward.

"Umbra . . . ," I breathed. My knees threatened to buckle. I wanted to scream with joy, but something stopped me. Its eyes connected with mine, and my throat closed up. Its eyes . . .

They were bloodred.

"I thought all umbra had gold eyes . . . ," Miles whispered.

That was what I had read. All the books said the same. Even Mum and Dad said it.

"You were right about the teeth, though," Miles said, gulping.

My body ran cold, like all the blood had drained away. I shifted Lucas on my back. What *was* this thing?

My gaze didn't move as the wolflike creature walked out from the trees, never breaking eye contact. A red aura pulsed around it, ever so faintly.

Danger. Danger.

When it opened its mouth, a loud roar ripped through the air, and I clutched my ears tight, screaming. Lucas cried out behind me. Was this really an umbra?

Miles looked as frightened as I felt, but he clenched his jaw and pushed me and Lucas behind him. "Stay back. Maybe I can tame it," he said, but I shook my head, stumbling as the shadow creature stepped closer.

"Don't!" I yanked him back, my palms sweaty. It took years of training to tame an umbra. The books never mentioned anything like this. I didn't know anything!

The wild hellhound umbra growled again and Lucas wailed, pounding me with his little fists. I sneaked a glance at him, and when I looked back, the umbra bared its fangs and I barely held back a scream. I'd never been so scared. The creature's bloodred eyes pierced straight through me, pinning me to the spot. Lucas's cries got even louder, and invisible sparks zapped from the umbra's mind to mine. I clutched my head and screamed again, feeling it invade like a virus. My knees gave way and I fell to the ground.

"We need to get out of here, Mia!" Miles yelled, clutching his own head.

I couldn't speak. I couldn't move. The pain kept me on my knees as panic took over and a voice invaded my mind.

"I'm starving. . . . You're a little small, but you'll do. . . ."

The shadow creature licked its lips, stopping just a foot away from me. I mentally shoved the voice out of my mind, blocking it out. As the creature's hot breath engulfed my face, a roar rattled the air behind us, and something leaped over our heads. It crashed into the wolflike umbra, and they tumbled across the field.

In a flash, the pain in my head disappeared and I scrambled to my feet, watching as another shadow creature jumped away from the wild umbra, snapping its head back at us.

"Bolt!" I yelled with relief as I recognized the panther-like shape of Dad's umbra.

Bolt's golden eyes shifted to us before facing forward as the wild umbra bared its fangs again. He smacked the wild umbra with his long, rattlesnake-like tail, leaping in front of us protectively.

"Be careful!" I yelled as the wild one prepared to pounce.

Bolt sprang at the wild umbra again and I gripped my hair, almost yanking it out as they clashed once more. If something happened to Bolt while he was protecting us, it would be all my fault. The hellhound growled. Its bloodred eyes connected with mine once again, and it leaped past Bolt straight for me. I turned around to run, but something snatched me backward. Lucas cried out, the blanket wedged between the umbra's teeth.

"No!" I yelled, yanking the blanket from the beast's sharp

fangs. I desperately tried to keep ahold of my brother as the umbra tried to get him.

Pushing the hellhound back, Bolt slashed at it with his claws, earning a cry of pain. Shaking its fur, the shadow wolf shifted its red eyes from Bolt to us, growling low. It gave me one last glare, before dragging its paw against the dirt, then turning around and racing away, deep into the plains.

"Mia! Miles!" a voice boomed, and I jumped as I turned to see Dad running toward us. His uniform and shoes were muddied, and the panic in his face made my stomach twist. Behind him, two more adults raced toward us with their umbra beside them.

"Why aren't you at home? What are you doing outside the gate?" he shouted.

I raced over and hugged him tight, those red eyes still burning in my head.

"Dad—"

"Mia! Miles! Lucas!" My stomach dropped even lower as Mum ran over to us, her lab coat swinging. "You could have been killed if it wasn't for Bolt catching your scent!"

She took Lucas from me, clutching him tight, part of the ripped blanket falling to the ground. Beside Mum, a huge shadowy bear with a spiked back looked at us with disappointment in his bright golden eyes. Spike, Mum's umbra.

"Not only did you put yourself at risk, but your baby brother, too!"

I hiccuped. It was true. That thing could have killed us. It could have killed Lucas. I couldn't even move.

"And you, Miles," Mum said, turning to the boy. "We are responsible for you now! Why would you put yourself in danger like that?"

He bowed his head. I scrubbed my sleeve against my eyes, sniffing back the tears the best I could. I just wanted to see a wild umbra. . . .

"Sorry, Mummy . . . ," I whispered.

Gently brushing one of my curls out of my face, Mum met my eyes.

"Promise me you'll never go beyond the walls again without permission," she said, resting her palm on my cheek. I leaned into it, sniffling.

"I promise."

After everything that had happened, I never wanted to go beyond the walls again.

Umbra weren't amazing at all. They were monsters.

ATTENTION: BLOOD MOON CURFEW

To all residents: This is your reminder that the Blood Moon is nearly upon us.

CURFEW: SKY CONNECT UNTIL SKY CONNECT

You must not leave your home under any circumstances.

If you see anyone outside alone, report it to a tamer via holo-phone.

Should you have to leave your homes for any emergency reason, contact a tamer and you will be escorted, where appropriate.

Be safe.

CHAPTER ONE

TODAY . . .

B o staff: *check.*

Hoodie: *check.*

Hair done in a tight, low ponytail: *double check.*

Bravery: *gulp.*

I stand in the hallway, staring dead ahead at the front door. Once I step through, there's no going back. I wipe my sweaty hands against my leggings as I inhale deeply and focus forward. Today's the first day of training. The first step in actually becoming an umbra tamer, one of the protectors of our city, and the first port of call for anyone who needs help beyond the walls. Soon I'll be one of them. If I pass training, that is. . . .

I hear a chuckle behind me and turn as a gentle hand rests on my shoulder. Dad smiles softly and runs his hand down my arm until he reaches mine, squeezing it.

"You'll be fine, baby-girl. I promise." I search his brown eyes, the very same eyes that me and Lucas have. There's nothing but honesty in them, yet I can't stop my arms from shaking. *Yeah, I'll be fine . . . I'm only going to be facing a creature capable of tearing me in two, but yeah. . . . No big deal, right?*

When I was younger, all I ever wanted to be was an umbra tamer. But after what happened in the Nightmare Plains, I never wanna step foot out there again, be a stinkin' tamer, or come anywhere close to a wild umbra.

I'm the only kid in Nubis being forced to be a tamer, and it sucks. I just want to go to normal school, to *be* normal. I guess that's not an option when your parents are the most famous tamers in the city, though. *Yay for me . . .* The only good part about being a tamer is the martial arts training that comes with it, but you do that at normal school too. So, what's the point?

Besides, if the other kids saw the same thing I did three years ago, they wouldn't dare dream of being a tamer either. It still gives me nightmares.

My eyes shift to the wall behind Dad as I distract myself by staring at the moving pictures that hang there. In one of the images by the stairs, a younger me is holding a newborn Lucas for the first time, looking from him to the camera in a continuous, wondering loop.

Another shows me and Miles with the biggest smiles on our faces, arms wrapped around each other as we sway side to side. I can't help but smile back at it. He squeezed me so tight that day, almost like he knew that was the last time we'd see each other. My smile wavers, and I hear a sigh.

"I miss him too. He was a good kid," Dad says.

"Was?" I ask, looking at him.

"People change, baby-girl." I catch the slight dryness in his tone, the knowing in his voice.

"Not Miles," I say, shaking my head. "He'll always be my friend."

Dad only smiles, which he always does when he doesn't agree with me but doesn't want to say it. But it's true. Miles will always be my friend. . . . Even if I don't know where he is right now.

"Why did they have to leave the town so quickly?" I ask, earning another sigh.

"We told you, Mia. His parents and a few others wanted to do something bad, so they had to leave."

Yeah, but *what* did they want to do? Every time I ask, he avoids answering.

A low growl makes me jump, and I whip my head around to see a curious creature made from shadow and stars walk in from the living room. Bolt's fur shimmers, and I hesitantly reach down and pet his fluffy head. Just like Dad, Bolt didn't like hearing or talking about Miles's parents and all the other people who had to leave Nubis too. The shadows play around my fingers, and his golden eyes stare up into mine, his huge fangs and sharp claws glinting, reminding me that he's far from a pet.

"Are you ready?" Dad asks, and I shrug, putting on my lilac gloves and tying the ribbon around my wrists.

Not really . . . , I think, tugging my sleeves down, but turning to him, I sigh. "I just . . . I don't want to let you and Mum down, and be that one kid who failed to follow in their parents' footsteps . . . but I don't want to be an umbra tamer, Dad. Why do *I* have to do it?"

In Nubis, it's tradition for kids to follow after their parents, but not *everyone* does. Besides, I'm only twelve. I don't get why Mum and Dad are so insistent.

Dad smiles, kissing my head and holding me close. His stubble tickles my cheek, but I hold him tighter, enjoying the warmth.

"You couldn't ever let us down, Mia," he says. I close my eyes, focusing on his gentle voice and not the twisting of my gut. "You're stronger than you think. This training will help you become the powerful girl we know you to be. Trust us. I love you, baby-girl. Always. You can do this."

He lets go, and the tiniest of smiles spreads across my face. I know it's not just about their legacy as the first-ever tamers of Nubis, in this forever-dark city. I *know* it's more than that, but . . . I just don't know what they're training me *for*, or why they seem to have more faith in me than they should. I'm nothing special.

Only a select few even make it as tamers, and I don't want to see any more shadow monsters than I have to, especially untamed ones. My heart pounds just thinking about it. Mum and Dad say all umbra are good, and that the one I saw was just an anomaly, something rare. But how can they know that for sure? There's a dangerous, terrifying side to umbra; there's no way that red-eyed umbra in the Nightmare Plains was the only one of its kind. No way. Even if no one else in Nubis has seen one, someone somewhere must have.

"Make sure to stop by the research lab on your way," says Dad. "Your mum wants to see you before your first class."

I nod, watching Bolt out of the corner of my eye. He just bows his head again, thankfully keeping his distance, but I could have sworn I saw a flicker of something in his eyes? Still, I shake off the thought as Dad squeezes me tight again.

"Do you have your bo staff?"

"Always," I say, patting my thigh, where the lilac staff is safely attached. Mum made it for me years ago in my favorite color.

"Good. Never be afraid to use it on those no-good boys in your class. Focus on doing well in your lessons."

I make a face. "Yeah, yeah, Dad. Love you," I say, walking to the door.

"Love you, too, baby-girl. Have a good day."

He steps back, and I suck in a deep breath as I open the door and it swings open, revealing our city, sparkling before my eyes. It's time.

I take a step out of the door, then spin on my heel. "I already gave Lucas a kiss, but tell him I said bye, okay? Wish me luck." *I'm gonna need it.* I force the corners of my lips up and wave as hard as I can. Dad waves back with a bright smile.

I break into a run, my shoes slapping against the pavement. *Here goes nothing, I guess. . . .* As soon as Dad is out of sight, my smile drops and the dread sinks back in.

The light of the forever moon shines bright over my head, making my brown skin glow as the stars dot and shift in the sky like crystallized fireflies. In Nubis, the moon is our sun and the stars are our time. Only in the City of Light, Stella, where that useless Queen Katiya lives, do the days follow the rays of the sun that she protects, far on the other side of the Nightmare Plains.

It's because of her that Mum and Dad have to go on dangerous missions to protect our city and others. Stella has all that technology—self-navigating travel pods, high-level security gates, and more—but they don't help anyone else outside their city. They even have a whole crystal, similar to the fragments Mum has in her lab, but when our scientists asked the queen if they could study it, she denied them. Even after all the years that Mum worked as a scientist in Stella, and trained to be part of the Queen's Guard, that was the stinkin' treatment she got. Every time the tamers asked Stella for help or assistance when it came to saving other cities from the Darkness, they were denied, for the "safety of the capital city." It literally makes no sense, but it's why my parents and most of the other tamers don't trust or respect the queen. They even shared their knowledge of the umbra, helping the queen tame one herself, yet they got nothing in return. They're all doing her job for her when it comes to fighting off the Darkness and the reapers, even though she's supposed to be the all-powerful one. Selfish gutterslug.

Slowly, the constellation begins to take shape overhead as the silver line that stitches the stars together fades, signaling the start of a new day: Sky Connect. Our version of morning in the city of Nubis.

I hop from rock to rock across the shimmering river, where blue fish splash and swim by my feet. Then I jump back onto the cobble path, where the floating travel pods are stationed. Before the Darkness took over the latest city, Lunavale, these pods would take groups of people across the Nightmare Plains to visit the other cities that were still lit for trade and festival events. Unlike the ones in Stella, our pods don't move unless umbra are pulling them. Now they're mainly used for rescue missions, and there aren't many cities left to save.

When I reach the market, rich smells of bread and sugar fill my nose. The place is already busy with people holding baskets, tokens in hand, as they shop for food and trinkets. Bright lights trail along the walls and across the ground, twinkling like magic in different colors.

I duck under Ms. Mabel's food market stall, a large wooden table decorated with beautiful blue ribbon, and a big sign hanging above with her name on it. The elderly woman jumps, laughing. Her braids are as pretty as ever, with the jewels in her hair glistening in the light. The cinnamon smell hits me, and I slow down as she knits her fingers together, nodding to me in greeting.

"Good luck today, Mia!" she calls out. She throws me a small pack of chewy honey drops and I reach up to catch it, nodding back in respect.

"Thanks, Ms. M! See ya later!"

I dodge through everyone, bumping into a man with a weird red cloak. I always see him around the market. He never really speaks to anyone, but he helps out with the food stalls sometimes. I wave a *sorry* to him before racing out of the market. I slow down as I pass the huge metal gate, the only way in and out of our city, and nerves hit me as they always do.

The wooden pallet that was once my secret exit out of the city with Miles is long gone, the hole under the wall patched up with cement so no one could sneak into the Nightmare Plains again. *Good.* It was for the best.

The walls keep us locked in from the outside world, and they also keep the outside world out. Cameras mounted at the top watch my every move, along with anyone else who passes within ten feet of the entryway. Beside them at the top are posts where extra guards and umbra birds now perch, watching the plains.

Sometimes you can hear the guards setting off fireworks, but I always seem to miss seeing them light the sky. Fireworks used to function as a warning to any reaper who threatened to get close, but after the fall of the Reaper King, they wouldn't dare come back. I imagine the only things the guards are scaring off now are bears and wolves.

Everyone's safe from reapers and those monstrous red-eyed umbra. That's what matters. There's no way there's just one out there.

I still don't know what caused that creature's eyes to go red, and I can't help but wonder if our own umbra in the city could do the same. The thought makes me shiver.

"Hey, Mia. Staying out of trouble?" one of the guards calls down, breaking into my thoughts. I look up and force a smile.

"Of course, Bently!" I yell back, jumping over a small crack in the ground before pivoting and backflipping over another one. "I'm always staying out of trouble!"

He waves me off, chuckling, and my smile drops as I glance at the shadowy rhinoceros umbra guarding the front of the gate, flicking their horselike tails. Their golden eyes stare ahead. I accelerate my pace until I pass the giant pictures engraved on the wall—a mural telling the story of the legendary battle between old Queen Lucina and the Reaper King.

I slow down to scan it, looking at her ancient staff ready to clash with the Reaper King's shadow claws. Each image is carefully chipped into the stone, with what look like tall towers engraved on either side of the two figures. The king's hooded minions are all around him, ready to attack, but what stands out the most is the sharp, jagged line that connects the queen and king together, with tiny umbra-like creatures beneath it. No one knows who engraved the story on the wall, but legend says that it depicts the moment umbra were created.

I carry on walking until the huge white research dome comes into view. When I reach the building's entrance, I stand in front of the scanner, blinking rapidly as a bright light blinds me.

"Welcome, Mia McKenna," a robotic voice says, and the doors slide open.

The room buzzes with energy as people dressed in lab coats race to and fro, some tapping away at computers and others examining things with mini microscopes. The ceiling is covered with lunar panels, drawing on the light of the moon for power, and the sterile smell of technology hits my nose as I make my way through. The walls are shiny white, covered with moving pictures of different types of umbra, some with long wings, some with sharp teeth, and others with fluffy tails. I keep my eyes to the ground, hoping I don't slip on the squeaky-clean floor.

A huge shadowy horse with twisted horns and a scaly tail suddenly charges at me, then *through* me, disappearing as I jump and gasp aloud.

"Sorry!" one of the scientists calls out as the holographic image appears again behind me.

I hurry past and see my mother perched on a stool with a book in her hand and something black swirling in a glass jar on the counter in front of her. I don't know half the stuff they do in this lab, but Mum runs all the umbra research. I gaze upon the star maps that shift and spin at a touch on the wall behind her. To the right of those, the crystal fragments discovered beyond the walls, said to hold the power of the founders, sparkle behind special glass cases. Mum says that the royal family found one of the crystals originally, and she thinks that's where their powers come from, but she's not 100 percent sure. One of them was destroyed into fragments, which is what we have, and the other is kept by Queen Katiya in the City of Light.

My eyes fall back to my mum, and my heart warms. Mum's pretty hair frames her cheeks, her curls showing off her beautiful brown face and hazel eyes, whereas my curly hair is tied back into a low ponytail with bangs. I wish I had her eyes, though—mine are much darker.

I'm mindful of Spike, the huge bearlike umbra with spikes all the way down his back, lying at Mum's feet. His fur glistens like midnight, and I twist at my sleeves nervously. He lifts his head, and as soon as our eyes connect, Mum looks over with a big smile.

"Mia, how are you, honey? Are you ready for today?"

Nope.

"Yeah, I think so," I say, rubbing the back of my neck, my eyes lingering on Spike. What if my first lesson is to ride on an umbra? Shivers tickle down my spine just thinking about it.

"Are you sure you don't want me to walk you to class?" Mum asks, and I blink at her, shaking my head.

"Nah, it's okay. TJ's meeting me at the bridge."

She nods, and I eye the jar on her desk, watching the darkness inside swirl and warp my reflection. Seeing me look at it, Mum leans closer and grins.

"It's called shadow matter, baby. It's what the umbra are made of. We're trying to find out its origin, and this is the first time we've been able to isolate a piece of it to examine. Hopefully, during this Blood Moon, we'll be able to see if our theories are right." Her eyes almost sparkle as she speaks, but I scrunch up my nose. It almost looks alive.

I glance down at Spike, and he raises his head. How did

Mum even get that stuff in the jar? Maybe the umbra pooped it out or something. . . . I've never seen an umbra actually poop, though. . . .

"Are you sure TJ will be there on time to meet you?" Mum asks. She arches her eyebrow, and I nod.

"Yep, he promised."

She kisses my cheek. "All right. Well, I'm glad you came here first. I have something for you."

Mum opens a drawer in her desk and pulls out a small blue box that's beautifully wrapped with a silver bow. She hands it to me, and when I open it, I gasp. Inside is a small glittery star bracelet, twinkling brightly.

"Wow," I say with big eyes. "But why?"

She chuckles, and I see Spike's shoulders shake, like he's chuckling too.

"Today is a big day for you, honey, and I know you've been on edge about it. It's made with real stardust, just like our family necklaces. Your nan gave me this bracelet when I first left home, and now it's yours. Think of it like an extra good luck charm," she says. I bite my lip, trying not to cry as I think of Nan and Grandad. They never visit anymore. Hologram calls just aren't the same, and we barely have those, either.

Mum says it's because they're still upset that we didn't live in Stella with them, but I think it's just because Nan doesn't like Dad. I don't know why, though. Nan always tries not to say things around me, but I still hear them. And lately Nan and Grandad both say that Nubis is getting too dangerous for me and Lucas, but it's always been the same here.

"We'll visit them soon. I promise."

"Thanks, Mum," I whisper. She helps me put the bracelet on and I give her a hug, breathing in the fresh smell of her perfume.

"I'll see you later, honey. Have a good day."

I head out of the lab, glancing up at the sky with my bracelet on my wrist. *Still on time.*

The paths light up with different colors from floating glow bugs and hanging fairy lights along the walls and houses. I count them, trying my best not to think about the day ahead.

The mini bridge comes into view, crossing over the tiny stream that flows beneath it through the city, and I sigh. No sign of TJ.

I stop when I reach the bridge, and as the stars slowly shift in the sky, I kick a rock into the water. *He promised.* . . . I twist and turn the ends of my sleeves, jumping from foot to foot, looking for the familiar Afro, denim jacket, and white sneakers. We'll be told off if we're late, and we could miss something important, like how not to be eaten or something. This is serious.

For the millionth time, I really wish Miles was here. He always turned up when he said he would.

I look left and right, spotting a few people getting their

floating lanterns ready for the Blood Moon that's coming soon. It happens every five years, and it always makes people nervous. During this time, both the Darkness and the umbra are at their strongest, and someone always goes missing. Snatched away in the night—by someone, or some*thing*. Some people think it's the reapers serving the Reaper King and bringing souls for him to devour so he can get stronger in the Spirit Plain, but others think the Blood Moon somehow puts people in a trance-like state, making them walk away into the Nightmare Plains, never to return. Honestly, I don't know which theory is worse. Both give me the creeps.

We release the colorful neon lanterns into the sky as symbols of hope and protection, and as beacons for all those missing and lost to find their way back home. But they never do.

I look farther, beyond the silver trees, to a small collection of houses. A particular white one catches my eye, just like it always does. Miles's old house. The violent carvings of the word "traitor" are still visible on the door, despite all the times Mum and I tried to scratch the word out or paint over it.

What could his parents have done that was so bad? My fingers drum against the bridge. Either way, Miles had nothing to do with it, I'm sure of it. He would have told me, and maybe he wouldn't have had to leave Nubis if he'd stayed living with us like he did whenever his parents went out on missions. . . .

I shake my head, looking back up at the stars.

The Capricornus constellation forms beside the Kay star and Ursa Minor—time is ticking and still no TJ. I can't wait any longer. *The jerk . . .*

I take off into a jog and skid to a stop as the bright purple field surrounded by low stone walls comes into sight. I hop over the wooden gate, panting as I join my classmates. Above our heads, a shadow circles, weaving and blending in with the night sky. I squint my eyes, but the braided-hair teen in front of me clears her throat with a smirk on her lips as she clasps her hands and nods to me.

"Glad you made it on time, Mia. I thought you'd chickened out for a second."

I force a smile. It's probably best not to tell her that this is the last place I want to be. Instead I clasp my hands, nodding back. She grins.

The girl before me is Jada Halliwell. At seventeen, she's the up-and-coming star tamer of Nubis. It usually takes three years of training before you tame an umbra, but she tamed hers after just two. She's especially cool because she always makes time to chat with me and the other kids. If any teacher is going to get me through this, it's her.

Tiny glow bugs flutter around the field, their warm light gently bouncing off her brown cheeks and highlighting her freckles as she paces back and forth in front of us. The space beside me where TJ should be feels especially large and empty.

I grab my hand to stop it from shaking, and we stay put as Jada turns and strides across the field away from us, her hair tied back in braids. In her thick combat boots, she trudges through the purple grass, wet with dew and glistening in the moonlight. I breathe in the sweet, earthy smell of pine as she reaches the middle of the field. *Deep breaths* . . .

She spins to face me and the other kids, who confusingly have *chosen* to be here: Mikasa, a short girl with jet-black hair and sparkly brown eyes, and Thomas and Lincoln, the oddly quiet but friendly freckled twins. My eyes shift forward. With her spiked choker, boots, and fingerless gloves, Jada is ready to kick butt . . . our butts.

I force myself to focus, pumping myself up. *I can do this.*

"As most of you know, my name is Jada Halliwell. You guys can call me Jada, though. None of that Ms. Halliwell stuff, all right? I'm not some old lady," she says. "Now, this isn't going to be easy. There's a reason only a few make it as tamers. It takes years to be a tamer, but the first thirty days are the hardest. Not everyone has the mental strength to do it, but if you continue your martial arts training too, then within the next two or three years, you should all be ready to try to tame your own umbra through the Spirit Calling."

My palms are slick with sweat, my throat dry. Beside me, Mikasa grins and jigs up and down, her silky black hair pulled up in two pigtails that bounce right along with her. On the other side of her, Thomas and Lincoln stand still as rocks with their eyes glued to Jada, not missing a single word.

"Most of you have chosen this path for yourselves, and your parents obviously believe in you or you wouldn't be here. So pay attention to everything from here on out."

I feel her eyes on me, but I can't help looking around for the last member of our class. TJ still isn't here. We were supposed to do this together. *He promised.*

Jada doesn't wait.

"All right, let's get straight down to business."

She raises her hand and snaps her fingers. The sound echoes in the wind, and we all flinch as a sudden bright light blinds us.

Blue blotches invade my sight, forcing me to blink until I finally see what's appeared in front of us, and jump back.

"Say hello to my umbra, Ruby."

Floating beside our teacher is a beautifully terrifying shadowy creature, about half her height. Her feathery wings shimmer like diamonds, black as the sky above, and my pulse races. I've never been this close to her before. Jada's umbra is definitely one of the prettiest I've ever seen, but that doesn't take away the fear that bubbles inside me.

Ruby, who is the shape of a phoenix, fixes her golden eyes on me, her feathery tail flaring out like a peacock's. The shadow matter that writhes around her body is a haunting reminder that she's a creature of the night, blending in and out of the darkness like she's one with it. My instincts scream at me to run, that one day those gold eyes will turn bloodred, but I force my feet to stay planted.

"Whoa! She's so cool! Can I touch her?" Mikasa yells. The twins' eyes are wide with awe. We've all seen umbra before, but Ruby . . . she's something magical. And horrifying.

"Listen up!" Jada's voice rings out. Her dark eyes don't leave us once. "As you know, umbra are the heart of our society here in Nubis. They protect us, and in return, we love and care for them. We bond with them and give them companionship, but remember: they are not pets. We must respect them. If you show mental weakness, they *will* eat your soul."

I share a glance with Mikasa, whose smile has dropped.

"However," Jada continues, "if you're both on the same wavelength, it'll be the best connection you'll ever have. You'll have a partner for life. Now, there are two standard forms of umbra. Three, once tamed."

I already know the three forms. When we were little, Miles used to think it was silly to study umbra so much, but all those hours in the library were definitely worth it. Aside from the reason for the red eyes, I know everything there is to know about umbra.

Jada looks at her feathery partner. Their love and trust hits me with a strange warmth, making my fingers tingle and putting a tiny smile on my face.

"Ruby here is in her baby form—the smallest she can make herself. It's believed that untamed umbra use this form for sneak attacks on wild animals and other umbra or to hide, whereas tamed umbra will use it to easily navigate cities and towns like ours," she tells us.

The shadow bird squawks, ruffling her feathers as Jada strokes the creature's back.

"Ruby, will you do the honors with the next form?"

Ruby's squawk pierces the air again, and she shakes her head before focusing back on her tamer. There's a moment of silence; then a flash of light blinds us once again and wild winds whip up, blowing my curls and ponytail all over the place. My toes crunch into my shoes as I try to stay upright.

In front of us now is a gigantic bird, almost the same height of a normal house, five times bigger than she was in her baby form. Each flap of Ruby's wings is powerful enough to create a mini tornado. I hold on to Mikasa to stop us from being blown away, but I'm frozen in fear.

The nightmare memories of bloodred eyes flash in my mind, and sharp canine teeth join the picture, making my fingers tremble. I remember my baby brother's cries, and Miles yelling for us to get back to safety. The hellhound umbra shakes her body, saliva dripping from her lips and—

"Mia!"

I jump, and my head snaps up to see Jada's worried eyes. "What's the matter?" she asks.

"N-nothing," I manage to say, forcing a smile, though I'm sure Jada sees right through it. "I mean it. I'm okay."

I push back the memories, locking them up in a box and shoving it all the way down into an imaginary bin, and remind myself that I'm safe within the walls. Jada gives me a knowing look before continuing.

"*This* is an umbra's natural form. The only time they really need to be in this form is to fight or if you're riding on their back."

Jada nods again and the shadow bird glows, turning into a shimmering dark shadow mass.

"The third form is the hardest of all to achieve. It's only when you and your umbra are truly connected, mind and soul, that you can become one powerful being."

Another blinding light flashes, and Ruby's shadows zap toward Jada's body, engulfing her. *Please be okay, please be okay!* The light burns my eyes for a second before clearing.

Then, standing before us and cased in a shadowy armor, our teacher smiles. A black shadow bow and arrow are in Jada's grip, and she twirls them playfully with her fingers. The other kids gasp in awe, but I just stare. She and Ruby have merged into one being. One entity. Their shadowy peacock-like tail swishes in the wind, along with huge shadowy wings that flap gently, completely morphed into a human-umbra being.

It's terrifying. I can't think of anything worse than having that shadowy darkness all around me.

Another blinding light flashes and they return to normal, with Ruby softly flapping beside Jada in her baby form. Why would anyone want to do that? To become one with a monster surely makes you a monster too. And what would happen if their eyes went red?

"Of course, you can't stay in that form forever," Jada continues. "I think the record goes to lead umbra tamer Daniel McKenna. He lasted four hours on one rescue mission."

Dad? I blink, unsure whether to feel proud or worried. None of the books said what would happen if you stayed in that form for too long. Although I can guess . . .

Jada's eyes darken as she walks closer to us, her boots flattening the grass. "Remember, any umbra can be tamed, but it's not easy. Although it's rare, there has been at least one incident where it has gone wrong during the Spirit Calling . . . but that's why I'm training you. I'll make sure you're safe."

Her eyes fall on me again, and I shuffle uncomfortably. One of the twins jumps for some reason, surprising me. Then I feel it too. An electric spark jolts through my brain, and a soft whisper enters my thoughts. I'm no longer alone in my head, as Ruby's lyrical voice softly sings to all of us:

"When you perform a Spirit Calling, we have no choice but to respond if we sense that we are spiritually connected to you. We don't know where this connection comes from, but most of us seek our tamer with curiosity and openness. Some, however, do not, and they will try and devour your soul if they don't deem you worthy, but this is rare. We trust that our tamers are strong mentally, even if weaker than us physically. If you're mentally weak, then . . ."

"Then what?" I urge, but she's stopped. All of us already know the answer.

Goose bumps dot up my arms.

"Listen," Jada says. "We've all heard about that incident from years ago. When Samuel Walker did his Spirit Calling to summon an umbra, he did everything right, but . . ." She pauses, searching for the right words. "He never woke up. We don't know for sure why or how, but it's safe to assume that either the umbra ate his soul, or he got lost in the Spirit Plain. It's the only incident of its kind that we know of, but he's being monitored every day at the lab until we can find a way to bring him back."

How could I ever forget? It caused outrage in the whole city. I only found out what really happened after my incident in the Nightmare Plains. Mum and Dad had wanted to wait until I was older, but after meeting that red-eyed umbra, they told me everything. People called for the tamer lessons to end, but Mum, Dad, and the other tamers insisted that we carry on because of the "bigger picture." What bigger picture was worth Samuel's life? Yeah, technically he's still breathing, but no one can wake him up. Just like that, an umbra took someone's soul and trapped them in the Spirit Plain with the ghosts and the Reaper King.

There is darkness in those creatures. Within all of them. Just because most of them choose not to eat human souls doesn't mean they can't just change their minds, and we still don't know much about the Spirit Plain. Bolt and Spike are all right now, but what if they decide to just switch on us? I wish I could stop thinking about it, but I can't. I'm a coward.

"*We don't need to eat human souls to survive, but certain umbra choose to. Some enjoy the taste, but not all,*" Ruby says, but it doesn't make me feel any better.

After Ruby finishes, Jada makes us run laps across the field, calling it "tough love" and "covering all bases" by making us physically fit. At the fourth lap I'm heaving, but I suck it up, trying not to think about Samuel Walker.

By the time we're through, my shirt's sticking to my back, and Jada smiles with satisfaction. She stands before us with one hand behind her and the other holding a rope gun loosely at her side. These rope-net-firers used to be used to capture thieves and bandits who chose to live out in the Nightmare Plains instead of in the cities. The criminals would often cause trouble, trying to steal things from houses and shops in our city. The reapers probably got them all now, though. . . .

"I've got one last challenge for you guys before we end class for today," Jada says. "All you have to do is take one of Ruby's feathers from her. Simple, right?"

I hold back a snort. It definitely isn't simple.

She grins. "Any volunteers? If you succeed, you get a cool mystery prize."

My hand stays down at my side. I'm not brave or anything special. *I can't do it.* I look around and realize everyone else is avoiding Jada's gaze too.

"All right," Jada says, smirking. "We'll have it my way, then." She scans each of our faces, waving her finger back and forth between us. "The first one up is . . ."

Her finger lands on me. "Mia McKenna. Let's go."

Umbra
A Lab Report by Lila McKenna

Umbra are creatures born of shadows and stars, a result of the clash between Queen Lucina and the Reaper King, according to the analysis of the mural.

They usually resemble a hybrid of different animals, with black shadow matter making up their bodies. While most have a black shadowy appearance, records show that there have been umbra with white shadow matter—but this is rare. There is no evidence to suggest that this change in color makes them any different from their counterparts.

For the most part, umbra still remain a scientific mystery. They do not generally live in groups, but appear to communicate telepathically with one another, just as they do with humans.

Means of Staying Alive

Umbra do not need food or drink to survive, and they tend to live peacefully among the wild animals of Lunis. However, there have been cases of umbra choosing to devour souls, be it animals or humans. According to our tamed umbra, a rare few umbra do it out of enjoyment—a dark trait caused by having been created partly from the Reaper King.

Connection with Humans

The connection many umbra have with humans, especially those who have made a connection through the Spirit Calling, is incredibly strong. Once an umbra is tamed, they and their tamer can transform into one ultimate being, granting them powers beyond even our own knowledge.

Additional Notes

After Mia's and Miles's report concerning an encounter with a dangerous red-eyed umbra, a covert investigation took place in which several tamers were caught experimenting on tamed umbra. Their methods were barbaric, and further evidence was found that said tamers were using the dark methods of the Reaper King himself. Those umbra are dangerous and must be avoided at all costs.

Any sightings of red-eyed umbra are now being reported. However, we have not seen any since those tamers were banished.

CHAPTER TWO

The rope gun is squeezed in my shaky grasp, my hoodie tied securely around my waist, as the shadow creature before me ruffles her feathers in her baby form. Ruby's golden eyes lock with mine, and everyone slowly comes out of focus until it is just me and her.

"I will not fly above your height, but you have only two shots with the rope gun. Good luck, young Mia. You'll need it," Ruby promises.

She bows her head, a few baby feathers fluttering to the ground as she stretches her wings, showing off the odd flecks of red among the black. I go to pick one up, but Jada toots her whistle.

"Nice try, but I don't think so. I said you have to take a feather *from* her. Not from the ground. Joker."

"Fine . . . ," I grumble, letting the baby feathers be.

Jada presses the whistle against her lips again and my shoes dig into the dirt, feeling the nerves bubbling. *Calm down . . . You got this. . . .*

"Three . . . ," Jada begins. "Two . . ." My legs start to jitter. "One—"

"Yo-yo-yo! I'm here! The king has arrived!"

Everyone's heads snap in the direction of the voice. Rapid footsteps skid to a halt next to me, and I slowly turn to the boy with moon-kissed brown skin standing beside me. His white sneakers glow in the moonlight, and he tugs at his black jean jacket, waggling his eyebrows at me. *This guy . . .* I nudge him back, making a face and fighting back the tiniest of smiles. TJ. Finally.

"Were you worried? Sorry about that," TJ says, flashing a toothy smile. "I had to make sure I had the right outfit and then I had to get breakfast and—"

"All right, you clown, don't push it. I actually have a test to do, ya know," I say, rolling my eyes, but I do feel much better now that he's here.

Only my best friend, TJ Johnson, would make such an entrance. Don't ever call him Tyler James, though. If he ever heard you call him that, he would literally explode, come back to life, and label you "No Name" for all time. No joke.

"You're late, Johnson." Jada crosses her arms. TJ winks at me and I can't help but laugh. Mikasa, Thomas, and Lincoln all shake their heads, not at all surprised. TJ is almost always late for our martial arts class too.

"You're lucky it's the first day. If you ever come to my class late again, I'll get Ruby to eat you. Got it? Now keep quiet and get in line." She jerks her thumb at Ruby, and the umbra snaps her beak at him.

Instantly, TJ zips his mouth shut and throws away an imaginary key. I copy him, my bottom lip still twitching. Little Mikasa giggles beside me, and Jada rolls her eyes, muttering some bad words under her breath before bringing the whistle back up to her lips.

"Right, McKenna, you're up." My smile drops and I turn back to the umbra.

"You can do it," TJ says, and I wanna believe him, but I can't stop the nerves.

I step toward Ruby. *Just one feather.*

I take a deep breath and nod.

"Three . . . two . . . one . . ." The whistle blows, and Ruby rises into the air. I leap toward her, firing off the rope gun straightaway, hoping to get this over with. The shadow phoenix zips left, and I pivot after her. I shoot another rope that she dodges again, effortlessly. Great—I've already wasted my two shots.

My fear dissipates as determination takes over. *I got this!* The wind swirls around me, but my eyes lock onto the far wall she's about to fly past, the one that blocks off the field from the rest of town. I pick up speed, pushing off the ground with more strength in every step. She flies right in front of the wall, going up, and I smirk. *Now!*

I leap, scrambling up the wall like a red-eared squirrel, then launch myself into the air. Adrenaline pushes me up, and I barely feel the cold breeze against my skin. My arms stretch. Her tail is just in sight.

"Yo, she's actually gonna get it! Go, Mia!" TJ yells.

My fingers brush against the sparkling tail and I clutch at it. A high-pitched squawk pierces my ears as I hold on with everything I have. "Got ya!"

Then I'm suddenly yanked high up into the air, still clutching her tail. My head snaps down as everyone shrinks to the size of ants, and cold air whips my body. Ruby thrashes and flails, trying to shake me off, and fear rushes through me. My body's thrown all over the place like a rag doll's. I grip on so tight my knuckles turn from brown to white and my arms cry for mercy.

"No! Don't drop me!" I scream, looking down as we fly farther up into the sky. My head whirls, and the bitter taste of vomit fills my mouth. My vision darkens. I feel like the wind is suffocating me. *I can't breathe!* "RUBY!"

A loud crash rattles the air and we both freeze, floating surreally in the sky. I look down, but the ground's blurry.

There's another bang, and my fingers slip from her tail.

I'm falling.

I scream, my lungs burning as the wind rushes past me.

The field hurtles closer. *No, no, NO!* An earsplitting whistle screeches. Then something grabs my body, yanking up and suspending me just a few feet from the ground. *What the flip!* I look up and realize Ruby has caught me in her talons. The frantic beating of her wings turns to slow, gentle flaps as she lowers me safely.

My legs crumple as everyone races over.

"Mia, are you okay? Did you hear that bang?" People are speaking, asking me questions, but I'm frozen. I'm lying on my side, and I notice a fuzzy orange caterpillar in the grass. Someone taps my shoulder and I flinch.

"Whoa, whoa, it's me, Mia." TJ puts his hands up as the others run over.

"That was so wild! Are you okay?" Mikasa says.

"Say something, Mia!" one of the twins says.

I swallow with difficulty and thrust my arm up, shaking. A single black, shimmering feather is trapped between my fingers, fluffy and soft.

Everyone erupts in cheers, but I can't bring myself to smile. My throat is so dry I can barely swallow. I let go and the feather slowly floats to the ground.

"Hey! Give her space, give her space! Mia, are you all right?" Jada says with a frown. "Sorry. That was really unlucky about the fireworks. You did well."

I barely register her words but nod anyway.

"Forgive me, Mia. Something felt off in the air. It was like a strange disturbance, and I acted on instinct . . . ," Ruby says, bowing her head. I slowly reach up and pet her black feathers, still shaky.

"It's okay. Erm, thanks for saving me." I look back up at the sky. Ruby was clearly as puzzled as I was. Because I didn't see any fireworks.

What was that noise?

"All right, class, we'll end it here, then. You guys have martial arts in a few hours, so get a little extra downtime. Tomorrow the rest of you will have a go at grabbing one of Ruby's feathers. Got it? Skedaddle," Jada says.

The others walk away, but I hang back.

Ruby bristles a little. She lays her entire body on the ground and Jada strokes her softly, thanking her for the help today. They are staring at each other, maybe telepathically communicating about that bang. What if it had something to do with the Blood Moon?

"Are you sure you're all right?" Jada asks me, catching me watching them. "Do you want me to walk you home?"

I shake my head, picking up the feather and giving it to her. She brings it to Ruby's tail and it blends back into the umbra's shadowy body.

"I'm fine." I force a smile, and her frown disappears.

"You're a tough one, McKenna. I knew you would be. You did really well today."

"Thanks," I say, rubbing the rough studs of the star bracelet. I was just lucky.

"This is just the beginning of your umbra training. Anything can happen when you do the Spirit Calling. You'll have to think quick on your feet when you're in that spiritual realm, and you'll be alone." Her words chill me, but she smiles, stretching her back. "But that's what I'm training you for. Now go on. I'll see you tomorrow—and here's your prize."

She chucks something at me, and I frown as I catch it.

"A ball? Are you serious?"

She laughs. "It's not just a ball." She leans in, cups her mouth to my ear, and whispers. "It's a smoke ball. Throw that and you are protected from an enemy's sight for a straight two minutes. It's a tamer's gadget, but you never know when it'll come in handy."

I quickly stash it in my pocket, thinking I could prank TJ with it or something.

"Catch you later, Mia!"

We wave at each other, and she and Ruby exit the field. Looking up at the stars as they shift, I gasp at the time. *Shoot! I'm gonna be late!* I'll have to run home to make it in time for dinner.

At our house, we always eat bang on at four o'clock. By then, Mum has usually finished her work in the research lab. Dad always makes the dinner when he's done checking the perimeters of the city.

As I'm crossing the bridge over the stream, loud feet stomp after me, and a heavy hand slaps my back. I whip round and punch on instinct. TJ doubles over as he grips his stomach, then laughs.

"That one almost hurt," he says, pretending like he wasn't just winded, and I smirk, shaking my fist.

"Don't sneak up on me, then, genius. Next time, I'm sending you to the stars."

"I was *waiting* for you, actually." *That's a first. . . .*

He starts walking next to me, and I raise an eyebrow. "Aren't you meeting your mums at the café?"

"Yeah, but that doesn't mean I can't walk you back, right? Besides, even supernovas like yourself—"

I stop listening as he carries on jabbering. *Supernova . . .* Miles used to call me that. His smile flashes in my mind. I still miss him so much it makes my chest hurt.

"Hey, race you to your house?"

I snap out of my thoughts. "You're on!" I say, dashing first.

TJ pounds after me. I jump left to right on the floating stones, across the small river. Little bunny-puppy umbra hop out of the way as I make it to the other side. Only a rare few tiny umbra live untamed within the walls. They usually hide in little holes or cracks in the walls.

The water splashes as TJ crashes through it, ignoring the stepping-stones, and I surge ahead.

He catches up at the trees, but I'm already in the branches. I swing and leap with TJ below me. He's the quickest runner in Nubis, but I'm the best climber.

Floating lamps made from solar glass in the city of Stella keep our path lit, along with the floating glow bugs. We make it out at the same time and weave through the market, and I catch TJ swiping a piece of sweet bread from Mr. Davies's stall. He gives a thumbs-up and yells, "One of my mums will pay you back later!" when the man protests.

My house comes into view, standing in a row among three others. TJ and I reach it at the same time, our hands pressing against the bright white front door as we huff and puff.

"Next time I'll win. Just you watch, Mia!"

"Whatever, mate. Just don't be late for class again."

"Yeah, yeah. Catch you later! Don't miss me too much."

He leaves, giving me a mini salute, and I smile, shaking my

head. Then I jump as another loud bang sounds in the sky, but there are definitely no fireworks. What *is* that?

I quickly ring the doorbell, activating the security scan. The light in the spy hole scans me, and I race inside as soon as the door clicks open.

"Welcome back, Mia." Spike greets me at the door, and the fresh smell of jerk chicken, fried dumplings, and pumpkin pastries fills the air. He stretches his spiky back and tail, standing up on two feet like a big cuddly black shadow bear. Even in his baby form, Spike matches my height with no problem at all.

"Did you hear that bang?" I ask him, taking off my shoes.

"Yes, there's a disturbance in the air. Your parents are sorting it. Do not worry."

"Disturbance?" It's the same word Ruby used.

I step back a bit when Spike moves toward me, getting too close. His golden eyes narrow, and just like with Bolt earlier, hesitation flickers in them as he bows his head. My heart tugs. Maybe he misses how we used to play together too, but it just wasn't the same after I saw that *thing*. Even Spike and Bolt couldn't explain why that umbra I saw had red eyes. . . . Or so they say, anyway.

Napping across from him by the stairs is Bolt, who remains unbothered by our conversation. His snakelike tail is wrapped around his black panther body, and he's purring like an oversized cat. Most of the time he's just moody, though.

I make an effort to walk around him and he rolls onto his side, watching me as I head into the living room.

Perhaps when I finish this silly training, I'll be able to completely find the trust again. After all, I grew up with Spike and Bolt.

The sound of cartoons invites me in, and I hear Lucas squealing. He's bouncing his little butt on the sofa to a theme song, so engrossed in the hologram TV that he doesn't even notice me. One finger up his nose, he's digging around for something up there, and it definitely isn't gold.

I cringe before leaping onto the sofa, and he almost flies off, whipping his finger out and hiding it behind his back.

"Why are you picking your nose? That's nasty! You're four now! No excuses!" I yell at him. His eyes open wide and he stands up on the sofa. Mum's *good* sofa—he's toast if she catches him.

"I wasn't!" he shouts back. He scrunches his nose, standing his ground.

I point my finger at the little booger eater. "Don't lie, pipsqueak! I saw you with my own two eyes."

He pushes out his bottom lip and crosses his tiny arms across his chest.

"Well, I didn't eat them this time!"

"You're gross. . . ."

"You're gross!" He sticks his tongue out, and I shake my head.

d ages," he says. "I asked for a cookie, and Daddy said he would get me one, but he *still* hasn't."

As I stand up to go find out, the door opens. My parents' normally smiling faces are replaced with frowns, their lips pressed firmly together. Mum's eyes soften as she looks at us, and she tries to smile, but there's only one time she ever smiles like that. My stomach drops as she walks over and pulls me into a hug.

"Sweetheart." I lean into her hand as she softly brushes the side of my face. "Your dad and I have to go. . . ."

She looks to Dad, and my heart squeezes. *Breathe in . . . out . . . in . . . out. . . . Don't think the worst.*

"Another city's been taken. People need help getting to safety," Dad says with a sigh.

Breathe. "Was that what the noises were? Spike said there was a disturbance in the air. So did Jada's umbra, Ruby."

Dad smiles gently, but it doesn't reach his eyes. "We're looking into it, baby-girl."

Lucas sniffles, his bottom lip trembling as he hops off t sofa and hugs Mum. She picks him up. I turn to Dad hug him as hard as I can, squeezing my eyes shut. need their help, I know, but sometimes I wish Mum didn't have to be the ones to leave all the time. F has to help, but . . . *It's not fair.* Two tamers sr time to protect the city, but it's never Mum ar Dad sees the expression on my face and

"You better sit down before Mum catches   a

the sofa."

Realizing what he was doing, he quickly plonk

on his bottom. *Baby clown.* He's so annoying some

he knows I'll always have his back. Even if he still

nose.

"How are you doing, Lu-Lu?" I ask, and quicker than

ning, he jumps on me, squeezing me tight in a hug with

booger hands.

"Where did you get that pretty bracelet from?" he asks

when he pulls away, admiring my wrist.

"Ugh, I can't move. Budge. Mum gave it to me." I wiggle

my body for more room, and he giggles, sitting back on the

sofa properly.

I can faintly hear Mum and Dad talking to someone on

the holo-phone in Dad's office. The serious tone in their voices

keeps my attention on the office door.

"Mimi . . ."

"Shh for a sec, Lucas," I hush him.

Mum and Dad must have heard me come in, and if they

hadn't, Spike would have told them telepathically, but they

aven't even come to wave hello.

"Lu-Lu, what's going on with Mum and Dad?" I ask, but

hrugs.

I don't know, Mimi. They've been on the phone for ages

"We'll be back soon. It should take only a couple of hours to get the people out of Ignis. It's not that far, so we're going to bring them back here to Nubis," he says softly, and I breathe in the smell of aftershave on his clothes.

They'll be fine. I know it. I just have to make myself believe it.

I let go of Dad as Mum puts Lucas down.

"Take your brother with you and go to class as normal," Mum says. I make a face, but she only smiles.

"By the time you both get home, we should be back. If not, bed by nine," she follows up.

"Nine thirty," I counter, and Mum smiles.

"Nine fifteen, and that's my final offer." I nod, and she wraps her arms around me, hugging me close. I feel the gentle rise and fall of her chest and my eyes close; I'm holding on to her just as tight. They'll be okay.

We pull apart and she brushes her fingers against my cheek.

"We'll be back soon, my loves. Be good," she tells us.

"Don't worry, children. It's a simple task," Spike says, walking into the living room with Bolt close behind, their golden eyes looking to our parents.

Dad hugs me one last time and kisses Lucas's head.

"What are the family promises?" he asks.

"Always do good listening," Lucas says, puffing out his little chest proudly.

"Always remember the good times," Mum adds.

Dad's smile widens. "Always stick together."

"And it's never goodbye, only see you later," I finish. We bump our fists together and show our necklaces to one another, the pendants flashing. On each of them are four silver sparkling stars, representing all of us.

A connection that solidifies our family promises and keeps us together. Always. The family necklaces are a tradition in Nubis. Each family has different necklaces, but our promises are the best.

Outside, a bright light flashes, and Bolt and Spike change to their natural forms. We all say goodbye once again, and they take off into the forever night with Mum and Dad on their backs.

CHAPTER THREE

Lucas cuddles against me as we watch TV and eat the jerk chicken with fried dumplings and rice and peas that Mum left us for dinner, making sure we leave no crumbs, or Mum will flip. When we finish, I go to wash the dishes, but Lucas calls me over before I can fill the sink with water.

"Mimi, look! Daddy left his door open!"

"What?" I call from the kitchen. "To his office? No way!"

I skid to a stop in the hallway beside the pipsqueak and gasp. Dad is *always* careful to keep this room locked. But it's definitely open now. Through a crack in the door, I glimpse the white wooden desk and smell caramel coffee.

I'm stepping forward when a tiny hand grabs me.

"No, Mimi! We're not allowed."

"I'm just going to peek. If you're gonna be a baby about it, then wait here, and don't snitch, okay?" There's no way I'm missing the chance to see inside Dad's office.

Lucas pushes out his bottom lip and I gently open the door. It welcomes me with a creak. The caramel coffee smell hits me again, and tingles travel up my arms and neck. I take careful steps, as if any second Dad could hear and catch me.

"Mimi, we could get in big-big trouble. . . ."

Ignoring him, I scan the two large bookshelves that stand either side of me, filled with books I've never seen before. So, this is Dad's hideaway world. . . .

Dad's holo-phone is on top of the filing cabinet, and I frown. Why would he leave it? He never goes on a mission without his holo-phone. I've always wanted one, but kids aren't allowed to have them. Without the help of Stella, we don't have the resources to manufacture enough of them. Only adults deemed important enough to carry holo-phones have them— or tamers, in Jada's case.

I pick it up, flicking the screen, but it's locked with an access code. *Of course.* I go to set it back down, but a big red cross flashing over a little bar icon in the top right corner catches my eye.

No signal. Weird. But that's probably why he left it. I place it on the cabinet and walk farther into the room.

The walls are covered with moving pictures, some of our family and some of different types of umbra. At the far end, a giant map of the kingdom of Lunis hangs above his desk. All six cities are displayed across the map, with Stella at the top and Nubis at the very bottom, making a sort of diamond shape. Colored pins are stuck in various places across the Nightmare Plains.

"What is it, Mimi?"

I jump, looking down at my brother. I hadn't even heard him follow me in. The sneaky little guy. I guess he gave up on the whole "we're not allowed" thing.

"It's a map," I tell him. "It shows you where all the cities are, but I don't know what all the pins in the Nightmare Plains mean."

"Why are some things crossed out?"

I clear my throat, staring at the four cities with red crosses over them.

"They're the cities taken by the Darkness. You see the one at the bottom with the cross? That's us. Nubis. We were the second city to be taken. Astaroth was the first. Lunavale—where TJ's from—was third, and Ignis is the fourth now. The two cities without crosses are Stella, the capital city, at the very top, and Nexus, just below it. They are the last two cities lit by a bright fireball in the sky called the sun."

"Mimi, why don't the other cities live in the nighttime too?" Lucas asks, and I smile softly at him. I remember asking

Mum that same question many times when I was younger. I didn't understand why we were the only city that lived in the dark. Why we were different from everyone else.

"Nubis never used to be dark all the time, like it is now. Before we were born, it was a mix of night and sunlight, until the Darkness came and took it away. Mum hasn't been able to prove it yet, but from the old books and the engravings in our city, she's sure that the smoke and darkness come from the Reaper King himself, but it's his minions, the reapers, who attack the cities."

He looks at me, confused. "But Mummy, Daddy, and the tamers stop the bad guys from coming into the city?"

"Yep. Mum and Dad made it possible for everyone to still live here. If it wasn't for them going against the queen's orders to evacuate when the attack happened, everyone in Nubis would probably all be living in Stella or Nexus." Those cities are only big enough to hold so many people, though, and a lot of people are homeless there after escaping the Darkness, but I don't tell that to Lucas.

"I don't think the dark is all bad, Mimi . . . ," Lucas says with a little sigh. I ruffle his hair.

"Same. Some people just don't realize there can be monsters in the light, too."

My eyes fall to Dad's giant desk, and I brush my fingers against the soft leather chair. A single book lies open in front of the computer. When I touch the pages, they feel fragile and a little flimsy—the book is old but has been well-kept for what looks like many years.

The image of a child glowing with a blue light—and holding what looks like a note—fills the right-hand page. Next to the child is a slightly taller child glowing in a purple light, with one hand on the other child's back and a long staff in the other. Beside them are two umbra-looking creatures—deerlike, but with foxtails and a single horn on their heads. Facing them on the opposite page is a creature with bony arms, a hooded face, and a raging red aura. My stomach churns.

The Reaper King.

"What are you looking at, Mimi? Let me see! Let me see!"

"All *right*, stop pushing." I shuffle to the side, and Lucas climbs onto Dad's chair.

"Daddy was reading a story? What's it about?"

"I don't know. . . ." I flip the pages to find some text, but it's in a different language or something. From the pictures, it reminds me of the bedtime stories that Dad tells us. About children with magical powers, who could control the light of both the moon and the sun. Like the old queen, Lucina.

I turn to the front cover and read out loud the sticky note underneath the title, written in Dad's handwriting: "The Umbra Tales: Legends of the Lightcasters. Author unknown."

"What's a lightca-ser, Mimi?" Lucas asks, scratching his head.

"I don't know. Maybe it's linked to the powers that old Queen Lucina had or something."

Lucas asks another question, but I tune him out, thinking of an idea.

"Wait here, okay?" I say, already racing out of the room as Lucas protests, and go upstairs. I come back down with my mini reading tablet and tap the button to make it expand. I focus on the front page of the book and request a search, but to my dismay, the system doesn't find the book in any library in Nubis. Instead I scan the cover and a few random pages, saving the images to examine more closely later.

Taking one last look around, I say, "Come on, we'd better go. And remember, when Mum and Dad come back, *don't* snitch."

"Okay, Mimi." I help him off the chair and tap the side button of my tablet, making it small again. I put it in my pocket and grab my bo staff.

We head out the door, leaving everything as we found it.

When we head out for my martial arts lesson, the town is a lot quieter than it was earlier. Or maybe it just feels that way because I know my parents and most of the other tamers are gone. The tapping of our shoes against the gray cobbled path echoes loudly as we walk the streets of our small city, my hoodie tied around my waist as always. Lucas hums by my side as he plays with the straps of his little bag, and I smile.

"Mimi, look! Sugarbelle flowers!" He lets go of my hand, running over and crouching by the small white bell-shaped flowers growing by a lamppost. He gently traces each petal, completely mesmerized. He takes his mini water bottle out and waters the little flowers before running back to me with a grin.

"Good job," I tell him. He gives me a thumbs-up and holds my hand again as we continue on our way.

In front of his sweetshop, Mr. Willis is cursing at his holophone. He spots us walking past and waves before tapping away at his phone again. I guess all the phones are acting up today. So weird. Lucas's small fingers squeeze my hand, and I smile down at him.

We come to a stop again in front of a huge silver tree in the middle of town with a small fence around it. A few people are on their knees crying before it, and I tug Lucas closer. This is the Missing Tree—a place of mourning for those lost during the Blood Moon. My heart sinks looking at the crystal stars dangling from it, each engraved with the name of a missing person. The silver stars are for the missing adults, and the blue for the children. Maybe this year we'll be lucky and no more names will need to be added. . . .

"Mimi?"

"I'm okay. Let's go," I say, tugging Lucas along.

Sometimes, I wish we could have seen the city before it fell to the Darkness—the bright blue velvet roses and rainbow tulips that

Mum said popped up in every free inch of soil. The giant solar wheels that would spin each time the light hit them, providing electricity for the city, and the huge greenhouse—now used for storing emergency supplies and transport pods—that was once filled with sweet pumpkins, carrots, strawberries, apples, and more.

The moon remains high in the sky, same as always, and hopefully Mum and Dad will be back by the time the stars all connect. You would have thought it was the queen's job to protect the other cities from the Darkness, but just as Dad says, it's "people for people" and "royalty for royalty." The city of Stella has all this technology, and a queen who supposedly has the power to fight off the Darkness, but she doesn't help in any way. She could at least send some of her guards to assist the tamers, but she doesn't.

If we don't save each other, then no one will.

Bently and the other gate guards say it's Queen Katiya's powers that are supposed to keep the cities safe and lit, like Queen Lucina did before her, but she isn't doing a good job, if you ask me. If the Darkness is truly just a leftover echo of power left behind by the Reaper King, then surely she could fight it off? It's been dark in our city for over fifteen years, and even longer than that for Astaroth. But what do I know, right? I'm just a kid born in said dark.

* * *

There's a chill in the air when Lucas and I reach the martial arts dome in the purple field, where our training is held. Tiny red birds with blue-speckled wings glide overhead. Before we join the others inside, I turn and crouch to Lucas's level. "You have to be good, okay? Don't do anything silly."

He gives me a thumbs-up and quickly nods. "I will, Mimi. I'll be really good."

I smile, taking his hand again and walking inside.

For once, TJ is here on time, sitting on the padded floor. When Miles was living with us, we'd save our tokens to spend and always grab a fresh chocolate muffin from Ms. Mabel's market stall before martial arts class, but that isn't happening with Mr. I-Can't-Show-Up-on-Time TJ.

He spots me and jigs his eyebrows at me. "Hey! So, your parents are out on the mission, then? My mum was the one to stay behind to protect the city this time."

"Yeah, hopefully they won't be gone too long," I murmur, but I can't help but feel jealous that his mum got to stay behind.

"Hey, little guy, you good?" TJ asks, and when Lucas nods, his eyes flick back to me. "Since the tamers are out of the city, do you wanna get some ice cream and play dodge-the-sword at my house after? I have to ask Mama, but maybe we can get Mikasa and the others to play too. Mama's made a new flavor of ice cream."

I grin. "Sure, if you don't mind getting your butt beat again. The robot won't hit me this time. Did she manage to fix it?"

"Yeah, last night—so don't break it again."

"I didn't break it!"

"Oh, so the robot just broke itself? It hit you through the sheet fair and square, and you smacked it back. You're only allowed to dodge, not attack." He laughs, and I roll my eyes. That boy is seriously so lucky, though. He gets unlimited ice cream from his mama's dessert café, *and* his other mum's a tamer plus an inventor. We aren't related or anything, but TJ's mums Carly and Lisa are the best and earned "Auntie" status real quick.

"Well, the robot thought it was slick with that last move. I had to put it in its place," I say, crossing my arms, making him laugh even louder. Lucas jumps up and down.

"I wanna play!"

"Sorry, Lu-Lu, you're too tiny," I say, ruffling his curls and flicking his bottom lip when he pokes it out.

"Yeah, sorry, buddy. There's a height requirement," TJ says, waving his hand over Lucas's head.

Mikasa, Thomas, and Lincoln arrive next, with Mr. Lin close behind, and we bow politely to each other. For once, I can just relax. Martial arts is always fun. We have two teachers, Mr. Walsh and Mr. Lin, who are the best martial artists in the kingdom and have mastered various styles and techniques over the years. They're seriously the coolest.

"All right," Mr. Lin says, clapping his hands together.

"Today we'll be focusing on the art of the eight limbs. Let's start with warm-up stretches."

Yes! One of my favorites. A powerful martial arts style that focuses on the eight points of contact: punches, kicks, knees, and elbows. Hard, but the best and most useful.

I can't help but grin as he continues. "Just like last time, we will quickly practice the strengths of both your kicks and punches specifically, then go straight into sparring, but remember to focus on your core, too. Now, who wants to be first?"

My hand and Mikasa's shoot straight up together. We both smirk. Mikasa is a beast at sparring and using a person's strength against them, but so am I. She's the best opponent.

"Okay, McKenna, Mizuhara, you're up first!" he declares. "Now warm up!"

I give Lucas my tablet to hold, and after stretching our limbs, everyone pads up with gloves and shin guards. I partner with TJ to practice my kicks and punches, and in no time the bell dings, announcing it's time to spar.

Everyone sits in a circle around us. I bow before Mikasa and she does the same. We touch gloves together and the fight begins. She goes straight for my legs with a low round kick, but I dodge with a jump, going for a jab to her stomach. We go at it, back and forth, toe to toe. Every bit of my pent-up anger at Mum and Dad leaving is unleashed behind every focused punch. Lucas cheers for me along with TJ, amping me up as

Mikasa and I stumble apart, ready to fight again. I'm determined to win no matter what. I can't lose.

A loud bang rattles the glass roof, and we all freeze. Something dark stirs in the air, and the hairs on the back of my neck and arms rise.

"What *is* that?" Mikasa asks.

A scream pierces the room, making my blood run cold, and TJ sprints to my side along with Lucas. I throw off my gloves and hold Lucas close.

"Everyone, stay here. I'm going to check it out," Mr. Lin orders. We all watch helplessly as our teacher goes outside.

The room is silent, none of us daring to speak. My heart's beating a thousand times a minute and the back of my throat itches, too dry to swallow. I tighten my grip on Lucas, and he hugs me. *We're safe. We're okay.* Nothing's happened yet, but I can't help a scary feeling in the pit of my stomach that something really bad happened to Mum and Dad.

TJ has the same worry in his eyes as he looks at me, staying close. "Why hasn't Mr. Lin come back?"

There's another scream.

"We've got to do something . . . ," Mikasa says, throwing her gloves off too.

"Let's get out of here!" one of the twins says.

Lucas is shivering, so I crouch down to his level and ignore the others. His eyes are squeezed tight and he grips his hair, no one saying a word, everyone else takes off their gloves and shin guards, and we race outside.

Screams rip through the air and giant wafts of smoke drift overhead from the direction of a row of shops. I can see the sign of Ms. Makin's cake and pudding shop go up in flames. My stomach twists as the once-sweet smell of pastry is replaced by burning that stings my nostrils. What in Lunis is happening? Are we actually under attack? Is it the red-eyed umbra? Reapers? I'm frozen to the spot in fear.

"What do we do? Where's Mr. Lin?" Mikasa cries.

Our teacher isn't anywhere in sight. TJ looks toward the gate, but I shake my head.

"No way, TJ. He told us to wait."

"We're useless here," he argues. "And exposed! Whatever's out there is gonna get us if we just stand here."

"He told us to wait here for a reason. We can't just run off," I say, refusing to budge.

Lucas stretches his arms and I pick him up. Another bang rattles the air, and a hole bursts through the wall behind us. Lucas cries, and I stumble back. Through the wafts of smoke, a figure slowly emerges. Mikasa screams, and the other kids scatter, running for their lives.

TJ grabs my arm. "Let's GO!" he yells.

I break off in a sprint with him, Lucas almost choking me as I hold him close. I glance back at the stranger, but I can't

trying to shut everything out. I gently place a hand on his h
like Mum always does.

"Hey, Lu-Lu, look at me," I say, trying my best to keep
voice calm. It takes a moment before he slowly peeks throu
one eye, and I force a smile on my face.

"What do we do when we're scared?" I ask, repeating tl
words Mum would say.

Lucas hiccups and points to his chest, then to me, an
clasps his little fingers together after.

"That's right," I tell him, my eyes prickling with tears. "You,
me, together always. If we stick together, we'll be all right."

I place my hands softly on top of his, and his eyes never
leave mine. "As long as you remember that, you'll always be
okay. I'll always be there for you. That's family promise number
three."

He smiles a little, hiccuping again. "Always?"

I nod. "Always. Do you have your whistle?"

He pulls a second necklace from under his shirt and shows
the small sapphire whistle attached to it. It's a gift I gave him on
his very first birthday. If he's ever lost or in any sort of danger,
all he has to do is blow it, and thanks to the special echo crystal
inside it, I'll hear it, no matter how far away I am. I open my
arms, giving him the biggest hug.

Another crash, closer this time, almost like someone is
blasting through the walls of the city. We all jump again. With

see them properly through the smoke. They only watch as we run off.

Down the street, bloodcurdling screams pierce the air. Doors slam shut, left and right.

"Where are we going, TJ? We should find Jada. She might know what to do," I say, struggling to keep up. Most of the tamers are gone. We have no way to protect ourselves!

We stop in an alleyway, and while I catch my breath, TJ walks to the other end to check out the route.

"Mimi . . . What's going on?" Lucas whispers.

"I don't know," I say. I try to keep my voice from trembling, so I don't scare him.

TJ gestures for me to join him, but before we can move on, we hear voices and footsteps approaching. Grabbing TJ's jean jacket, I pull him and Lucas behind some bins and trash lining the alleyway.

"Mimi, it smells. . . ."

"Shhh!" I put Lucas down and place a finger against my lips.

Two men dressed in dark red cloaks with their hoods up stroll past, exiting the alleyway and turning away from us. Two huge cobra-like umbra with spiked tails and spider legs slither and skitter beside them. My stomach lurches.

They aren't from Nubis.

Beside me, TJ looks worried. "You guys wait here. Mama's shop isn't too far. I wanna see if she's there."

I shake my head. "We should stay together. We have no idea who those people are or what they want. If you're going, we're coming too."

He turns to me and smiles. "I'll be all right. You have to stay here with Lucas. It'll be quicker if I go alone."

As much as I hate to admit it, TJ's right. "All right, be quick." *Be careful.*

TJ nods and slips out of the alley.

Lucas tugs at my shirt. "What are we going to do now?"

"I don't know."

"What—"

"Lucas, I don't know!" I whisper-shout. "We have to be quiet!"

His bottom lip trembles, and I immediately feel bad. I hug him tight. "I'm sorry. When TJ's back, we'll go and see if Mum and Dad are back." They have to be safe. They're the best tamers in the kingdom. Maybe they're back and looking for us right now. That has to be it.

We crouch in silence by the bins. Up ahead, at the end of the alley, someone yells, and there's an abrupt clang that echoes through the alley.

"Put them here, right in the middle. This should get those kids to show themselves!"

Dread washes over me. I take Lucas's hand, and we creep closer to get a better look.

A enormous cage has been brought to the square by a wagon and slammed on the ground. Inside it are a group of people, adults, but two scarily familiar faces stand out in the crowd.

Our parents.

CHAPTER FOUR

Mum and Dad and the other tamers are caged like animals. I can tell from here that Mum is raging, her eyes darting everywhere as she bashes the bars, rattling them. Lucas's eyes widen.

"Ma—" My hand claps over his mouth, and I pull him into the shadows as one of the red-cloaked men walks in front of the alley.

One of the adults in the cage yells, "Let us out!"

"What did you do to all those people in Ignis?" another demands.

"Not so tough now you're all locked up, are you?" a man

in a red cloak says, laughing. "Calm yourselves. That city was gone long before you got there."

What?

I examine his clothes. I can't see the white fox symbol of the queen's crest on their cloaks, or a badge of honor, and I frown. If they're not from Stella, then where?

The adults continue to carry on in the cage, and behind us, at the other opening of the alleyway, children are screaming and crying as they are snatched from the streets by the red-cloaked men and women. Still hidden, I watch in horror as a weird black smoke wafts from the red-cloak guards' hands, engulfing the children's faces.

"These are clear," one of the guards says, releasing two kids who look to be around Lucas's age. The smoke vanishes and the children drop to the ground, coughing violently.

"Keep checking! They're here somewhere."

One of the men in front of us guarding the cage moves behind the structure, and I scurry closer with Lucas, keeping him by my side. On the other side of the metal prison, I can see Spike, Bolt, and all the other tamed umbra standing with weird blue collars wrapped around their necks.

"Why aren't they transforming?" I mutter.

I get my answer when Bolt growls and tries to pounce at one of the red-cloaked men, but an invisible force yanks him down, pinning him to the ground.

Mum spots us just as one of the guards walks over to her, and she averts her eyes quickly. The guard's back is to me, his cloak flapping in the wind. Whatever he says makes her mad enough to try to kick him through the cage. Dad reaches through to grab the man, but he jumps back, swearing and cursing. Mum mutters something to Dad, and he disappears from sight. Seconds later a loud banging and clanging from the other side of the cage captures the gutterslug guard's attention.

"What are you doing? Keep it down!" the guard in front of us yells, walking out of sight to investigate the noise. Mum snaps her head back to us, clutching the bars.

Crouching down, I take Lucas's hand and we quickly, carefully, make our way over to her. Her hands shoot through the bars to caress our faces.

"My babies." Her eyes fill with pain and mine sting as I grab her hand tight. Her palm warms my cheek as I cling to it, and Lucas sniffles, rubbing his cheek into her other hand.

"Listen to me," she whispers. "You have to get out of Nubis and go to Stella. It's your best chance."

I shake my head, unable to take in what she's saying. She can't expect us to just leave without her and Dad? No way!

"Take your brother and go, sweetheart. The City of Light is the only place that will be safe now," Mum continues.

"No. We can't leave you," I say. Nubis is our home, the only place that's ever been safe. Because of our parents. And the rest of the tamers. Stella only has the queen, and what can she do?

The guards are still distracted, and my hand tightens around hers. None of this makes any sense. I'm not ready to leave the walls yet.

"You *have* to go. To keep yourself and your brother safe. Only you two can stop this. Don't let any of the guards grab you, and don't let their smoke touch you. If their smoke touches you, they'll know."

"Know what? Mum, what's happening? Are they reapers?" I'm close to crying, but I try to hold it in. The last time I cried was the day I found out Miles was gone, and the tears feel foreign in my eyes.

"No. Not yet, but, Mia, we don't have time. You know where to go now," she adds. "Go and get the bag. Find your grandparents. They'll take you through the next steps."

The bag. The one they packed in case of an emergency outside the walls. The only other time I had ever gone out into the Nightmare Plains was to see where they buried it. But it was meant for all of us—not just me and Lucas. I shake my head again, trembling.

"I'm not ready, Mummy."

She holds my face tight, staring me straight in the eyes with a confidence that I don't deserve. "You must, Mia. I wish you could have been trained longer, but you can do this. You have the power in you."

"Hey!"

Mum's head snaps left. One of the men has spotted us.

"Go, sweetheart. Reach the City of Light and you can save everyone."

"Get those damn kids!"

With blurry eyes, I snatch Lucas's hand and pull him away. We run, not looking back.

"Mama!" Lucas yells, but I don't let go.

We have a head start, but the stampeding feet of the men are not far behind. My hold on Lucas's hand only gets stronger and he yells out, digging his feet into the ground in protest.

"We don't have time for this, Lucas. COME ON! We have to get out of here!"

I scoop him up as he thrashes about, doing my best to run with him. He weighs me down and I almost lose my balance. I shift him in my arms, but he keeps flailing. Pivoting, I grab a bin lid and throw it behind us. I hear it clang into the men, but they're only slowed down for a moment, and I hear their footsteps begin again, even more pounding and determined.

"I want Mummy!"

"We have to *move*, Lucas! They're after us!"

We race across the street, into the midst of crying and yelling. The men and women in red cloaks are still dragging children from their homes, their parents and grandparents clinging to them, but to no avail. *Why are they taking kids?*

The red cloaks stare into the faces of each child they take, forcing the strange smoky shadows in their hands to engulf them.

"Got you!" A hand yanks me from behind, and I scream, letting go of Lucas. He tumbles to the ground, and I whip my head around, staring straight into the angry eyes of a red-cloaked man.

"Lucas! Run!" I slap and thrash against my captor's arms. I elbow him in the gut, scraping the heel of my shoe against his shin. He hisses but refuses to let go.

"Hold still, you little brat!"

Mum's words ring in my head. *Don't get grabbed; don't let the smoke touch you!*

I've already failed her.

The man raises his hand to my face and I scream, twisting and turning, my heart pounding. Then I freeze.

A shadow puffs out of his hand and slowly creeps toward my face. I thrash my head around, squeezing my eyes shut, expecting to choke.

Panic sets in, and what feel like little electric sparks spread across my body like wildfire, and I scream so loud the back of my throat burns. "I SAID GET OFF ME!"

My eyes fly open and his hand snaps back. The shadows blow away, as if repelled by an invisible wind. The man gasps, yelling in pain, and his grip on me loosens.

In that split second I grab his arm. I wrap the back of my leg around his and force myself forward, just as I've learned in martial arts class. I throw the man over me, using his own weight against him, and he crashes to the ground, yelling and cursing. Rolling forward, I strike him straight in the stomach.

"Take that, you gutterslug!"

He cries out, winded. "You're the one! Get back here!"

"Mimi! What—"

Snatching Lucas's hand, I make a dash for it back through town, leaving the man yelling for help on the ground.

Screams continue to fill the air, and I almost crash into Mr. McKinley's door as I race down the street. I round the corner, but a red-cloaked woman stands at the other end of the narrow street. I turn back around and see two more guards behind us. *No, no, no!*

"There's nowhere to run," one of them laughs, and they start to close in. I cuddle Lucas close to my chest, and he buries his head in my neck. The weight of him forces me to my knees, but my arms refuse to let go.

"Get away!" I scream, and I look up at the red-cloaked guards as they approach. Maybe I could take out the two behind us, and Lucas could run—but what if she grabbed Lucas before he could get away? We're trapped.

Someone clears their throat noisily. The men and women surrounding us hesitate, roll their eyes, and come to a stop, stepping aside to let someone through. I narrow my eyes, trying to see who it is, but with the smoke filling the city, the person is hazy, the face unclear.

"Hey, Supernova."

I freeze. As he approaches, a pale boy dressed completely in black from his shirt to his sneakers becomes clear, standing before us with his hands in his pockets. I have no idea what to think or say as recognition hits me like a punch to the gut.

"Miles?"

CHAPTER FIVE

His short black, wavy hair is just how I remember it. And that familiar lopsided grin and chill stance make me feel weirdly warm all over. The guards fade into the background, and if it weren't for Lucas, I'd be sure this was a dream. *Miles Tanaka is here. . . .*

"What? You're not gonna say anything?" He chuckles, his voice a little different than I remember. Deeper.

It's so . . . weird.

My lips curve into the biggest smile, and memories rush into my brain. My best friend is actually back.

There's so much I want to say, *need* to say, but all the words turn to mush. The chaos of whatever is happening falls away and I race over to him, squeezing him tight.

The warmth of his body is real. My eyes sting. It feels like only yesterday we were playing in the city. *Miles.*

My vision blurs, but I hug him even tighter, remembering all the adventures we had. Scared that if I let go, he will poof into thin air and this really will be just a dream.

I can almost hear the squeals and laughs of our little-kid selves. For hours, we would play in our secret garden, a small lot filled with flowers that glowed every Sky Connect, all the stars in the sky bound by a single silver line, signaling a new day. He could spot all the pictures in the sky, even when I wouldn't see one, only the normal constellations in the sky that were there all the time. He always had starlight in his soul.

My eyes slowly open as I realize . . . he's not hugging me back.

"I've missed you, too, Mia." Miles's voice throws me, soft as the wind, but empty. No excitement, no . . .

"Mimi! Be careful! The bad people aren't leaving!"

I whip my head up and stare at the men behind Miles. Lucas is right. Something is off.

"Wait . . ." I feel a sudden chill in my spine. I look at the red cloaks, then to Miles.

They moved out of the way *for* Miles. I start to pull away, but he snatches my wrist.

"Stay still." His voice is a whisper, meant for my ears only, but I shake my head, noticing that all the red-cloaked men and women take a step closer. "Don't move."

I look back at Miles. His face is serious.

"Miles, my mum and dad are captured right now," I say. "Those people behind you trapped them in a cage like animals."

"I know."

I freeze again. This isn't making any sense. "Let go."

"No." His words slice through me as I realize the awful truth—Miles is part of the invasion.

I don't know what to do, what to believe, what to think, but my gut screams one single thing as I look at the enemies around us:

Run. Now.

"Lucas, come here." My throat is dry as I stare Miles in the eyes. I hear Lucas scramble to his feet and feel him gently crash into my side.

I take his hand.

"Mimi . . . Who is that?"

Miles's eyes shift to him.

I ignore him—how can I explain that he used to live with us sometimes, that he once was practically family?—and instead whisper, "What are you doing here, Miles?"

My eyes fall on a creature stalking behind him in the shadows, just out of sight. How in Lunis does *he* have an umbra? *None of this makes sense! What the flip is going on?*

"We're looking for someone," he replies, smiling down at Lucas, before shifting his attention back to me.

"Who?"

"Don't know." He shrugs. "That's why we're checking everyone. But once we find them, they'll be able to free the true king. Now keep still. I'll be quick. I promise."

The true king? He couldn't mean . . .

He squeezes my wrist tighter, breaking into my thoughts, es his other hand toward my face. I snatch my hand ck as lightning, and stumble away with Lucas. Rage rough my veins as I glare at Miles, and he shakes his

"Don't be like that, Mia. We won't hurt any of you. We're just looking for—" He cuts off with a startled look and puts a hand to his ear. I glimpse a small device there and frown. Whatever the person says makes Miles's nose scrunch up. For a split second, his face looks troubled before he sighs and looks at me.

"Well, Supernova, looks like you're the one we're looking for. Typical."

"What are you talking about?" I ask. I wonder if it had omething to do with that man who grabbed me earlier. That moke . . .

"I should have known it'd be you." He smirks, but for some reason, his eyes waver. Hesitating. "Mia, make this easy and just come with me, okay?"

Over my dead body.

I spot the mystery umbra again and hover my hand over my bo staff. The guards seem uneasy at the creature's presence, but it's still just out of sight for me, blending with the shadows and the night. I swallow down nausea as I wonder where Miles has been and what's happened to him these past three years. Was it his parents? He always seemed happier when he st with us, or maybe Dad was right, and he . . . changed.

My fist shakes. *No.* Something happened to him have to save him, too, then so be it. Starting with who the other end of that earpiece.

There's a low growl, and fear squeezes me as I realize the shadowy creature has now moved up right behind Miles. Its floppy, bunny-like ears and doglike form strike a chord, and my knees almost give way when I spot the red eyes.

"Guess you remember Shade, huh?"

Miles brushes his pale fingers against the black fur of the hellhound umbra and laughs. It's the very creature from my nightmares. From the Nightmare Plains.

"Funny story," Miles says with a chuckle that makes m blood run cold. "Turns out my parents and some others we experimenting with new ways of taming umbra to help fr

"I should have known it'd be you." He smirks, but for some reason, his eyes waver. Hesitating. "Mia, make this easy and just come with me, okay?"

Over my dead body.

I spot the mystery umbra again and hover my hand over my bo staff. The guards seem uneasy at the creature's presence, but it's still just out of sight for me, blending with the shadows and the night. I swallow down nausea as I wonder where Miles has been and what's happened to him these past three years. Was it his parents? He always seemed happier when he stayed with us, or maybe Dad was right, and he . . . changed.

My fist shakes. *No.* Something happened to him, and if I have to save him, too, then so be it. Starting with whoever's on the other end of that earpiece.

There's a low growl, and fear squeezes me as I realize the shadowy creature has now moved up right behind Miles. Its floppy, bunny-like ears and doglike form strike a chord, and my knees almost give way when I spot the red eyes.

"Guess you remember Shade, huh?"

Miles brushes his pale fingers against the black fur of the hellhound umbra and laughs. It's the very creature from my nightmares. From the Nightmare Plains.

"Funny story," Miles says with a chuckle that makes my blood run cold. "Turns out my parents and some others were experimenting with new ways of taming umbra to help free ows, just out of sight. How in Lunis does *he* have an umbra? *None of this makes sense! What the flip is going on?*

"We're looking for someone," he replies, smiling down at Lucas, before shifting his attention back to me.

"Who?"

"Don't know." He shrugs. "That's why we're checking everyone. But once we find them, they'll be able to free the true king. Now keep still. I'll be quick. I promise."

The true king? He couldn't mean . . .

He squeezes my wrist tighter, breaking into my thoughts, and raises his other hand toward my face. I snatch my hand back, quick as lightning, and stumble away with Lucas. Rage pulses through my veins as I glare at Miles, and he shakes his head.

"Don't be like that, Mia. We won't hurt any of you. We're just looking for—" He cuts off with a startled look and puts a hand to his ear. I glimpse a small device there and frown. Whatever the person says makes Miles's nose scrunch up. For a split second, his face looks troubled before he sighs and looks at me.

"Well, Supernova, looks like you're the one we're looking for. Typical."

"What are you talking about?" I ask. I wonder if it had something to do with that man who grabbed me earlier. That smoke . . .

the king. Shade here was a test run when we came across her. But it didn't go down well in Nubis when the other tamers found out."

What? I stare at the shadowy beast, fighting against the fear.

She snarls, baring her sharp canine teeth at us, making Lucas whimper.

"Anyway, we don't have time to waste." Miles walks forward and I find my feet, stepping back until I hit the guard behind me.

"What happened to you, Miles?" I whisper.

The huge shadowy hellhound walks up behind him, each step calculated, like a predator stalking prey.

"You don't have to be afraid. Just come with me, Mia," Miles says, reaching his hand out again.

"What makes you think I'm afraid of you?" I ask, keeping one eye on the umbra.

"Because you're shaking."

He grins, staring down at me, and suddenly the fear leaves me and a strange calm takes over.

"Lucas, go wait by the wall." I push him a little behind me, and after some resistance, he does as I tell him.

Miles reaches out to touch me and I flinch away. The red cloaks begin to move in, but Miles stops them with a wave of his hand. He thinks he can take me on his own.

"Look. You can trust me," he says, walking closer.

I can't help but laugh. "Bog off with that . . . You're *with* them."

He sighs. "Mia, you're going to have to come with me, so you might as well just follow now. Nothing will happen to you. I promise." He starts walking off, expecting me to follow, but my feet stay planted to the ground.

"Do I look like Pippy the Clown to you? You can't just turn up with your earpiece and cages and expect everyone to bow down," I say. "You better free my parents and everyone else right now." I wish my voice sounded stronger, but it's the best I can manage while keeping my hands from shaking.

He laughs, but I'm unflinching, and his smile drops.

"Come on, Mia, and bring your brother."

"I think you need to fix your hearing problem, mate." Old best friend or not, every instinct inside me warns me not to follow.

His eyes glance to his umbra, Shade. She looks back at him, and I realize they're communicating.

Before they can get the jump on me, I yank my bo staff from my thigh and click the button, and it bursts out to full size. At full length, it's taller than me, ready to fight off any red-eyed umbra. It shakes in my grip, but I turn toward Miles's hellhound, concentrating fully on the beast. She snaps her jaws at me, teeth as sharp as a shark's, licking her lips like I'm her next meal. She paws the ground, feeling it out, and I spread my feet apart. My heart is thumping, my palms sweaty. *Don't be scared. Don't be scared.*

My body stiffens as her voice seeps inside my mind, a whisper that works its way into my very being.

"This will be fun . . ."

Determined not to let her get to me, I shove the voice out my mind and close the door shut, just like I did that day.

Miles's voice rings out. "Shade—get her."

The shadow dog pounces on Miles's command, and Lucas screams. I step back and use my staff to smack the umbra with full force. She skids and I jump away, twirling the staff with my fingers.

"Try again, you creepy mutt," I tell her. I try to stay calm, feeling the strength flowing from my hands. I can do this. A growl rumbles from the beast's chest, and she launches at me again. I jerk the pole up with both hands, jamming it between her teeth, feeling her hot breath against my face. Face-to-face, brown eyes to red eyes. My toes dig into the ground, but she pushes me back. Lucas cries out, and in the corner of my eye, Miles moves. My ex-friend's face is so red with anger that I can almost see flames flickering in his eyes.

"What's—the matter—Miles? Can't fight me yourself—so, you send—your puppy?"

My heart's ready to leap out of my throat, but something else stirs too, like a spark rising up inside. He might have an umbra, but it doesn't mean he's better than me. I won't let this monster haunt me anymore. I snap my head back to the red eyes that have haunted my dreams all these years and push back.

"Mimi! Look out!!" Lucas gasps.

My focus shifts as I spot Miles taking a rope gun out of his pocket.

The hellhound bites at the pole and I hiss. I'm pinned. A crackling sound hits my ears as the rope gun fires a net, trapping me.

"Mimi!"

"Lucas, run!" He jumps, his little legs shaking as he looks down the path and back at me. All around us the red cloaks still ready to grab him if ordered. "Now!"

"I don't think so," Miles says. "I need both of you."

He's about to grab my little brother when a loud squawk screeches through the air. My eyes widen as a familiar shadow-feathered beast swoops down.

"Ruby!"

With a mighty flick of her tail, she sends Miles and Shade flying.

"Get going. I'll catch up!" Jada calls out from atop the shadow bird as someone else jumps off.

I can't quite believe my eyes as TJ runs over and cuts the rope with a dagger. He helps me up as relief washes through me and I grab my bo staff from the ground—I've never been so happy to see the goofball.

"Mia, let's go!"

The red cloaks spring into action, rushing toward us. Ruby squawks and pushes them back with her tail, just in time.

I step over to Lucas and grab his hand. "Can you run?" I ask him, and he nods.

"I think so, Mimi. . . ."

The three of us make a break for it.

I can hear Miles yelling, and I flinch as the umbra collide and fight behind us, the ground rumbling from the impact.

"Get out of my way! Stupid bird!"

TJ grips my other hand as our city burns with fire and chaos around us.

"Did you find your mums?" I ask.

TJ's eyes narrow. "They weren't at the shop."

Dread swirls inside me.

"Where now?" I ask as we round a corner and take a moment to catch our breath. TJ rests his hands on his knees.

"Yeah . . . about that," he says, puffing. "I didn't really have a plan past this point."

Mum's words echo in my mind. *Get out of Nubis.* I almost don't want to repeat what she told me, but I force myself. "Mum said to go to Stella. My grandparents live there. She said if we get there, we can stop this somehow."

"The City of Light? All right, got it. Let's go!" He picks up the pace, making me race after him carrying Lucas, but trusting without question.

"Wait, you clown! We can't go yet. Do you even know how far it is? Besides, we have to get Mum and Dad's emergency stash first."

"Okay, and maybe we can find a travel pod too."

"But we don't have an umbra."

Whether he hears me or not, he keeps running. It takes like a day to get to Stella on an umbra or in a travel pod, and on foot—forget it! We need a proper plan first. The Nightmare Plains are called that for a reason—they are dangerous. Still, determination is written all over his face.

Our shoes echo on the cobbles, and the giant metal gate comes into view. It's the only thing keeping us from the monsters on the other side, and my skin crawls as I skid to a stop.

"What are you doing? Come on!" TJ says, but I hesitate. We have no means of protection, only my bo staff and TJ's dagger and slingshot. No Jada, no Mum and Dad, but a four-year-old little brother to look after. A shiver runs down my spine. What if Mum is wrong? Maybe we should wait it out until the red cloaks leave, or until Jada finds us.

"Mimi, TJ. There's someone at the gate." Lucas points.

We both look ahead and see one of the red-cloaked men

now standing in front of the gate with a giant umbra. It's the shape of a rhino, with a huge horn and a long, horselike tail. Its eyes are as red as a Blood Moon, just like that hellhound. I gulp. But still . . . I got lucky against Shade. I don't think I could best another like her again.

"Great," TJ says. "So all we have to do is grab the man, beat him up, then lock him and his stinkin' umbra in Mr. Willis's sweetshop. Easy. I can do it with my eyes closed."

I shoot TJ a look, and he zips his lips with an awkward grin.

I stare ahead, drilling every inch of my brain for an idea.

"TJ, go distract him. Lucas and I will make a break for it and open the gate for you."

The boy whips his head around, looking at me like I just told him to run around naked or something. "No way!" He presses his arms together to make a cross. "You want my butt to be on the line? Get out of here. You do it!"

I quickly make a cross with my fingers. "If I get caught, who'll protect Lucas?"

"I'll look after him. Right, buddy?"

Lucas smiles gently and bumps his tiny fist with TJ. *Traitor.*

"He's little, he's confused ninety percent of the time."

Lucas wiggles out of my grip and frowns.

"I'm not confused, I'm intelli-gunt." He shakes his little fist, and I blink at him.

"It's 'intelligent,' and you don't even know what it means."

"It means a good word." He sticks his tongue out at me, like he's the smartest kid in the world or something. I shake my head, focusing on the gate.

The guard doesn't move an inch. His eyes slowly scan back and forth, but he hasn't seen us yet. His umbra is sniffing the ground. My bo staff wouldn't even dent that beast, and it's made with steel bolts from Mum's old crossbow and arrows.

"There's always plan B," TJ whispers, giving me the side-eye.

"What's that?" I ask.

"We run for it."

"That's basically plan A," I tell him. "Okay, forget it. You only live once. Let's go!"

"GO, GO, GO!" Lucas yells as I grab his hand.

"They'll never take us alive!" TJ screams.

We break out in a sprint, screaming at the top of our lungs. The guard snaps his head round, dipping his hand into his pocket, and I grab my staff and click the button. It shoots out to full length, and I ready myself.

"Don't even think about it, gutterslug!" I let go of Lucas's hand and pivot left, twirling the staff and smacking it into the guard, yelling at Lucas and TJ to keep going.

The man hisses, rubbing his arm as they slip past him to

the gate. I hit the man's stomach, rolling out of the way as his umbra stampedes after me, thrusting his horn.

I duck as the man tries to grab me, bringing my weapon up and striking him square in the chin. My body feels electrified as I jump away from the shadowy rhino, but my legs wobble.

"DO IT NOW!" I yell.

TJ races to the lever that works the gate, and I take another swing at the guard. The staff collides with his umbra's horn as his shadow partner protects him, making me growl. TJ pulls the lever up and the gate rumbles, slowly sliding up.

"You little brat. Enough!" The man's eyes rage. He jerks forward, trying to grab me again, but I backflip out of the way and swat his legs with my staff, rolling away from his stampeding creature. *We're so close!*

As soon as there's enough space, TJ shoves Lucas under the gate before squeezing under himself, watching through the gap. The adrenaline keeps me moving, as I dodge every lunge from the umbra's horn and attempted grab from the man, waiting for the right moment.

A whinny screeches through the air and something collides with the red cloak's umbra, forcing the beast back. From out of nowhere, a tall shadow creature the size of a horse but with flower antennae and butterfly-shaped wings has swooped in and floored both guard and umbra.

I hear TJ gasp. "Mum!"

Auntie Carly runs up to me, her clothes in tatters and blood staining her shirt.

"Mia, you and Lucas need to go to the City of Light," she says breathlessly. "Take TJ with you too. Jada will find you. Now run! More are coming!"

"Mum! Where's Mama? Is she safe?" TJ calls out as I sprint for the gate.

Auntie Carly attacks the guard, who is back on his feet. Both of them transform into their third forms with their umbra. Their weapons clash, sending out a shock wave that rattles the ground, throwing me toward the gate.

"Just. Go!" Auntie Carly yells through clenched teeth.

"Come on, Mimi!" Lucas shouts.

"Let's go, Mia! Super ninja! You can make it!" TJ yells.

I flick down the gate lever, reversing it, and slide under the gate before it shuts. I spin around as a bright light explodes from Auntie Carly and the red-cloaked guard, blinding us. The shadows of their umbra surround them as the gate slides shut.

"Mum!" TJ yells. Loud bangs rattle the gate from the inside, and I pull him back.

"We need to go!"

"But my mum! She can make it."

"We'll come back for her. I promise! We'll come back for all of them!" *Even Miles.*

With one last look, I grab Lucas and we run as fast as we can.

My legs feel heavy as bricks as reality kicks in. We're actually out in the open. We're in the Nightmare Plains, among the monsters . . . with no protection.

CHAPTER SIX

You're never alone in the Nightmare Plains. I learned that three years ago.

Everything's alive.

The air's cold as we slow down. With each breath, I feel like we're about to be jumped by monsters that are waiting in the shadows. Foxes and badgers run away at the sight of us, and every step is like we're treading on eggshells, waiting for something to happen.

Bony trees twitch in the wind, with crooked-branch arms and holes in the trunks that look like faces. Bloodred carnivorous plants snap at our ankles, and this time there aren't any

flowery rosy-dill plants to comfort me. The smell of dirt and pine fills my nose instead.

My eyes sting from the oni-weeds that hide among the grass, and memories of that shadow dog haunt my mind.

"Maybe we should go back," I say. I'm not ready for this. "We could sneak back in and figure out a way to open the cage. Maybe one of the red-cloak guys has a key or—"

TJ shakes his head. "We can do this, Mia."

"But we just left them there. . . ." *What if they're being hurt?*

He takes my hand and squeezes it, staring me dead in the eyes.

"You didn't leave them. Your mum told you to go. Just like mine did. Don't look back now. Only forward."

"I'm scared . . . ," I whisper, and grit my teeth. Of all the places to be, why did it have to be here? TJ squeezes my hand tighter, but my eyes burn with tears.

"I know. I'm scared too," he says. "And I want to save my mums too, but to do that we have to find help. Okay?"

For the first time in a while, TJ's face is completely serious. Not a joke or anything in sight. The severity of the situation is almost suffocating the both of us. We're really out here alone, with no one else to help us.

I nod, wiping my eyes, and look down as Lucas holds my other hand.

"Don't cry, Mimi. You can borrow my safety whistle," he offers. I force a smile, wiping my eyes again as the tears fall.

"Thanks Lu-Lu, but you keep it." I stroke his head and he smiles back.

TJ is right: we've come this far. Mum and Dad are counting on me. A loud bang sounds by the gate, and we jump.

"Let's get the bag! It should be this way!" I yell, hiccuping. There's no going back now. I force my feet forward.

As we carry on ahead, we slow our pace to a brisk walk. I jump at every snap of a twig, twisting and turning my long sleeves, just waiting to get jumped by those red cloaks, but overall it's quiet. TJ sniffs beside me, but I don't think it's the oni-weeds that are bothering him.

"I bet your mum kicked that guy's butt," I say.

He nods, quickly wiping his eyes and forcing a smile.

"Yeah, maybe she's saving everyone right now. . . ."

I nod, but gently sigh, and so does he. We both know there's a scary chance that she didn't win. That she's probably joined my parents in the cage. Trapped. A metallic taste of blood fills my mouth from chewing my lip. Maybe, just maybe, if we reach the City of Light somehow, we'll be able to save them all. But what are we supposed to do when we get there? And . . . what if we fail?

"This is something else . . . ," TJ mutters under his breath. "I don't remember the plains being so . . ."

". . . scary," I finish, and he gulps, nodding. *I never forgot.*

"Do you think they're still after us?" he asks.

"Yeah," I whisper, looking over my shoulder, hearing another bang.

TJ had traveled to Nubis with his mums when his home, the city of Lunavale, got taken by the Darkness over a year ago. I'll never forget the day we met. It was at the old dessert shop that his mums decided to buy and fix up. He snuck me an extra scoop of honey-crunch ice cream after I had shown him how to flip someone over his shoulder onto the floor, and we've been friends ever since.

"Hey, Mia?" TJ says, serious. "Do you think everyone in Nubis is going to be okay?"

He looks down, and I nudge him. It's my turn to comfort him.

"Of course. Everyone in our city is superstrong, and they'll look out for each other. Plus, we have tamers. Those red-cloak guys are gonna lose." He smiles, nodding softly as I try my best to believe my own words. I spot three silver trees with oddly twisted branches and dark blue leaves in the distance and point at them.

"Look! We're almost there. This way, quick!" I offer my hand to Lucas, and we're off.

"Hey, slow down!" TJ calls.

"It should be over here somewhere! Come on." I wade through the high grass, which is nearly as tall as Lucas.

"What should be here?" TJ calls out.

"My mum and dad's emergency pack, you goofball. I told you."

He blinks, before grinning. "Oh yeah . . . Why do you guys even have an emergency pack anyway?"

"They made the bag and hid it the day Miles and the others left Nubis. Maybe they saw all this coming. I don't know." I just wish Mum and Dad hadn't kept so much from me. Then again, maybe all the signs were there, and I just missed them.

Apart from that day three years ago, Lucas and I have only been on the plains once with Mum and Dad, and that was just to show me where the emergency bag was hidden. I remember joking about them being overprepared for anything, but I never imagined we'd actually be using it, especially without them. They always seemed to have a plan.

I fall to my knees in front of the middle tree. It's a little shorter than the other two, with a slight shimmer to the branches in the moonlight.

Right in the middle of the trunk are small *L* and *D* engravings entwined in a heart. Many years ago, Mum and Dad met under this very tree. I can't help but smile at the story Mum's told me so many times.

It was before Darkness had taken over our town, when the sun would light the lands, disappearing for only a few hours before coming back. There wasn't a need for any walls to protect us back then. Mum said the houses would shimmer and all kinds of plants and flowers would grow—red and pink apples, and vines with grapes as sweet as sugar. I wish I knew what it was like. Now all our fruit comes from the city of Stella. When they decide to be generous, that is.

The umbra existed during those times too, as Nubis was still lit for a long while after the Reaper King's fall, but no one knew you could tame them. Mum grew up in the city of Stella and trained to become part of the Queen's Guard and part of their scientist program. She was traveling to Nubis on an errand as a newly appointed scientist of Stella when she met Dad, right here under this tree. His transport pod had malfunctioned, and she stopped to help. Dad fell in love with her at first sight. It took Mum a little longer, though. She said she wanted to make sure he was worthy of her time.

I find myself grinning as I tap at different parts along the bottom of the trunk. After a few tries, something pops, and I pull the camouflaged panel from the tree, revealing a gap inside. Tucked away behind is a big brown backpack. "Got it!"

TJ helps me yank it out with one good tug. He wipes away the dirt like we've found an ancient treasure. "This is so cool. What's inside?"

But when I go to open it, the sounds of chains clanging and metal scraping screeches through the air.

"Those brats can't have gone far. Find them and bring them back!" a man's voice roars. Something about it is familiar, but TJ's tugging breaks my attention.

"Let's go," he whisper-shouts, swinging the backpack over his shoulder.

In the distance, the men and women in red cloaks file out the gate. Some are riding their umbra, and others are on foot. We make a break for it through the tall grass. Lucas's hand squeezes mine as I scan the surroundings for a place to hide.

"There!" In a panic, I point to a giant howling tree. "All of us can fit in that."

It stands taller than any other tree, and a giant hole gapes at the bottom of the hollow trunk. Back in Nubis, Miles and I used to play in these types of trees all the time. I would climb to the top and Miles would stay at the bottom, whispering something in the hole and letting the tree carry his voice all the way up to where I was. He always made everything fun. . . .

Lucas crawls in first, then me, then TJ. We huddle together as voices yell for us to show ourselves. Hooves trample the ground outside and I hold Lucas tight, feeling the anger boil. Maybe we shouldn't have left. We should have found Jada, and she could have helped us save Mum and Dad, and we could have all escaped together.

Boots stomp right by the tree and I flinch, squeezing my eyes shut. *Please don't find us. Please don't find us.* I get ready to run, but then the footsteps begin to fade. When they're nothing more than a gentle pitter-patter in the distance, I let out a heavy breath. TJ sighs and wipes his forehead.

"That was close. . . . You cool?" he asks. I nod. How the flip are we going to get to Stella with a search party after us?

"Are we gonna be okay now?" Lucas asks.

"I don't know. Maybe," I say. I couldn't lie. He needs to be alert just as much as me and TJ.

When everything sounds quiet, we file out of the tree and look around. TJ places the bag down and I crouch beside him, opening it up and pulling everything out. There's a star scope that lets us see all the way to the stars. An address compass, lunar torches, well-preserved food packs, water, a blanket . . . My fingers pause over a photo.

"What's that, Mimi?" Lucas asks, leaning on my leg. He almost makes me topple over, but I steady myself and show him. It's the four of us: Me, him, Mum, and Dad. It was a day at the lake, the one part of the city that has still water you can swim in. So pretty, and clear like a mirror. We're standing in front of it; Mum has her arms around me, while Lucas sits on Dad's shoulders with a big cheesy grin on his face. My chest tightens from the memory. Mum was wearing her favorite perfume that day, and I can almost smell the sweet rosy-dill scent. She looks like a true queen. Dad was freshly shaved. Me and Mum had ganged up on him to shave off the beard that always made our faces itch whenever he kissed our cheeks.

The backs of my eyes start to sting, so I stuff the picture back in the bag, zipping it up along with my feelings.

"Mimi . . . ?"

I give Lucas the best smile I can muster up, but something tells me that even a four-year-old can see right through it.

"Look, there's a map," TJ says, scrolling it out. I quickly wipe my eyes with my sleeve and look at the map of Lunis, similar to the one in Dad's office, but with much more detail.

"There!" He taps his finger on the one spot that's been circled, and the three of us look at each other. Just as Mum said, our destination is clear . . . Stella, the City of Light. The distance from Nubis to Stella stretches overwhelmingly over the paper. *Oh boy* . . .

"So, your parents really do want us to go there. . . ." TJ groans.

"You've changed your tune. Weren't you the one saying, 'Let's go. Let's go'?" I say, eyeing him.

"Yeah, I was just caught up in the moment. These sneakers aren't meant for long distance. They're premium."

"So now they're about to be well-loved and walked in," I say. "Let's go."

I pack up the map and everything else in the bag, then swing it over my shoulder and take hold of Lucas's hand. At least we have an address compass, so we'll know exactly where to go when we get to Stella.

As much as I don't like it, Mum made it clear. We don't have a choice. We have to survive. She said we'd be able to save everyone if we went to Stella. I have to try and believe that at least, especially since I ran like a coward. Nan and Grandad might be able to help us, though I can't believe that gutterslug queen is an option.

Anyway, we have a plan, and that's what matters. A new-found determination fuels me, and the doubts of before are slowly buried, for now.

The three of us make our way deeper into the Nightmare Plains. Definitely past our bedtime. We travel for what feels like hours, but checking the stars, it can't actually have been more than one. We take it in turns carrying Lucas, who drifts in and out of sleep, and ration the water to only a few sips when needed, but it's hard to stop Lucas drinking more than he should.

"Are we even going the right way?" TJ asks, and I nod.

"If we keep going this way, we should eventually reach Ignis—" I cut myself off, feeling a sudden chill. A twig snaps and I whip my head around, but nothing's there but a little green red-eared squirrel that scurries in the grass. We haven't seen one of the red cloaks since we started walking, but they could be anywhere.

Then the wind stirs around us and an ear-piercing squawk shatters the silence. Before we can hide, something thuds in front of us, making me stumble backward. A huge, shadowy bird stands before us, her wings glistening like diamonds in the moonlight.

"Ruby!" Lucas squeals, letting go of me and running to the black phoenix, who is four times his size. She lowers her long neck down to his level, gently bumping her head against his, letting him brush his fingers against her feathers. I hold my trembling hand still. Great, even Lucas is braver than me.

"You guys made it out. I'm impressed."

I sigh in relief as Jada slides down from Ruby's back, landing silently in front of us. Despite her confidence, the tiredness in her eyes is obvious. The bruises and scratches on her arms suggest that the fight with Miles was brutal. But weirdly, I hope he's all right too.

"You guys had me worried there," Jada continues. "Guess I trained you well."

"You only trained us half a day, mate," TJ says.

She shoots him a look. "I wasn't talking about you, lackey."

I laugh and we bump fists. For the first time since escaping, genuine hope fills my heart.

TJ puffs out his chest. "Well, everything happens for a reason. Besides, it was close, but I saved us."

I jab my elbow into his side, and he hisses.

"Mimi saved us," Lucas says. I grin and TJ rolls his eyes.

"That's a minor detail," he says, flicking his wrist.

Jada looks at Ruby, who takes off into the air, flying over our heads into the distance. Everyone is silent for a moment. TJ and Jada are trying to keep the mood light, but the reality of the situation is sinking in. Our parents are captured. Our city is taken. And it's down to us to save it and everyone inside.

"Where's the birdie going?" Lucas asks.

"I asked her to scout around to make sure there's no one close by. It was tough getting out," Jada says. Her eyes lock onto my bag, and I take it off my shoulder.

"But I didn't hear you say anything," Lucas says.

"I spoke to her through my mind," she says, smiling at him as she walks over to me.

Lucas drags out an *ooh* and smiles. "Mummy and Daddy does that sometimes, I think."

I show Jada everything in the emergency pack as quickly as I can. I feel better with her here, but being out in the open like this still has me on edge. It's like something is constantly watching us.

"Mum told us to go to Stella. I have grandparents there who may be able to help," I explain, zipping the bag back up and giving it to TJ. He can take a turn to carry it.

Jada grabs the map right from my hands. "You bet they can. And we have to tell the queen about this. All the holo-phones are down in Nubis, so no one could call." She looks behind us. "I don't think anyone but us managed to get out, but you guys are all that matter."

I arch an eyebrow. "What do you—"

"Yeah, but we can't just rock up and ask to speak to the queen," TJ interrupts.

"We don't need her. My grandparents will know what to do," I say. The queen hasn't exactly done a good job of helping the other fallen cities. Mum and Dad and the other tamers did that.

"No offense, but how are your grandparents gonna help?" he asks.

I don't actually know. "Mum just said we can stop this if I find my grandparents."

"And she's right," says Jada. "But we don't have time to talk about that right now. We need to focus on getting out of here and finding a place to rest."

I can't help but want to ask more about Miles. About what he meant when he mentioned the true king rising again. In the pit of my stomach, I have a feeling I know who he means, but for now I keep my mouth shut.

Jada focuses on the map as we begin walking, drawing pathways with her finger from the plains to the City of Light. "The quickest route to Stella is through Ignis, Bone Valley, and the swamp. . . . It's not going to be easy, especially with only

Ruby to fight if something gets in the way . . ." Her head snaps up to us, and I blink, not liking the look in her eyes.

"Sorry, guys, we're going to have to skip a few lessons. If we're going to survive, you guys are going to have to become tamers."

The Taming of Umbra: A Guide
The Spirit Plain

The Spirit Plain is a world that exists outside our own, a realm that has been much speculated about, but little is known in certainty. It is where the Reaper King is held, barred from our world, but it is also the home of the umbra, although some of them prefer to also wander the land of the living.

They are the only creatures who can freely cross into both realms for as long as they wish, unharmed.

As proven by umbra tamers, through skill and meditation, humans can enter the Spirit Plain, but it comes with great risk. If they stay in the Spirit Plain for too long, they can lose their soul to the ghosts and some of the umbra that live there.

There are still many things unknown about this place. However, it is the only known place you can call your destined umbra to you.

If you choose to send your soul into the Spirit Plain to tame an umbra, be sure you have at least two fellow tamers guarding your body and anchoring you to this world. And make sure to protect your mind.

Do not attempt it alone.

Always remember that you have a life to return to. Do not allow yourself to be convinced to stay in the Spirit Plain for any reason. No matter what you see, you must always leave.

Under no circumstances should you stay in the Spirit Plain for longer than you have to. The tamers with you will keep track of time, and one of their umbra will help guide you there and back.

CHAPTER SEVEN

TJ and I glance at each other. I don't want my soul to be devoured, or be lost forever in the Spirit Plain like Samuel Walker's, and I'm pretty sure TJ doesn't either. *Great.*

I remember once when I thought I was so ready to tame an umbra. Miles and I were seven, and just like every other kid, we had to go through the trial of "Becoming One with the Darkness," to test the strength of our minds and get us used to fighting the Reaper King's Darkness, should he ever invade the city again.

The haunting images of being put in a room without sight, smell, hearing, or touch come back in full force. So dark that your eyes play tricks on you and you see creatures move and feel invisible things around you. It's the closest thing to the Darkness that Mum and the other scientists could create and use to test our mental will. Some kids cry, some are fascinated, and many just fall asleep. I was a crier. I cried like a big baby the whole way through until my eyes and face were puffy, red, and sore. Miles took it in his stride. Lucky guy. I was so jealous, but he gave me some sweets when I came out and it made me feel better. But after that, I felt like I could handle anything. Oh, how wrong I was . . .

I look over at TJ. Nervousness is written all over his face, right behind that awkward smile that tries to mask it.

"What do you think my umbra will look like?" TJ asks as we wade through the tall purple grass.

"A shadowy penguin with horns and wings," I say, jumping over some snapping carno plants and prickly sticks.

"Haha, very funny. You know I hate those winged flipper creeps." He shivers, and I stifle a chuckle.

TJ was much older when he did his trial. He didn't come to Nubis until he was eleven, when Lunavale got taken over. He came out of the room looking fine to me, but he refused to speak about it after. Even to this day, he'll just make a joke or change the conversation if you ask about it. I don't know about Jada's trial. She probably did it like a boss, without breaking a sweat.

We walk for a few more hours, the air growing icy as the stars shift way past bedtime. When we find an abandoned hut, Jada announces that's where we'll rest for the night. Its battered walls and old makeshift bed show signs of having belonged to a bandit once. TJ sets up a fire in one corner, fencing it off with a few muddy rocks so it doesn't spread. I double-check that the door and windows are secure and look out, silently twisting the ends of my sleeves.

Tomorrow we'll be risking our lives to tame an umbra.

Jada continues to busy herself with the map as we all huddle round the fire, enjoying the heat as it warms our fingers and faces. I pull my knees to my chest, staring at the flickering embers, but Mum's face keeps flashing in my mind. Her worried eyes and Dad's determination to distract the guards and keep us safe . . . I wish I could rewind the clock and tell them not to leave the city, and not to go to Ignis. We'd be at home, laughing and dancing to music during one of our jamming sessions. I'd still be plotting ways to sneak into Dad's office, and Lucas would be playing with his building blocks. I just want to go home, but Mum said we can stop this. What if she's wrong, though?

"Hey, Jada, have you ever heard of the Lightcasters?" I ask, trying to focus on something else. She blinks at me, raising an eyebrow. An awkward silence falls.

"Who told you about them?" she finally asks.

I shrug. "No one . . . I, erm . . . I read about them in one of Dad's books."

"We sneaky snuck into his office!" Lucas chirps. *Little snitch!*

She nods. "Yeah. I've heard of them, but I don't know much. Lightcasters are said to be people who hold the powers of the moon and the sun. They can literally conjure light with their hands, and they can battle against the shadow magic of the Reaper King and his reapers."

"Why have I never heard of them before?" TJ jumps in, and I'm just as curious to know.

"You have, just not by name," Jada says. "The old Queen Lucina had powers to banish the Reaper King to the Spirit Plain all those years ago, right? It was because she was a Lightcaster. Once every generation a child in the royal family is born with the power. That's why Queen Katiya is important. She's a Lightcaster too, keeping the kingdom lit."

"So that's why Mum said she could help . . . ," I mutter. It makes sense with what I first thought when I read that book.

If she is a Lightcaster, then she really sucks at keeping the kingdom lit. She probably doesn't even have any powers. . . . I kinda wonder why Mum and Dad never mentioned Lightcasters, though.

"Why do you ask?" Jada presses, but I shrug again.

"No reason, it's just something I remembered just now. I

actually have some of the pages from the book on my tablet," I say. "Lucas, do you still have it?"

He nods and opens up his tiny bag. My little tablet is tucked away inside.

"The term 'Lightcasters' is known only by tamers, the queen, and her guard," Jada says.

But why keep it a secret? Everyone in the kingdom knows already that the queen has powers. Why keep the fact that she's a *Lightcaster* a secret? It doesn't make sense.

Jada scrolls through the pages on my tablet, then suddenly pauses. "Mia, back in the city . . . did Miles or anyone put their hands over your face with black smoke?"

Her voice is low, and for some reason I find myself gulping. She stares expectantly, and as I slowly nod, her face turns grave.

"Miles said that I was the one they were looking for. One of the red cloaks did too. But they were rounding up all the kids, so I might not be the only one."

"Jeez, all right. We need to get a move on. As soon as it's Sky Connect, we leave. They're still after us."

"Wait, why?" I ask. "Do you know why they're after us? Why me?"

She pauses. "I'm not a hundred percent sure."

I sit back, confused. I know I'm nothing special, but then why did Miles say I was the one they were looking for?

"They know we're going to get help. We leave at Sky Connect," she repeats, putting a full stop to further questions. I frown, glancing at TJ, who shrugs. Something isn't adding up, but Jada isn't ready to discuss it.

"Do you think we're going to make it to Stella?" I ask, watching her search through the bag for something.

Jada smiles, but it doesn't reach her eyes.

"We have to," is all she says.

An arm wraps around my shoulders, warming me up again, and I look to see TJ's smiling face.

"We're going to be the best tamers, right? So, of course we're going to make it," he says, and the moment our eyes meet, I almost believe every word. He'll make a great tamer, but I'm not so sure about me. Still, I take a deep breath.

"You're right." I nod. "We've got this."

"And, even if *you* don't got this, be happy that you have a friend who does." He winks at me, and I shove him with a laugh.

We fall silent when we catch sight of Jada's serious expression.

"We can't make it to Stella without at least one more umbra. Ruby won't be enough to protect us, if even half the rumors are true about this place. If we ever have to run, she can't carry all of us either. You guys will have to try the Spirit Calling soon."

"Great . . . ," I mutter, watching Lucas play with the star scope.

"So," TJ says, changing the subject, and I'm grateful for it. "Are we gonna talk about who that kid with the umbra mutt was?" He looks straight at me, and that gratefulness evaporates.

"You mean those red-cloak guys? I don't know . . . ," I say, scratching my cheek. I'm not ready to talk about Miles.

He knows I'm trying to play dumb. What was I even supposed to say? Even if I told TJ that I know Miles and there's no way he's truly the enemy, he wouldn't believe me. My heart hurts just thinking about it.

I look to Jada for help, but she's staying out of it, "fixing" Ruby's feathers.

"Just spill, Mia. He tried to capture you and Lucas. Who is he?"

I sigh.

"His name is Miles. He used to be my best friend."

My only real friend at the time. He didn't laugh like the other kids when I said I wanted to be the best tamer in the kingdom, and then later a teacher after the incident happened. It wasn't a fancy dream, like wanting to be a part of the Queen's Guard, like TJ, or live in the Royal Circle in the City of Light, but it was mine, and Miles dreamed it for me too.

"So how come he's now part of this evil scheme with those red-cloak guys?" says TJ.

"He's not bad!" I yell, and both TJ and Jada shoot me a startled look. I shake my head. "It's not like that. He's being used."

"You really believe that?" TJ asks, and I nod. "You're a clown."

"I'm not. You're just jealous." TJ huffs, but I haven't stopped thinking about what happened with Miles since we left. The more I think about it, the clearer everything becomes. He's being used by someone. Probably his parents. They've always treated him horribly.

"All right. Where's your proof, then?" TJ says.

"Huh?"

"Proof. What makes you think he is innocent?"

"Someone was speaking to him through an earpiece," I tell him. "They were giving him orders. I think it might be his parents. You remember how his parents used to be, right, Jada?"

She nods, but she's obviously turning something over in her mind.

"Look, Mia, you need to consider that Miles might have changed," she says eventually. "Controlled or not, you need to be prepared to fight if he gets in the way of saving Nubis. Do you think you could do that?"

"I'm not wrong . . . ," I say instead of answering, staring hard at a tiny crack in the floor, but I can't deny the little niggle of doubt that she's caused in the back of my mind. What if Miles *is* the enemy now? Would I actually be able to fight him?

TJ hums, as if debating whether to ask more questions, but I'm relieved when he doesn't. He's letting it go, for now.

"Either way, we've got bigger problems to focus on," Jada says. "Tomorrow we'll do some practice exercises before you attempt your Spirit Callings. Get some rest, guys."

We all settle down on the hard wooden floor of the hut. The gentle flicker of the fireplace warms me as I lie down next to Lucas, and to my surprise, it doesn't take long for me to fall asleep.

"Mia . . . MIA!"

I jump up, whipping my head left and right. The hut is empty and the walls seem higher than I remember—I'm barely able to see the ceiling.

"Guys?" I call out, looking around. Where in the galaxy did everyone go? It's almost pitch-black, but something lights up ahead. The door is glowing bright white.

"Mia!" someone yells, and the door creaks slowly open. My heart is pounding a million times a minute.

"Mum!"

I race through the door and I'm suddenly in our living room, with the picture of me as a baby trying to eat one of Mum's research books over the fireplace, our TV, and our gray curtains. The sweet smell of rosy-dill fills my nose. *What?*

"Mia!"

I spin around. Mum is standing there, her hazel eyes locking with mine. She snaps her hand up, stopping me before I can run to her, the star necklace around her neck glowing.

"Mia. You must reach the City of Light. It holds the answers you're ready for. If you don't—"

Her words are cut off as bony hands reach out from behind and snatch her. I scream as her beautiful eyes turn black.

She can't speak, but I hear the words: "It's all your fault. You left us in Nubis. You left us!"

She struggles to free herself as the hands pin her to the spot, and suddenly her body morphs into that of a thirteen-year-old boy, his skin pale white and his dark hair disheveled.

"Miles?"

Panic fills his eyes as he reaches out to me, fighting against the bony hands that grip him.

"Mia, you have to turn to the Darkness. . . ."

I try to grab his hand, but then a sinister chuckle echoes from above.

I look up to the ceiling, where a hooded figure with a crown made of bones on his head grins, and I scream. His hand jerks out, grabbing my neck, and I squirm, gasping for air.

"I . . . will . . . return."

"Mia, wake up!"

I sit up, screaming. My back is drenched and sweat is dripping down my face. Jada, Lucas, TJ, and Ruby are hovering over me, shocked and concerned. I touch my burning throat, still feeling the bony fingers. *It was just a dream.*

"You were having a nightmare. Are you all right?" Jada asks, and I nod slowly.

"Yeah, I'm fine," I say, clearing my throat. I can't stop thinking about it. *I left them. . . .* Lucas throws himself at me in a tight hug, but I can't bring myself to smile. "I'm okay, Lu-Lu. Promise."

I turn to Jada again, and when her eyes catch mine, I ask the question I've been meaning to ask since we left Nubis.

"Hey. Back in the city, I heard some of those red cloaks say that Ignis had already fallen to the Darkness when all the tamers left. How is that even possible?"

"Wait, what?" Jada says, confusion written all over her face. "Just before the holo-phones went down, there was a holo-call to all the tamers from the people in Ignis. They were asking us for help. You're telling me that was all a trick?"

"That's what I heard the red cloak say. Miles also mentioned the rise of the true king. You don't think—"

Jada's face pales and I cut myself off. The fear in her eyes makes me too nervous to finish.

Miles seemed too confident. Those red cloaks planned all this. Tricking our parents and all the tamers. Capturing them and taking over the city. Everything until now has been a calculated plan.

"Let's just focus on the mission, okay?" Jada says, interrupting my thoughts. "One step at a time."

Through the window, the thin silver line once again connects the stars, signaling that it's almost Sky Connect, the start of a new day in our ever-dark slice of the kingdom. It's time to move.

We pack our things and put out the fire before setting off. Still shaken, I think of Miles as we run across the purple fields. Am I right about him, or has he betrayed us?

Wild, golden-eyed umbra of various shapes and sizes race across the plains around us. I roll my shoulders and yawn. My back aches from the hard floor last night, and TJ groans.

"Let's push for at least an hour, guys. Take a snack from the bag too," Jada calls, taking the lead, with Ruby flying overhead.

Something's in the air. We're all feeling it. More than once, I shake Lucas off as he grabs me a little too hard. He's extra fidgety, and despite the lands being mostly empty aside from some umbra, it feels like eyes are on us, hidden between the crooked trees and the snapping carno plants.

"Mimi . . . is the scary Reaper man gonna get us?" I look down at Lucas. His voice is a whisper and his bottom lip is trembling.

Of all the stories Mum and Dad used to tell, the story of the Reaper King was the worst because it was real. *Beware of the Reaper Creeper, creeping in the night. When innocent children meet the tragic ends of their short little lives.*

"Relax, the Reaper King is sealed away in the Spirit Plain. The old queen made sure of that. The Darkness is just the aftermath of his reign," Jada says, almost too certainly.

That must have been like a hundred years ago, though. . . . Surely the light should have returned by now if he was truly gone like we once thought? Those red cloaks know something. It's the only explanation. I glance at Jada, unsure, but she only stares back. Even she can't deny that there is a reason why people don't camp out or live in the plains anymore, despite the Reaper King being gone for so long. His minions can get you. Outside the walls you always have to keep moving, because not all of them are trapped in the spirit world. Besides, who knows how many red-eyed umbra are out there, tamed or not, randomly stalking the plains like Shade once was, thanks to those red-cloaked gutterslugs' experiments?

After going scouting, Ruby returns in her baby form, flapping gently beside her tamer.

"There's no one within several miles of our location. Most of the tamers are still prisoners in Nubis, though it would appear that some of them are being relocated to the Lost City of Astaroth."

The first city to be taken over, before I was even born. Is *that* where Miles and those red-cloaked soldiers came from?

"What about my mum and dad?" I call out, squeezing Lucas's hand.

"And my mums?" TJ chimes in.

"They are all still in Nubis."

Thank Lunis, they're still alive, but why are some of the tamers being moved? Something else is going on. Something we're all missing.

"All right, take a seat, kids," Jada says, sitting on the ground. She crosses her legs, resting the backs of her hands on her knees.

Lucas plonks himself down at once, tugging at my leg, and I do the same. TJ raises an eyebrow but does it too.

"Why do we have to sit, Mimi?" Lucas whispers, but I shrug. All I know is that I'm not going to like it. At all.

"You guys are going to do a calming preparatory technique called meditation. It tests your mind for your Spirit Calling."

"So we're really doing this, huh?" TJ says, sounding nervous. Lucas pats TJ's leg, and I shove my hands against the dirt to stop them from shaking. Jada gives us a look that's a mix of sympathy and determination.

"Roll your shoulders back and take a few deep breaths. Close your eyes and listen to my voice. Picture yourself away from here. Away from the Nightmare Plains, in a place where you feel the safest."

I close my eyes and take a deep breath, then slowly release it, silencing my mind. My shoulders gently rise and fall as I inhale and exhale. I picture myself back home with Mum, Dad, and Lucas. The aroma of sweet hot chocolate fills the air, and I lean back against the comfy sofa, feeling the heat from the mug in my hands.

"Listen to my words." Jada's calm voice echoes, sounding so far away. "Focus on your safe space. You can't be harmed in your safe space. Breathe in and out."

In . . . Out . . .

With every exhale, my shoulders loosen and calm washes over me. I'm in control. I'm safe. I'm not afraid. My mind wanders. I imagine TJ sitting beside me with a goofy smile on his face, probably daydreaming about being the best chef and Queen's Guard in the world. *Goofball.* I imagine Lucas daydreaming about playing with his favorite puzzles and building blocks.

"Just let the thoughts pass. You are safe."

I think of Miles and my smile drops. Mum and Dad. My shoulders tense. I left them all behind.

My breath quickens and my chest tightens.

"Now open your eyes."

When I do, the purple grass and vicious carno plants of the Nightmare Plains greet me.

"Okay?" Jada asks, and I nod. Beside me, Lucas yawns, stretching his little arms in the air.

"That made me sleepy," he says, rubbing his eyes.

"More like that was weird," TJ says. "I kinda feel relaxed, though."

"You guys did well, but that was the easy bit," Jada says, standing up. She brushes herself off and ushers us to our feet as well. Above our heads, Ruby circles, phasing in and out of the dark sky.

"What's next?" I ask.

"The hard bit. Lucas, I've got a big job for you," Jada says, and my brother jumps up and down.

"What is it?" he squeals.

"We're going to partner up, and I need you to help TJ," she says. "Mia, TJ, I want you two to close your eyes. Lucas and I will try to poke you, and you need to try and sense when and where we're going to do it, and dodge. Simple."

I raise an eyebrow. "Wait, what?"

"We've got this, Mia. It's basically dodge the robot, just like how we play at home," TJ says, jumping from foot to foot, and I nod.

"Close your eyes and focus," Jada orders. "I'm about to poke you."

I squeeze my eyes shut. My shoulders tense, but seconds pass and nothing happens.

"You didn't—" I start as a hard finger suddenly pokes my forehead, and I hiss, looking at her. "That's cheating!"

"Keep your eyes shut," Jada scolds. I grumble under my breath and do it. "Try again. Focus. When you're in the Spirit Plain, you need to keep connected with your senses. If you lose yourself in there, you won't come back—umbra or not. Lucas, keep poking TJ."

"This is hard . . . ," I hear TJ complain.

I roll my shoulders back. *Okay, I can do this.* I imagine a white silhouette of Jada in front of me. I squeeze my eyes harder, concentrating. Her finger rises and I focus on it, waiting. Her glowing finger jerks forward and I throw my head left, slapping her hand right. Someone gasps, and I open my eyes to see Jada frozen, gripping the hand I just slapped. Her jaw has dropped open, and I blink. I did it. *I actually did it!*

"I can't believe it . . . ," she mutters.

I find myself smiling for a moment and she does too, and yet I'm still tense. There's no way I'm ready to do a Spirit Calling. I don't even want to try it. What if I end up lost forever in the Spirit Plain? *Maybe I could fake it. . . . There has to be a way.*

"All right, let's go again."

For a while, we go at it, Jada's pokes turning to punches and kicks. We swap partners, too, Lucas giggling each time I dodge him. Then I go against Jada again. I almost forget my eyes are closed as I weave left and right, dodging every kick and punch.

"Okay, we're done. You guys did great," Jada pants at last. I open my eyes to see her puffing for breath with her hands on her knees. *Maybe I'm not so useless after all. . . .* Across from us, TJ flawlessly dodges Lucas with his eyes closed as Lucas gives up trying to poke and instead tries to grab him. He actually looks pretty cool.

"All right, that's enough, you two!" Jada calls.

Lucas huffs, crossing his arms and stamping his foot. "It's not fair. He cheated!"

"I didn't cheat. Thanks for helping me, little buddy," TJ says, and Lucas's sulky pout vanishes into a bright smile.

The moment of triumph is shattered as a deafening whistle sounds. A blazing trail of light jets across the sky and bursts bloodred above us.

"A firework?" TJ asks, looking at us confused, but my eyes stay pinned upward as the color fizzles out. I squint as a single blue light pierces the night sky from the direction of home, and my throat dries up as a holographic image of a man's face comes into view. I've never seen a holo-image so big before.

A large purple crown is on his head, and his hair is dark and disheveled. There's something familiar about him, but I can't put my finger on it.

"Shoot . . . ," Jada mutters, but before I can say anything, the holo-image speaks.

"We know you children have escaped. If you don't return, your parents and every single person in this city will perish. We are coming for you. Do not resist. Do not fight back. The ritual begins in three days—and then he will return. I repeat. You have three days."

The image vanishes, allowing the night to take over once again, but we're all silent. In the distance, in the sky above Nubis, the number three is projected.

"What's that?" Lucas asks.

The hairs on the back of my neck stand on end and my palms sweat. "It's a countdown, Lucas."

"A countdown to what, Mimi?"

I lower my arm, struggling to swallow the lump in my throat.

"To when something really bad happens to our city . . ."

CHAPTER EIGHT

O kay, so that just happened. . . . The sooner we get to
Stella and talk to the queen, the better," TJ says, pacing
back and forth across the violet grass.

"What makes you think she can even help us? Don't you
think she would have done it already?" I ask, frowning.

"She's the *queen*, Mia. Plus a Lightcaster, too, apparently,"
TJ says, throwing his hands up. "Of course she can help. Your
mum even told you to speak to her, right?"

"She said go to Stella and find my grandparents, not just
talk to the queen," I correct him. She might serve as a symbol

of hope for some people and that's it, but the queen could kick a stick for all I care. She's useless to us.

"Maybe she can help us save Mummy and Daddy!" Lucas says, and I sigh.

I wish I knew why Mum wants us to go to the City of Light. It's more than just keeping us safe. What am I supposed to *do*? She said we could stop all this, and that Nan and Grandad will take me "through the next steps . . ." What does that even mean? There are just too many questions with no answers. We're literally running in the dark, and if we take a wrong step, we'll never see our families again. It's too much.

I think back to that book in Dad's office. It might have some of the answers we're looking for. Then there was that gutterslug red cloak who grabbed me. . . . He and Miles both said that I was the one they were looking for. Maybe it has something to do with the ritual. Do I have special blood or something that they need, or is that too far-fetched?

"What kinda ritual do you think he was talking about? And why three days? What's so special about that?" TJ asks, interrupting my train of thought.

"I don't know. They need us back in Nubis for a reason, though. It can't just be to stop us from getting help . . . ," I murmur, racking my brain about what could possibly be important about three days from now.

Jada and I look at each other as we both work it out.

"It's the day of the Blood Moon," I say.

TJ's jaw drops. "The day the moon goes that creepy red color? The day that literally means 'the day of death'? Well, that's not at all scary. . . ."

"The Blood Moon is when we umbra are at our strongest, so I can only imagine that applies to other shadow beings as well. It has a link to the Spirit Plain," Ruby says.

"You mean like the Reaper King . . . ," I say dryly, and she nods.

"It's why we send up lanterns, to try and cast the evil away," Jada says. "But people still go missing, and those already missing still don't return."

"That man said 'he' will return," I mutter, and TJ shuffles uncomfortably. Miles also mentioned the return of the true king. . . . It all confirms my thoughts. As much as I hate to even consider it, there's only one answer to who it could be, and it makes my skin crawl.

"They're trying to bring back the Reaper King," I blurt out.

"We can't think about that right now," Jada says. "You two have a more important mission, and we don't have time to mess about. You have to do a Spirit Calling."

Jada sits on the ground again, crossing her legs, with her hands pressed firmly on her knees. She's determined not to talk about it, but the fear is written all over her face.

"We'll try it one at a time," she says. "It's a risk, but just remember the meditation. All your training, including martial arts, survival classes, and schooling, has strengthened your minds, whether you realize it or not. I'll be your voice guide to help you. Now Johnson, come here."

With a grin, my cocky friend slides on over to Jada with a swagger. This all feels wrong. I hum in annoyance. Why is he so happy to do this? I tug and twist at my sleeves, torn between wanting him to succeed, so I don't have to, and wanting him to be safe by not doing it at all.

"Jada obviously knows *I'm* the most likely to tame an umbra," he says, knowing he's winding me up. I almost tell him to shut up, but hold myself back, swallowing the frustration.

Lucas lets go of me and sits down close to Jada to watch. I fall back on my butt beside him, ruffling his curly locks.

"What's he doing, Mimi?" he asks with big, curious eyes.

"He's going to try and tame an umbra, like Mum and Dad. It's called a Spirit Calling," I tell him, kissing his head.

Lucas smiles and nods as TJ sits down in front of Jada, cross-legged like she is.

"This ain't . . . gonna hurt or nothing, is it?" he asks. I hear a hint of nerves in his voice that makes me feel a bit better. Maybe he *is* taking this seriously.

"Nah. Well, not unless you mess up and summon a monstrous umbra that claws you to death, or you don't come back at all, because you lose your mind to the spirits," Jada jokes, and I narrow my eyes.

Lucas gasps and TJ laughs, but the way his fingers drum against his leg tells a different story. I don't blame him at all. I'm terrified too.

"That rarely happens, though, right?" he asks, then pauses. "Right?"

"Take a deep breath and relax. You can do this," Jada says, her tone setting my teeth on edge. She places her hands gently on either side of TJ's face, her fingers barely grazing his skin, and I cross my fingers.

He'll be all right. He has to be.

He closes his eyes and suddenly falls back. I jerk forward, but Jada catches his head before it hits the grass and gently lays him down. She mutters something, whispering things to him that I can't hear.

"What happened? Is he sleeping?" Lucas asks.

"Yeah, he's sleeping," I tell him, hugging my little brother close.

"Why is he sleeping? It's scary here. What if the monsters come?" Lucas asks, always finding the worst time to ask questions. My anxiety has me scrunching up my sleeves and chewing my lip, constantly looking around to make sure we're safe.

The Spirit Calling can only be done on the Nightmare Plains because of all the potential umbra roaming in and out of the Spirit Plain. It's usually done outside the walls of the city, with a group of tamers around to be safe in case it goes wrong. Unlike now . . .

Mum believes that there's an umbra for everyone. That a bond was created the day that old Queen Lucina clashed with the Reaper King. Come to think of it . . . if umbra can travel in and out of the Spirit Plain through the Nightmare Plains . . . then maybe that really is how the Reaper King's powers seep through. Either way, it doesn't make much of a difference or help our situation now, and I gulp, looking at TJ and Jada.

TJ is literally calling the spirit of a shadow-beast-monster and bringing it back into the physical world to tame it. But today we only have one girl, one tamer, and my four-year-old brother.

"We'll protect him. Don't worry, little man. He'll wake up soon," Jada says, with so much hope I almost believe her.

I look at TJ's face, so peaceful under the moonlight as his chest slowly rises and falls, and I find myself smiling, scooting closer to gently hold his hand. *You've got this.*

"Hey, hey, listen," Lucas says, rustling in his small strapped bag. "Mummy and Daddy showed me how to pre-tect myself with this." He whips out a small boomerang, and I blink. "I can pre-tect TJ, too."

Jada smiles, and I do too. The kid is too much sometimes, but I love him all the same.

"It's 'protect,'" I correct him. "And hopefully, you won't have to use that. At least not until you're bigger. Now, keep it safe in your bag, pipsqueak."

He puts it back in and I take out my mini tablet before he zips it up. While we're waiting, I decide to try to make sense of some of the pictures in Dad's book. I don't get far. It's hard to concentrate. More than once I feel as if eyes are on us, and I shuffle in my seat.

We all sit there, feeling the wind blow against us and listening to the pitter-patter of small creatures. There's no sign of any Reaper King, the red cloaks, or anything scary, but a few harmless umbra come up to us and sniff us before going about their business.

I jump out of my skin as TJ's eyes burst open, and he jerks up to a sitting position. Jada and I quickly stand up, looking around for the umbra he's summoned, but there's nothing. The field is quiet and empty.

We look at TJ. He's smiling, but his eyes . . . I don't know what to say as it becomes painfully clear what happened. He didn't manage it.

I wrap my arms around him, feeling every inch of his pain. Even though I don't want an umbra for myself, he did. Jada places a hand on his shoulder. I wish I could give him some sort of comfort, even just a little bit, so he doesn't feel so sad, but I don't know what to say. Not understanding what's going on, but feeling the quiet sadness as well, Lucas hugs TJ's legs.

TJ sighs. "Guess, I'm not the best after all, huh?"

I squeeze him tighter and rack my brain for anything that will make him feel better, but inside I'm feeling sick for another reason. If he couldn't do it . . .

"I'm sorry, TJ. But it was only your first time. And you survived. Focus on that. You'll be able to be a part of the Queen's Guard. Umbra or not, your mums will be proud," Jada says.

He clears his throat. "Yeah . . . I guess."

Jada turns to me, but I can't bring myself to look at her.

"Mia, I'm sorry, but you're next. We can't stay here too long. Those red cloaks are still after us."

Ruby confirms this, circling above our heads, still keeping a lookout. But if TJ couldn't do it, with all his confidence, then how in the Kingdom am I going to? Doubt seeps into me and spreads like an infection. I think I'm going to throw up, when I feel TJ's hand on my arm.

"You've got this, Supernova. . . . Oh, sorry, I know you don't like it when I call you that." TJ gives me the brightest smile, and it warms me up a little bit inside. "Go get 'em, Superstar."

He slowly lets go of me, and I clench my jaw. I wish he was right, but I'm not brave like him. I'm nothing. Mum and Dad, TJ's parents, Auntie Carly and Auntie Lisa . . . they're all captured and counting on me to help, but I can't. I'm scared.

Jada sits cross-legged again and I join her, sitting with my hands pressed into my knees, digging my fingers into my skin. *I just want to go home.* I chew my lip and focus on her face.

Her braids move with the wind, and the freckles that decorate her nose and cheeks are faint in the starlight. In the corner of my eye, TJ gives me a thumbs-up, and Lucas copies him. I manage a small smile. But I just . . . can't do this. The thought of being face-to-face with an umbra I don't know, trying to keep my soul from being taken, sounds terrifying. I twist my hands in my sleeves to cover their shakiness. I'm not brave enough. I have no choice but to fake it, and I'm terrified.

"Get ready, Mia," Jada says quietly. "You're about to enter the world of the Reaper King. You won't be there long, and the queen froze him in that world so he won't be able to get you, but you have to be careful. The Spirit Plain will try and trap you there with the other ghosts and spirits. You get in, call your umbra, and get out. If you get scared, think about your safe space, just like we practiced. Focus on your goal and you *will* come back."

But what if I don't? What if I end up like Samuel Walker? What happens if I don't wake up?

I take a deep breath, then slowly release it and close my eyes. Jada's fingers rest delicately on my face, pressing against my cheeks, and I tense up.

"Relax," she whispers.

I take another deep breath, trying to take control of my mind and focus. I picture myself back home, Mum and Dad chatting away about the adventures they had when they were my age, while Lucas and I sit and listen to every word. The fireplace in our living room crackles, making our shadows dance on the walls, and the smell of Mum's sweet perfume wafts to my nose. . . .

"I'm about to send you to the deepest realms of your mind. Is your mind calm? Ruby will lead you there, but she can't stay. Are you ready?"

I nod, giving her the signal to begin. Suddenly my body jerks back and I'm falling into a dark abyss.

My eyes snap open, but I'm alone. Everywhere is pitch-black, except the glowing purple floor I lie on. I let out a shaky breath and stand, testing my arms and legs. Everything's functioning, and I look around. This is *my* mind. I have the power.

"Mia."

I spin around to see a pair of golden eyes and the sparkling outline of flapping wings. "Ruby?"

"Follow." She turns around and I run after her.

"Wait up!" I yell, but with each step, she gets farther away until a bright light flashes and I find myself alone. I can hear an eerie wailing cry, and a strange mist surrounds my body. I wrap my arms around myself, looking around for Ruby, Jada, anyone. I want to go home.

I take another deep breath to calm my mind. I release it, and my body floats up. I focus on every thought, opening myself up to an umbra, any umbra, finding me. Energy surges through me and I thrust my hand forward. The fireplace from home appears ahead of me. Familiar photos emerge on the mantelpiece, and four people begin to take shape.

"Mum, Dad, Lucas . . ." I stare at the final shadow . . . *me.*

My eyes well up. I want to reach out to the image, but I force myself to look away and face the darkness. I stare into nothingness, swallow, and squeeze my eyes shut, forcing myself to say the four words that could change my life forever.

"Umbra. Come to me. . . ."

Something shifts in the dark, and my eyes burst open. A faint spot of light glows like a lunar lantern ahead. It floats up and down, getting brighter, but makes no move to come closer. I reach out for it, pushing through the darkness. *"Wait. Don't be afraid. Come closer. What are you?"*

I beckon it closer to me, reaching out to the light as it grows bigger and bigger. Suddenly it splits into two. Electricity zaps through my body, throwing me back. The wind is knocked from my stomach, and my muscles seize up from the force, as a strange voice enters my thoughts.

"We found you."

I'm sucked out of the dark world, screaming. The blackness surrounding me shatters, and I gasp, sitting up. The purple blades of grass and starry sky return, and my chest heaves. I'm back on the Nightmare Plains. I rub my eyes to see Lucas, TJ, and Jada staring, shocked.

My frazzled mind takes in their faces, and I realize their wide eyes aren't aimed at me. They're looking *behind* me. I rub my eyes again, jump to my feet, and turn to look.

Two umbra are standing there. Their heads and tails are long and fluffy, like foxes, but their legs and bodies resemble shadowlike deer. Each has a horn on its head, curved toward each other, as if they were once one, instead of two creatures. The one on the left is black, but the other is white, like yin and yang, and they have the most amazing golden eyes I've ever seen. Dread twists my gut, and yet they pull me to them like a magic spell.

Two umbra? And one of them *white*? Something sparks my memory, but I can't quite remember.

"Mia . . . ," Jada whispers. "What have you done?"

Someone grabs my arm, and I turn to see TJ frowning at me. The umbra stand there silently, and the pull to go closer tugs at me like invisible hands. I pat TJ's arm and pull out of his grip. My palms are sweaty as I quietly approach.

They bow their heads when I reach them. I slowly hold out my hand to pet their snouts, but their heads jerk up, and a sharp force pushes against my stomach, throwing me across the field. My body bounces off the ground and I hiss, clutching my stomach. Their horns didn't touch me, but it felt like they pierced through me. I roll over as the pain shoots up my body.

"Mimi!"

"I'm okay, Lucas," I wheeze, stumbling to my feet, waving at the others to stay put. My teeth clench as pain stabs my stomach, but I hold in the ache and force myself forward. I focus back on the two beasts, reaching for them with my senses, but five words alone enter my mind.

"We will devour your soul."

CHAPTER NINE

My knees buckle and I want to run, but my feet are glued to the spot. Even though I'm petrified, there's something familiar about these umbra, like I know them already.

I force my feet forward again. Each step jabs my stomach. My hand clutches at the bo staff on my thigh belt. These umbra are trying to scare me, but I have to tame them. Lives depend on it.

There's no going back now.

I stop in front of the umbra again, and this time anger bubbles inside me. I clench my fists. I'll earn their respect. They will be my partners and help me fight through the Nightmare

Plains to reach Stella. I will make it back to Nubis in time to save Mum and Dad.

I am not prey.

Energy rushes through me. The black umbra tilts his head to the side, inspecting me, while the white one's shadowy fur bristles as he also watches my every move. I snap open my bo staff and their heads jerk back, not breaking eye contact. This is only going to go one way; I can't lose.

"Look!" I yell. "I never wanted to tame you, but right now, I need your help, so come at me with everything you've got! I'm ready!"

My legs threaten to wobble again, but I dig my feet into the ground. I harness every bit of my martial arts skills, but there are two of them and one of me. *How in Lunis am I supposed to do this?* I feel a drop of sweat run down my face. It's all on me. I picture Lucas, Mum, and Dad . . . I can't afford to lose—I *won't* lose, but if I do, I'll at least go down fighting.

The umbra lower their heads again, and I brace myself for the attack. Quick as lightning they spin around, kicking out their back hooves at me, and I dodge, swift on my feet, twirling my staff and smacking their legs. *Got ya!* The white one growls.

I jerk my staff toward them, baiting them to try again. Their hooves tap at the grass, but I spring off my feet first, zeroing in on them. They throw their heads back, then suddenly forward, and a high-pitched screech pins me to the spot. The ringing pierces my ears and they launch forward, but I backflip, bouncing off the ground with my hands as their horns try to hook me, barely grazing my clothes. I stumble the landing but whack their horns away. My breathing's heavy as I try to regain focus, but the two charge at me again. They're too quick. Most of my energy is sapped, and I falter.

"Mia!" TJ yells. Digging deep inside myself, I throw my bo staff up into the air, planting my feet into the ground.

The umbra turn, but I'm ready. I brace myself, stretching out my hands and catching their horns. My shoes skid back against the grass, building a mountain of mud and dirt around me. My arm muscles burn as I hold on as tight as I can, refusing to let go. They jerk about, trying to escape, but I force my head down between their horns, headbutting them both as hard as I can. I scream as pain stabs through my head, and I pull back to look at them.

"I may not be brave, but I'm not completely weak. I just need your help! Please!" I yell. They cry out in pain, and I hiss as my forehead throbs. Against my hands, I feel their bodies vibrate through their horns, but I refuse to go down. *I need you. Just for a little bit, please.*

Their golden eyes lock with mine once again, and something twinges inside as a strange sense of calm washes over me. The aggression in them is replaced with a softness that makes my heart skip with the tiniest bit of hope. Then I feel it, for the first time, and relief fills me up. I'm no longer alone in my head.

"We accept you as our worthy tamer, Mia McKenna."

My knees give out and I fall to the ground, panting. *I did it. I actually did it!*

A cold muzzle presses against my forehead and I shriek, scrambling back against the grass. The two umbra look at each other, confused.

"Sorry, just . . . personal space," I tell them, standing up. They're still monsters.

"No . . . way! How come you have two and I don't even get *one*?!" TJ's protest cuts through the awkward moment.

Lucas chuckles and cheers, racing over.

"Honestly, I don't know what's going on," I say.

Jada walks over to my new umbra and examines them in disbelief. Apart from the color and the direction of their horns, they are identical.

"How is this even possible?" she mutters.

"How is one even *white*?" TJ adds.

Lucas giggles and pats their legs gently. The black one blinks, while the white one bats him away with a hoof.

"They're so tall. They're like horsies, or foxes, or both! What's your name, horsey-foxey?"

"I am neither of those, tiny human," the white one grumbles. *"But I am Lux."*

"My name is Nox," the dark one says with a much calmer vibe than his twin.

My instincts tell me they're both boys, and they're my partners for life now, whether I like it or not.

Starting today, I'm a tamer.

I stand before Lux and Nox, filled with strange pride and nerves as they both stare at me. If Miles or those men in red cloaks find us, we can fight back. I can protect Lucas and save Mum and Dad now—but am I really capable of being a tamer? So far it feels more like luck than skill. . . .

I turn to TJ, who tries to smile, but his failure clearly still burns him. I glance back to Lux and Nox and frown. *Why did I get two?*

"What happened in the Spirit Plain?" asks Jada.

"I don't really remember," I tell her. "It's kinda like a blur. At first it felt like I was at home, then it went dark and I called out for an umbra, and then this happened. How is this even possible?"

She shakes her head. "I don't know. Nothing like this has ever happened before."

But it has. . . .

I think of the storybook in Dad's office, with the picture of those kids and two umbra. I thought it was one umbra for each kid, but . . . maybe not. That's why these seem familiar.

"Lucas, can I have my tablet?" I ask. He scrambles in his

little bag and hands it to me, and I press the button to make it bigger. "Look."

Everyone gathers around as I flick through the holograms of the pages I copied.

"No way . . . ," TJ mutters as I show them the image of the two children and the umbra.

"They're the same umbra," Jada confirms.

I almost drop the tablet. It's too much to take in.

TJ looks at the pages over my shoulder. "Wait . . . You don't think . . ."

"It might not be," I interrupt, "but if it is, then is there a way to reverse the spirit calling?"

"Charming," Nox, the dark umbra, says. *"Our tamer wants nothing to do with us."*

"It's not too late to eat her," Lux remarks, and I shoot him a look.

"No, you can't reverse it. These two are your partners for life now. You'll learn to depend on each other," Jada says.

I scrunch up my nose, glancing at the umbra.

Let's see how that goes.

"But . . . if that's actually your umbra in the picture, then . . . you could be one of the kids in that drawing," Jada says.

"Trust me, I would know if I had light glowing around me," I say. I couldn't even protect Lucas years ago when he needed me the most.

"But it would make sense with what your mum said," TJ says. "Mia, if you have powers—"

"Mum would have told me if I had powers, and Jada said it herself. The only Lightcasters are in the royal family, and trust me, I'm not royalty. I'll even draw you a family tree later to prove it." There's just no way. I'd know if I had some sort of special power. Mum and Dad wouldn't keep something that important a secret. I refuse to believe it.

He throws his hands up, giving in. Jada sighs. "Let's just focus on one step at a time. First, we need to get to Ignis. Okay? Let's go."

We continue through the plains. I catch Jada looking at me weirdly a few times and I chew my lip, tugging at my sleeves. I can't help but think about what TJ said. I'd know if I had powers. Plus, if I did, I would have actually used them instead of being a coward and leaving Mum and Dad behind.

Stay focused. I try and clear my head, focusing on getting to Ignis. I have to keep strong or these two beautifully monstrous creatures could turn on me.

After a while, Lucas tugs at my arm and whisper-shouts, "Hey, Mimi, listen-listen. If you rub TJ's back like this, he'll feel better." He rubs small circles on my back with his tiny hand.

"What are you talking about?"

"Shhhh!" He presses his finger to his lips and checks to make sure TJ isn't listening, even though his whisper-shouts can basically be heard by everyone.

"You clown. Why would I rub his back? You do it," I tell Lucas.

The little kid puffs his cheeks, shaking his head firmly. "I'm not a clown. I'm a boy, and I can't do it, because I can't reach his back. I'm too short."

I roll my eyes.

"All right, genius. Fair enough. Maybe later."

He balls his small fist at me. "Listen-listen, I told you. I'm a boy, not a genie!"

Little mini umbra resembling a mix between a hedgehog and a mouse scurry around us. It's quiet for now, but something tells me it won't be for long. We're heading for Ignis, where we can stop for the night, but in the back of my mind, that red-cloaked guard's words ring. This city fell long before anyone knew, so who knows what to expect? If all goes well, though, we can reach Stella tomorrow evening. But that depends on our new companions. . . .

"It'll be quicker if we go by umbra," Jada says.

I shuffle uneasily and eye my new partners.

"Hey, um, Lux, Nox. Can me and TJ ride on you?" I ask.

"We're not pets to carry you around all day," growls Lux.

"Why do you want us to carry you?" Nox asks.

I'm learning that he's the voice of reason, more so than Mr. Grouchy beside him. I glance at Jada, but she keeps her mouth shut. *Oh yeah, I forgot. They're my problem.*

"We heard that." I jump as Lux speaks to me, and I grumble under my breath, having completely forgotten that tiny little detail: our thoughts are now permanently connected. That is definitely gonna be a pain in the butt.

"You fear us. . . . Why?" Nox asks, his eyes curious.

"I just had a bad experience with an umbra when I was younger," I mutter, trying my best to think of anything but that red-eyed hellhound.

"We will not harm you," Nox says, and I look up. His golden eyes are as gentle as his voice. I want to believe that this shadowy beast speaks the truth, but it's hard.

"I don't know what kind of umbra you saw, but we are not weak. We control our actions, unlike some," Lux scoffs, headbutting me.

I hiss, rubbing my forehead. *What was that for? Jerk.*

"For your foolish thoughts," he answers, and I ball my fist at him, making the umbra snicker.

I clear my throat and try again. "Please help me, guys. We need to get to the City of Light. My home's been taken over and my mum told me to go there."

"But that doesn't answer the question. We said, why should we carry you?" Lux asks.

His attitude is starting to get on my last nerve.

"Because we're supposed to be a team, and umbra are faster than people. I wouldn't ask if we weren't in such a hurry. Please, can you help me?" I say through gritted teeth. They tilt their heads together.

A voice chuckles inside my head.

"Fine, calm down. You're loud and bossy for such a little thing. We know we're better than you humans at everything," Lux says.

"I see why we were drawn to you now . . . ," Nox adds. *"This will be interesting. A human who fears umbra and yet tames two. Yes, as you ask so politely, we will carry you and the one named TJ."*

My face goes red with embarrassment, but I brush it off, trying to ignore it. I crouch before Lucas, putting my hands on his shoulders. He looks at me curiously with those big eyes of his, and I smile. "All right, Lu-Lu. You're going to fly with Jada."

"No!" he yells, shrugging off my hands, and I look at him, confused. "I wanna go with you, Mimi."

"You're probably too heavy to be on Lux's back with me. Stop being difficult." I already decided to ride Lux, since he seems to be the grouchy one. At least I know Lucas will be safe with Jada.

Lucas flails his arms and stamps his feet in protest.

"We don't have time for your tantrums. You're gonna draw attention to us!" I tell him, but he yells louder.

"No! You're being mean. You know the number one family rule and you're breaking it!"

His words almost tear my heart in half. We already broke that family rule once when we left Mum and Dad in Nubis. As much as I hate to admit it, the pipsqueak is right. He crosses his arms, waiting.

"The main family rule," I begin, "is that we'll always be together . . ."

"And . . ."

". . . never leave each other's side. No matter what."

"So, I'm coming with you on the horsey-fox!" He stamps his foot one last time, and I sigh.

"They don't even look like horses—they're more like deer," I mutter.

A warm hand presses against my back, and I look up to see TJ smiling, but it's not his usual goofy one. I can't help but return it with a cheesy grin.

"Come on, let's go," he says, and we bump fists. "Besides, you got hustled by a four-year-old. There's no coming back from this."

I punch his arm and chuckle. *Jerk.* But at least it's cured the butterflies in my stomach.

I help Lucas up on Lux, then climb up myself, settling behind my little brother.

Lucas grins as he grips Lux's fur.

"Not too tight, tiny human. You'll rip the shadows out," Lux says.

He flashes to his full height, and we're off. I almost scream as we race across the Nightmare Plains. I try my best not to grip Lux too hard, but my pulse is racing. The shadows beneath me swirl against my thighs and fingers, like a gentle blanket, and little electric sparks tingle up my arms and legs. Through the sparkling purple specks of grass and vicious red carnelia weeds, we run under the starlit night. The pounding of Lux's shadow-hooves echoes in my ears as the wind whips my hair, yet there's a warmness that fills me up. Replacing the fear, for the first time, I feel relief . . . and hope. *This is what it's like to ride on an umbra.*

It's nothing like I expected.

At some point my fingers relax and I see that Lucas has fallen asleep. Then my eyes spot an unfamiliar and magical glow ahead. Far, far in the distance, a yellow ball of fire lights a small patch of the kingdom: Nexus and our destination, Stella, the City of Light.

"We're not far from Ignis now, guys! Hang tight!" Jada calls from above.

It's then that Lux and Nox suddenly slow down.

"What's the matter?" I ask, but they're quiet.

I look ahead. Six umbra are gathered on the plain, devouring something I can't quite see, and I'm pretty sure I don't want to either.

One looks up and spots us. Its eyes are bright red, like the blood that drips from its fangs and pincers. It must have alerted the others, because the rest of them look up too, their eyes pinned on their next meal.

Us.

Since when do umbra feed on animals?

"What the . . . ?" TJ mutters.

I swallow a sick feeling as Jada swoops down beside us on Ruby.

"Everyone, stay together. We might have to fight it out," she orders.

My heart's racing, and I thank Lunis that Lucas is still asleep.

The wild umbra approach, pincers snapping, horns ready to attack. The leader is a giant spider-crab, while another is like a monstrous hedgehog with claws and horns all over. For a split second I think its eyes flicker gold, but as I continue to study them, they remain red.

"Anyone got any bright ideas? You know . . . Your boy hasn't exactly got much protection," TJ says.

"They must be more of those experiments. Like Miles's umbra. They all have the same eyes," I say. "The red cloaks might be close."

"You're right," Jada says, putting it all together. She must have heard about the experiments from the other tamers but never saw one for herself. Until Shade, and now this bunch.

Lux, Nox, can you fight them? I ask, and Lux snorts.

"Why should we fight them?"

Gee, helpful, thanks.

Ruby screeches and flares her wings, lifting off into the air and pecking at the huge crab as a warning to back up, but it doesn't. The creatures continue to move in, blood dripping on the grass, and my umbra just *stand* there.

"Guys, come on. Please," I beg. They came to *me* during my Spirit Calling, so why are they being so difficult? Now, of all the stinkin' times!

"Why aren't you helping?" I yell, getting desperate.

A loud laugh echoes in my mind, and I glare down at the glowing white umbra. He turns his head, staring me dead in the eyes, but I don't back down, giving him the toughest look I can muster up. I'm not gonna be a pushover.

"Just because you tamed us does not mean we must follow your every command. Remember that, child."

We don't have time for this. I look to Nox and he blinks at me, yet I swear I can see the faintest of smiles on his face. It's clear that neither is gonna make this easy on me.

I gather all the inner strength I have, clenching my fist as my thoughts explode. Enough is enough!

Don't you guys dare let anything happen to Lucas! Protect him and I'll protect you! I promise!

Energy bursts from my mind straight to theirs, making a connection I never felt before, and suddenly, Lux and Nox stand alert, eyes snapping open wide. They launch forward, releasing a deafening scream as the wild umbra roar out and fall back, then begin to retreat.

"Let's make a break for it!" Jada yells, and without a single word, Lux and Nox race away with us on their backs before the wild umbra can recover. In the back of my mind, the buzz of the connection between me, Lux, and Nox echoes. For a split second, we felt like one.

We don't slow down until we reach a broken, moss-covered gateway, smiling with relief as we stand before Ignis.

TJ jumps off Nox to take a look around.

"Don't go too far," Jada warns, landing on her feet beside me, and Ruby transforms into her baby form. I hop off Lux and help Lucas down after. He whines, grumpy after waking up, and much to my annoyance, I end up carrying him on my back.

We walk cautiously into the derelict city, and I try not to think about what happened here when it fell. All those poor people. Ash and rubble cover the once-clear diamond path that ran through the town. Shops with busted windows and houses with caved-in roofs surround us, with no signs of life. Our footsteps and the gentle whistle of the wind break the silence, but the abandoned ghost town sends chills through my spine. We are truly far from home.

"This is proper weird, man . . . ," TJ mutters. "I mean, I don't know what I was expecting, but . . ." He suddenly stops and I glance over. He is staring at something on the ground. It's a small bunny rabbit doll, torn and abandoned.

"Jeez," TJ says, but his eyes give him away. They always do. "I wonder if the little kid got away."

I shift Lucas on my back and place my hand on TJ's shoulder. "They did," I say. But who knows? I can only hope.

Mum told us about the huge, beautiful trees with ruby red and silver leaves that were once a feature of Ignis, but they are no more than skeletons now. How long ago did this city fall to the Darkness and no one knew a thing? We continue walking until something familiar catches my eye and I pause. I feel Lucas shift on my back, but my eyes are pinned to the spot.

"Mia, what's up?"

TJ walks over and freezes when he sees what I'm staring at. Hundreds of crystal stars with names engraved on them litter the ground, trampled and covered in mud.

"It's just like our Missing Tree at home," he murmurs.

"But there's hundreds here. . . ." Just how many people went missing during a Blood Moon in this city?

Mum, Dad, and the tamers were supposed to come here to save people, but there was never anyone left to save. The distress call they got had to have been a trick from those red-cloaked gutterslugs. Everyone's already gone.

TJ picks up one of the stars. "I guess some of these look kinda new, but . . ."

"This place was taken by the Darkness long before Mum and Dad got that distress call," I finish. "It was all a trick by those red cloaks."

These people were gone or missing long before that.

"Mia, there's someone here." Nox's warning sends a chill down my spine and makes me whip my head around. TJ nearly jumps out of his skin as a man in tattered clothes suddenly appears, standing in the street ahead.

"Whoa! Hey, okay! Old man! You can't be sneaking up on people!" TJ says.

"What are you doing here?" the stranger asks in a creaky voice. His shoulders are hunched, and his messy gray hair barely covers the round bald patch at the top of his head. A crooked smile spreads across his face, showing his gums and the few teeth he has left.

I yell as TJ zips behind me and peeks over my shoulder. "No way! You're not hiding behind me, mate!"

How is this man even still here? How long ago did Ignis fall? I set Lucas down, and he grumbles, but stands without making a fuss. That's when I notice that Jada's nowhere to be seen. *Where the flip did she go?*

"Young one." Nox's voice brings my focus back to the old man. We don't move, but he drags his feet closer, his wrinkled old bony hand dipping into his pocket.

He speaks again. "Those are some pretty umbra you have there." His eyes examine Lux and Nox, and their shadow fur bristles.

Be careful, I tell my umbra telepathically. *Something's up with this guy. I don't trust him.*

"Neither do we," Nox replies, and I'm glad we're on the same page on that at least.

"What happened here?" I ask.

The old man stops a few feet away, keeping his distance, but his hand is still in his pocket. Does he have some sort of weapon? Device? Either way, he couldn't exactly outrun us if we made a dash for it.

TJ's fingers are hovering over his slingshot. I feel Lucas's hand slide into mine, and I squeeze it.

"I see you've found the stars. I engraved each and every one . . . ," the old man tells us, ignoring my question.

"Okay, good to know," I say, making up my mind. "We'll just be on our way now."

"We've been in the dark for so long. . . ."

I pause. *We? Who's we?*

It's getting creepier by the second.

A big crooked smile spreads across his face again. "But it's just the way he likes it. He wants us all to embrace the Darkness."

I open my mouth to speak, but TJ grabs my other hand and beats me to it.

"Hey, sorry, but we really were just passing through. Gotta go! See ya!"

We speed-walk away, but when we reach the corner, something yanks me back. The wrinkly old man grins, inches from my face, gripping my arm with a wild look in his eyes. I scream. Lucas yells, and I let go of his hand as he runs behind Lux.

"He's coming, you know."

The old man's eyes are full of glee. I try and yank my arm away, but his grip tightens.

"LET GO!"

Nox charges at the man, and I scream again as he releases me. My heart is racing. The old man's chaotic laughter pierces the air, and I realize he might have lost part of his soul to the Darkness completely. A piece of him forever taken by that monster trapped in the Spirit Plain.

"The Reaper King is coming!" He throws his hands to the sky, and suddenly winces as something flies past his nose.

"Okay, it's time to stop playing around. Mia, let's go!" TJ orders, brandishing his slingshot. I hadn't even realized he had let go of my hand. "Don't make me do it, old man!"

"He'll get you! He'll get all of you!" the man yells over and over again. We jump on Lux and Nox and race through the town, taking a different route, never looking back.

We eventually stop in front of some small houses, their color faded and their busted windows all boarded up. I help Lucas off Lux, but he's still shaking as I put him on the ground. I touch my arm where the man grabbed me—I can still feel the indent of his fingers. Lucas grips his hair, pulling at his curly locks and squeezing his eyes shut.

"I don't want to see the scary man again. . . . I don't want to . . ."

"Where did Jada go? She literally just dusted out and left for no reason," TJ says.

"I don't know," I say, starting to get worried. "That old man seemed alone, but do you think someone got her?"

"But Ruby would have squawked or something," TJ argues, and it's a good point.

Lucas whimpers and I take his hand, while TJ and Nox search for a safe place to camp. Breathing slowly, I kneel down by my little brother.

"Lu-Lu, look at me." He slowly opens his watery eyes, and I smile. "What do we do when we're scared?"

He points to his chest and then to me, and clasps his hands together.

"Yeah. You and me, together always. Remember, remember, remember," I say, clasping my hands the same. "As long as you do, you'll always be okay. I'm here. That's family promise number one."

He sniffs and smiles, and I reach over and ruffle his hair. "Thank you, Mimi."

"I'm your big sister. I've got you, Lu-Lu. Always. Now come on, let's catch up with TJ and Nox."

He takes my hand again, and with Lux, we walk past the broken and abandoned houses. Little smudges of color on the roofs are the only reminders of how amazing the city once was. Mum said that Ignis used to hold fire festivals every year before the Darkness began to take over the cities. Fire spinners would dance up and down the streets, and the festivities would last all night. Apparently, Ignis was always known as the party city, but now . . . lampposts that once shone blue and yellow are busted and broken like ancient relics, and parks are now ash.

Everything is gone.

Despite it all, I smile, seeing little pockets of flowers blooming in the odd bits of soil. Maybe they are a sign of hope.

"It's so pretty," Lucas says, pointing to one of the flowers, his other hand squeezing mine. I squeeze it back, but I can't relax. There's still no sign of Jada.

"Guys! There you are!"

We spin round to see Jada and Ruby. I race over and pull her into the biggest hug.

"What's got into you lot? I wasn't gone for *that* long," she says as Lucas hugs her too, jumping up and down.

TJ reappears as well. "You're kidding, right? We just got

harassed by this creepy old man ranting about the Reaper King, and we had no idea where you were. We are *not okay!*" he says, throwing his hands in the air. I couldn't have said it better myself.

"He was a mean old man," Lucas adds.

"Where did you go? You can't just ditch us like that," I say.

"Sorry. I heard something weird, so I went with Ruby to check it out. Turns out there's a few people still living in this town," she says.

"Took you long enough," Lux grumbles.

"Didn't know you needed protecting," Ruby snipes back, flapping her wings, and Lux growls.

"Well, new rule!" I yell, interrupting. "No one is allowed to randomly disappear. If you want to go check something out, you tell the group!"

"Anyway, guys, come and take a look at this." TJ points to a tiny bungalow with no second floor. "I checked it out. It's free of creepy old men, women, and creatures." He grins and bows his head, ushering us in like a doorman.

"Good job, Johnson," Jada says, smiling.

We take out our lunar torches from the backpack, flashing the light along the walls and up at the ceiling. Despite the floors being creaky and bare, and the paint peeling from the walls, the house still looks strong. The air is thick, musty and dry, but nothing a couple of open windows can't fix.

But the longer we're there, the more it seems like something else lingers in the air, and it follows us down the hall like a shadow, stopping when we stop and looking where we look. I almost jump out of my skin when I catch sight of my reflection in a dusty mirror. At least I can't see any spiders. . . .

Nubis is safe from the Spirit Plain and the Nightmare Plains because the tamers made it so, but what protection do we have here?

Lucas sticks close to me, and Nox and Lux have turned into their baby forms, no bigger than foals. I'm definitely more comfortable with them that size. Doesn't stop them from being rude to me, though.

Something catches my eye out the window. I could have sworn I saw something red float by, but it's quiet out there. There's only the other broken houses on the opposite side of the street and dust blowing by. I blink, but whatever it was is gone as quickly as it came.

"Mimi?"

I force a smile down at Lucas. "It's nothing. Come on."

We all decide to stay together in the living room. Safety in numbers. We grab blankets and pillows from the bedrooms, one of which looks like it belonged to a girl my age. I hope she's now safe in the city of Stella.

Given that Ignis fell without the aid of tamers, though, I can't deny the tiny bit of worry in my heart for her.

We have fun creating a giant makeshift bed on the floor by the fireplace. Then I'm in charge of getting the fire started. Jada checks the area outside again, and TJ puts his chef skills to work, rustling in the emergency backpack for food. He's literally the best chef in Nubis. No joke. He could make a meal fit for Queen Katiya with a slice of bread and a couple of berries. Lucas decides to help him in the kitchen, and when I check on them, I can't help but notice a dusty baby bottle resting on its side on the counter.

I leave them to it and go back to Lux and Nox, though my smile falters when I hear them complaining.

"This is our life now. Living on the run . . . ," Lux grumbles.

I chuck a pillow at him and it bounces off his head. "Can you take your grumbling elsewhere? Outta my brain would be nice."

Nox chuckles while Lux snorts and looks away. I give them a small smile and get back to work on the fire, clicking and rubbing the flint and steel from our emergency pack, trying to get a spark. A snicker echoes in my mind once again, but I ignore it. Little sparks fly, but no fire follows, and I throw the rock and steel down, irritated.

I'm such an idiot. . . . Mum would be able to do it if she was here, but she isn't, and neither is Dad. I wrap my arms around myself and sniff as the bridge of my nose burns and my eyes sting. *I just want to go home. . . .*

"Mimi!"

I quickly wipe my eyes with my sleeve and pick up the flint and steel again.

"Mimi, come see what me and TJ are making." Lucas runs over and pulls at my arm. I ignore him, focusing on the wood already in the fireplace and tapping the flint and steel together, but every word feels like a poke in my chest. I bash with more force, ignoring the jolts of pain and my stinging eyes. *I want to go home. I want to go home.*

"Mimi! Listen to me!"

"Lucas, get off!" I yank my arm out of his grip and glare at him.

TJ runs into the room, looking shocked.

"Whoa, what's going on? Mia, calm down." His words fuel me up even more. I bash the rock one last time and finally fire erupts, blasting heat into the room.

"No!" I yell, standing up. "I'm sick and tired of everything. I haven't showered, I'm hungry, and I'm scared Mum and Dad are being tortured, or worse. I'm tired of pretending everything's going to be okay when it isn't! These people, the ones who lived here? The girl my age and the baby whose bottle is still in the kitchen? They're probably *dead*. They're gone. And that's exactly what's going to happen to us!"

Jada returns in time to catch my outburst, and everyone goes quiet. I feel terrible when I see Lucas's face. For a moment he stands still, completely shocked. Then his eyes squeeze shut and he bursts into tears. Instant regret rushes through me. My own eyes blur with tears again and I reach out, but he bats my hand away.

He runs over to TJ, who picks him up, making me feel more of a jerk.

"Lucas, I'm really sorry."

He doesn't even look at me, and the tears finally unleash and flood down my cheeks.

So much for being a good big sister . . .

"It's probably best you leave the small one be," Nox says, and with no other choice, I do. TJ takes him back to the kitchen and I sit down in front of the fire, staring into the flames.

Jada sits down beside me. "It'll be okay." She wraps an arm around my shoulders, and I let her. For a moment, I close my eyes, imagining she's Mum.

"Hey, what happened to the positive, nerdy girl I know and love?" she says. "We'll do everything we can to save everyone. Don't worry. You'll soon go back to being teacher's pet."

"I'm not a teacher's pet. I don't suck up to you. I'm my own woman," I protest. Jada laughs, gently punching my arm.

"You're nowhere near grown yet, girl. You better chill with that talk. Besides, I'm the teacher, so I know a future teacher's pet when I see one. It's not a bad thing."

That makes me laugh too, and soon the tears that stained my face dry up.

"Seriously," she says, "you'll be all right, and so will everyone else. If worst comes to worst, we go to the queen's citadel castle and tell her what's going on, and she'll be able to use her own powers to stop all of this. They might not even know what's happening right now."

"How can you know that?" I ask. How can anyone?

"Trust me, I know," she says, tapping her nose. "We've got—" She cuts herself off.

"Got what?" I ask, and she smiles.

"Each other."

"Well, yeah, I guess. I'm definitely glad I'm not alone," I say, cradling my knees. That would've been way worse. "How did you know you wanted to be a tamer anyway, Jada?"

"Honestly? It was your mum who inspired me."

My lips part in shock, and she laughs gently to herself, continuing. "I didn't know my parents growing up. My mum went missing during the Blood Moon when I was three, and my dad wasn't around, so I lived with my grandparents until they died. But I . . . I've always wanted to have a big family, and the tamers seemed to be just that. And your mum was everything I wanted to be: strong, smart, a tamer *and* a scientist. She was amazing at everything she did, and she was always nice to me and my grandparents."

Jada's eyes look so far away, lost in memory as she speaks about Mum, and a warmth fills my heart and stomach as she continues.

"I remember one day, after my Becoming One with the Darkness. I had helped some of the other kids prepare for it. . . . Everyone was nervous and on edge. I came out of the room and your mum brought me and the other kids the biggest cake ever. With ten words, she calmed everyone."

"What were the words?"

"'You can do it. You can do anything and everything,'" Jada says. "From that moment, I wanted to be able to do the same. To be able to encourage and help others like she did, but not just with words—with training, too, and here I am. Tamer and teacher."

My mouth opens to speak, but no words come out. Pride wells up in me with thoughts of my mum, and I grip my legs harder.

"Don't tell anyone else that story, though. I don't want you ruining my tough image," Jada says, winking.

We both chuckle as the kitchen door clicks open and TJ stands there with a big grin on his face. I sigh happily as the faint smell of thyme wafts to my nose, making my stomach growl.

"All right, hungry kids, the chef is done. Dinner is ready. Come and grab your bowls. Today's special is an awesomely delicious pumpkin soup with tree cress, and magi plants for a nice spicy kick. We got crackers to go with it too." He kisses his fingers at his masterpiece, and I get some bowls from the kitchen. Glad the taps still work, I give them a quick rinse and set them down between us on the blankets.

TJ sets the pot on the fire.

Later, as we eat, my eyes flick to Lucas as he prods at his food. Our eyes meet and I give him a little smile, but he doesn't return it, instead looking back down at his bowl. Lux and Nox glance at each other, but no one says a word. TJ suddenly clears his throat.

"Well, this is a little awkward," he says. Jada gives him the deadest look and he grins, shrugging. "I mean, things could be worse, right? We could be out in the wilderness with no toilet, no food, and naked. *That* would be so peak."

"Shut up. . . . Just please, shut up," I say, and he winks at me. At least he's managed to break the tension, and the atmosphere *has* cleared a little.

"Still, we are definitely lucky we haven't bumped into those red-cloaked people yet," Jada says. *Reapers, too . . .*

"Yeah, that's a point. What *are* we going to do if we bump into the red cloaks and that other kid again?" TJ asks.

"Miles?" I ask. I set down my bowl, ignoring the little bit of soup still at the bottom. "Nothing. I'm not going to fight him. I told you, he isn't bad. Someone is *making* him do this."

TJ makes a face. "But what if he attacks us?"

"He isn't our priority. Getting Mia to Stella is. If we see him, we try to avoid conflict at all costs," Jada says, and I raise a brow at her. We're *all* going to Stella. Why single me out?

After dinner, we settle down for the night. Lucas lies next to me, pulling the covers over his head, but I can't sleep. The fire crackles softly beside us, and I gently reach out and pat him.

"Lucas, I'm sorry, okay? I didn't mean to make you upset," I whisper. Lucas wiggles a bit, still awake. "I'm just . . . a little scared, but I'm your big sister, so it's my job to look after you and save Mum and Dad, all right?"

He peeps out of the covers with a serious face, and I give him the best smile I can.

He pulls the covers all the way down and looks at me.

"Mimi, it's okay. I'll look after you, too."

My eyes well up and I hug him close to me, glad we have each other.

I've just closed my eyes when his quiet voice calls to me again.

"Mimi?"

"Yeah?"

"How did you do that?" he asks.

"What?"

"The fire."

"Magic," I muse, and he scrunches up his face.

"It's not magic."

"It is."

"Isn't."

"Is!"

Jada starts to snore, and we both clap our hands over our mouths, sniggering. The noise is strangely calming.

Lucas sighs. "I miss Mummy and Daddy." Small tears run down his face, and I brush them away with my thumbs and kiss his forehead like Mum does.

"I know. I miss them too."

He cuddles into me and I close my eyes, keeping him snuggled against me as I run my fingers through his curls. "We've got a plan, and it'll work."

It has to.

Then there's Miles. I have to find out what's going on with him. I have to save him as well.

An Account of Everything Known about the "Darkness" and the Attack on Nubis
A report by Lila McKenna

When a city falls to the Darkness, a thick smoky mist created by the Reaper King takes over. The smoke numbs the senses of the citizens and anyone who might try to protect the city, and then the Reaper King's minions, the reapers, attack—harvesting souls that will be devoured by the Reaper King.

The Darkness cannot be penetrated by the sun, and it seems only those who hold the power of light and dark within them, such as the queen, can pierce it.

After the initial attack on a city, the Darkness hovers over it like a dark cloud, sucking the joy and hope from anyone left behind or overlooked by the reapers. The cities never see the light or the warmth of the sun again.

However, a few of us found a way to make our dark city habitable again. Daniel, Magnus, Maria, and I were the first to find a way to connect with the umbra, becoming "tamers" who fought off the reapers. With the use of moonlight, we embedded reflecting moon crystals into the main walls of the city. This appears to keep the effects of the Darkness and any potential reapers at bay. Using the power of the moon, we illuminated the city with artificial lamps and lights.

So far there has been no sign of the Darkness penetrating our defenses. Only the Blood Moon every five years continues to be a threat. Through either the weakening of our protections or the strengthening of dark power during that time, when the Blood Moon rises, our fortifications seem to falter, resulting in mysterious disappearances and—perhaps—deaths.

Nubis is the one city that has been able to recover from the effects of the Darkness, although it remains forever under the light of the moon.

CHAPTER TEN

I wake up at Sky Connect, and through the window the city is briefly illuminated by the silver light of the stars. I get up and look closer, and right beside the moon, the giant number three in the sky changes to two. Two more days to save Mum and Dad.

I stretch my arms and pat Lucas to get up, but my hand falls on an empty space. I look around and realize I'm alone in the room. I panic as I scrabble through the blankets and bedding. "Lucas!"

Jada and TJ come in from the kitchen. "He's exploring the house," Jada says.

At least he stuck to the rules and told her. I take a deep breath, calming my racing pulse. I fix my hair the best I can after the second time sleeping without a bonnet, and drink some of the leftover soup for breakfast while TJ and Jada explore the house again. Afterward, I pack one of the blankets in the rucksack. Almost ready to go.

We scavenge for anything else useful in the house, and I sneeze as dust tickles my nose.

"Man, I hope we can sleep in a proper bed again soon. The floor was so hard," TJ complains, stretching and clicking his neck.

I'm scooping up the last of the bedding from the living room when Nox and Lux return from the hallway.

"It's a straight line for Stella now. We should make it before the next Sky Connect," Jada says. Music to my ears.

"I can't wait to see the queen," TJ says. "I wonder if she's actually as awesome as people say."

I roll my eyes.

"I know plenty of people who say the opposite," I grumble. "If she was so great, then the whole kingdom would have light again by now."

I turn away and start calling for Lucas, but TJ is annoyed now. "Hey, watch your mouth, you muppet. That's the queen you're talking about."

"Exactly, a queen who can't do anything. And I'd rather be a muppet than a clown," I retort. I walk out into the hallway,

looking around. Lucas never usually takes this long to answer.

I cup my mouth with my hands and yell out one last time at the top of my lungs: "Hey, pipsqueak! We're leaving without you, if you don't come!"

Silence. My stomach lurches, and panic rushes through me. "Guys, where's Lucas?"

Nox pauses for a moment, his snout in the air. *"Mia, I do not smell the little one's scent."*

Something catches my eye in the bedroom that belonged to the little girl. The curtains are swishing back and forth, and a deathly chill blows through a wide-open window.

Anxiety crawls all over my skin. I can barely breathe or even think. A hand rests on my shoulder, but I don't know whose it is.

"He might still be in the house. We'll find him," Jada says, and everyone rushes around me, calling for Lucas with fuzzy voices. I walk back into the hallway in a panic.

"We can feel your anxiety rising, and your heart is beating too fast. Don't worry, Mia. We will find him."

He wouldn't have run off. He must have been taken, and he could be anywhere by now. Something brushes against my cheek, and I snap out of my thoughts to see Nox's head near to mine. I realize it was his nose that touched me.

Jada and TJ run back to me by the front door, and my anger boils over. I knew something was wrong!

"You said he was in the house!"

"He was, I swear!" Jada says. "I saw him playing in one of the bedrooms a few minutes ago."

But it's not good enough. *He's gone!*

"Everyone, relax," TJ says, and I shoot him a look.

Jada starts, "Look, I'll go—"

"No!" I cut her off. "He's my brother. My responsibility. Stay here in case he comes back."

I burst through the front door, running out into the street before they can stop me. They call after me, but I don't hear what they say.

Mum and Dad trusted me to look after Lucas, and I failed.

I look to either side of me, searching for any sign of him. Every alleyway and street is empty, and the buildings all start to look the same. It feels like I'm running in a maze full of tricks.

"Lucas!" My throat burns, but I keep at it, screaming out his name. "LUCAS!"

What if he's hurt somewhere? What if he's captured? What if those red cloaks were here all along? My legs feel like lead and begin to ache, and then a jolt shoots through my brain, and I'm no longer alone in my thoughts.

"Mia, we are with you."

I hear the sound of hoofs, and Nox and Lux are at my side in their normal forms.

"We'll help you find your younger sibling," Nox says.

"Thanks for leaving us like that. You threw that little rule of yours out of the window. It was a pain to find you," were Lux's less generous words. *"Besides, the little runt probably just wandered off."*

Despite the relief I feel at seeing them, I know Lucas wouldn't go anywhere without me. The longer he's gone, the worse I feel. The air's cold, and the emptiness of the town grows, with my little brother out there somewhere.

A loud bang sounds ahead, and I round the corner, stopping with a skid when I see my brother.

"Mimi!"

My heart leaps hearing Lucas's voice, but my smile drops as he scrambles to escape the clutches of the creepy old man with bad teeth. My anger bubbles up afresh.

"Let him go!"

"I can't let him go," the man says. "I needed him to get you to come. All of you. And now they're coming."

He's talking so fast I barely understand what he's saying. Lucas continues to kick and squirm.

"Who's coming? What are you talking about?" I step forward, but he pulls Lucas back, farther away from me.

"The Elite will bring about the change that will purge this damned kingdom!" His laughter shrills through the air, and I snatch my bo staff from my thigh belt. He clutches Lucas tighter, making him yell out, and I lunge forward.

"Wait, Mia." Everything inside me is screaming to attack, but Nox's words force me to stay put. *"One wrong move and he may hurt the little one."* I nod slowly and slightly lower my staff.

The old man continues to rant. "I'll get a nice reward for the two of you."

Money. You've got to be kidding me. We're being given away for *money*? My bo staff shakes in my grasp.

Lux, Nox, you can hear me, right? I've got a plan.

The umbra absorb my thoughts, and Nox slinks off in the darkness. Lucas cries out again and I spring toward the man, bo staff ready.

"I said let him go, you gutterslug!"

I'm about to swing my staff when a howl sounds, stopping me. The old man cackles and I look behind him to see another man, this one in a dark red cloak. On his head is a purple crown, and a shiny badge with a purple eagle is pinned to his cloak.

I freeze, recognizing him as the man who gave the message in the sky, but something else about him strikes me. I *know* him from somewhere. . . .

He sits on a huge umbra that's a mix between a shadow lion, a tiger, and a wolf, with white stripes streaking across its black fur and a long, scorpion-like tail. Lux growls, and the hairs on the back of my neck stand on end. Five more men appear at his side, riding on normal horse-looking umbra.

There's no mistaking it—the red cloaks have been following us, and now they have a name—the Elite. I search for Miles among them, but he's not there. I don't know if I feel relief or disappointment.

"I've got them! I've got the two of them," the old man trills. "Where's my reward? I did exactly what you said!"

The leader smirks. "We never *promised* you anything."

The old man's eyes widen as the leader stretches out his hand to him. *The smoke!*

Nox slowly walks out from the shadows. Our eyes connect for a split second as the cloaked men get closer.

"NOW!" I scream.

Instantly, Nox leaps forward, biting the old man's shoulder with his sharp teeth. Lucas flails his arms, forcing the man to let go. Nox grabs Lucas by the back of his shirt with his teeth and throws him up on his back.

"Don't move!" the purple crown man yells, and they all surge toward us.

I leap up on Lux's back and point to the men. "Ram right through them!" I yell. "We have to get back to the others."

Lux taps the ground twice before sprinting toward them. He and Nox bow their horns down together as the cloaked men pull out their rope guns.

"Full speed through these clowns!"

"I'm starting to like you, Mouse," Lux says.

They ramp up their speed and I lean forward, clutching tight. Side by side, Lux and Nox blast through the men. They scatter and shout, and some are thrown off their umbra, but we don't stop until we're back at the house.

TJ and Jada are there waiting for us in agitation with the emergency bag in tow.

"Hey, you found him. Are you all right? What happened?" Jada asks.

"I'll tell you later. We really gotta go!" I yell.

I pull Lucas onto Lux with me.

TJ opens his mouth, but the sound of furious yells draws closer. Quickly, he jumps onto Nox. "Okay, I get it. Go now, talk later. Let's get out of here."

As the red cloaks come into sight, Jada jumps onto Ruby and we leave Ignis, hopefully never to return.

CHAPTER ELEVEN

Under the bright white moon, we venture through the
Nightmare Plains again. The wind is behind us as we leap
over the snapping carno plants and slip through the crooked trees,
breaking through the wooden branches that scrape against us.

Jada and Ruby grace the forever-night sky above our heads.
I wish Lux could fly, but leaping through the air feels close to
it. The air rushes through my fluffy locks, and I feel scared and
excited at the same time. Beneath my fingertips, Lux's fur is
as soft as a bunny umbra. Once I catch Jada glancing down at
me, but she quickly looks away with a smile on her face. I find
myself smiling too, with a weird sense of pride.

Not for long. Lux interrupts my thoughts.

"Don't relax just yet. I can still smell their disgusting scents," he says, looking behind us, and I actually sense them too. In my mind, I see six cloaked men highlighted in red, riding on their umbra, fueled by their ferocious drive to find.

What the flip is going on? I can feel them.

Nox chuckles, brushing off my slight panic. *"We are connecting more. You can sense and see what we can, if you choose to."*

I can't help but smile a little more at that.

The trail seems endless, and we lose track of time. Lucas has fallen asleep against me, and Jada is above with Ruby. I can no longer sense the pursuers, and neither can my umbra, but still we have to keep going.

TJ groans loudly, resting his head on Nox's neck.

"How long have we been going for?" he moans. Anyone would think he's the one carrying Nox. I'm tired too, but we have to push on.

"Lux, Nox, how are you guys holding up?" I call out to them.

"We're all right for now, but we should rest soon," Nox says.

"Well, I've been carrying you two for hours. A break would be nice," Lux responds with his usual snark. I pat his neck.

"I know, sorry," I tell him. When we reach Stella, I'll look after them properly and start getting to know them better. After all, they're going to be my partners for life.

"Lux, before I called you and Nox in the Spirit Plain, what did you guys do?" I ask.

"We traveled far and wide from kingdoms and places far beyond Lunis," he says, wiggling his back for a second. *"Some were islands, small pieces of land surrounded completely by water. Others were very mountainous."*

My eyes widen. A place completely surrounded by water . . . that sounds so cool.

"But you . . . ," Nox chimes in. *"Your spirit called to us. It's something we've never felt before."*

A warmth spreads through me at his words, but I still can't help but wonder if I'll ever be a good tamer. . . .

"We had heard tales of umbra finding counterparts. . . . Tamers, who would lead us to the light, and together, we would fulfill each other's lives with more purpose and meaning than we ever imagined. We just never thought ours would be a child," Lux says.

Yeah? Well, I'm not just a kid.

Lux snorts, leaning back and bumping his horn against my head. *"We'll soon see about that. That was brave, what you did for your brother, but it was reckless and foolish as well."*

I had you two backing me up, didn't I? I guess we'll find out together why we were meant to be partners.

I'm determined to at least find that out. I wonder again what the pictures in that book mean, if they really do have anything to do with me.

"Guys! Up ahead!" Jada yells from above.

A roar rips through the air and Lux skids to a stop, jerking Lucas and me forward. I grab him before he's thrown off, and his eyes burst open. Nox stops beside us with TJ as Ruby swoops down, landing close by.

"What the hell was that?" TJ yells out, and Jada points ahead.

A group of red-eyed umbra stand across the way, a reddish aura coating their black shadowy fur. They have manes like a lion's, and their faces and bodies are those of giant lizards, with razor-sharp teeth. They're in their normal forms—and they're *big*.

Behind these umbra stand their gutterslug red-cloaked tamers with their hoods up and their leader with them.

"This is why they stopped following us from Ignis," Jada mutters. "They had backup."

"We're not doing your stinkin' ritual!" I yell. "So can you please just leave us *alone*?" TJ gives me a look, like he wants to laugh at me. But I'm just so exhausted of running. Of being afraid.

The beings ahead, who ignore me, are like distortions in the moonlight. There, but not there, like human cutouts made from shadows, with their blazing red cloaks flapping in the wind. Shadow power, I realize. Just like back in Nubis. They used those same powers to cover my face in that shadow smoke. Now they're projecting themselves. With every blink, they twitch a little closer to us, making me jump. Could they still harm us? Even if not, the umbra definitely could.

"Warning. Danger," Lux and Nox growl.

Bony skeleton fingers pop out from long sleeves, and the leader with the crown speaks.

"Our powers are strengthening. He will be awakened, and we need the Lightcasters. Come now and you won't be hurt."

I grip Lux tighter, but my hands won't stop shaking.

Beware of the Reaper Creeper, creeping in the night. When innocent children meet the tragic ends of their short little lives.

The poem repeats over and over in my head.

Is this the end for us?

"Yo . . . The red cloaks have big shadow powers now? How is that even possible?" says TJ. "We need to go! Like NOW!"

"Let's get them." The words tumble out of my mouth before I can stop them.

"No, fall back," snaps Jada. My jaw drops, and she gives me a hard look.

"We can't keep running all the time," I tell her. "They'll just follow us, and then what? Those Elite or red cloaks, whatever they are, won't stop coming for us."

"You and your umbra are no way ready to fight full-out yet. And we don't know what these things are capable of," says Jada. "Bone Valley is close by. We'll lose them there."

The figures twitch closer.

"I agree. Yep, a hundred and a billion percent," TJ says quickly. "Let's dip."

Despite my frustration, I do as Jada says. Ruby's cries pierce the air as she flies up, and we fall back, breaking off into another run. The hooded figures stare after us, but they don't give chase. The image haunts me. Why aren't they following us? Unless they know they can capture us elsewhere . . .

We keep running, and the feeling that eyes watch our every move grows stronger by the second.

"What the hell were those things?" asks TJ. "They can't have actually been the red cloaks—they seemed to have some kind of . . . shadow power like reapers. But the Reaper King was sealed away. You don't think they're actually his new minions . . . new reapers?"

His voice is filled with worry.

"*We've seen beings like that on our travels near the city of Astaroth,*" Lux says.

"*There are some places in the Spirit Plain that even we umbra do not go. The Reaper King is sealed there, but that doesn't mean he is powerless outside it. Maybe it's their reward for helping him escape. . . . They have shadow powers, and the closer they are to releasing him . . . the stronger they get,*" Nox adds.

The poem is still echoing in my mind, along with the engraved images on the wall of Nubis. I think they're right. The Elite are the Reaper King's new minions, and together they are going to finish the job and plunge the entire world into complete darkness, so they can bring the Reaper King back and rule a new dark realm . . . and this time, we don't have a strong queen to save us.

"The old man back in Ignis called them the Elite," I tell TJ.

"Red cloaks, Elites, gutterslugs, they're all the same to me," he snorts.

"Guys, hold up. There's something in the ground!" Jada calls out. Ruby lands with a heavy thud and Jada jumps off, racing ahead.

"Hey! Wait!" I yell, running with Lux to catch up to her. I hop off, helping Lucas down after. Jada stops among some blue lava buds—small flowers that pulse with light—where one patch of grass is darker than the rest. I walk over, hearing an odd thud under my shoe. I brush my foot over a little mound and tap it again.

"I think I've found something," I call out. I crouch down and claw at the dirt. Jada joins in, and we scramble to dig up the dirt. It flies everywhere and I stop, spotting something.

"Look!" Buried within, a little brown handle pokes out.

"Is it a trapdoor or something?" I ask.

TJ runs over with Nox, and upon seeing the handle, he shakes his head.

"Nope, don't do it," he says, and I give him a look, snapping a finger to my lips for him to zip it.

"Is it scary, Mimi?" Lucas asks, and I shrug.

"Not sure, Lu-Lu."

"Wait a sec. I remember seeing something weird here on the map. Let me check." Jada digs out the map from the bag and spreads it out, then points to a cross with the word *Beware* scribbled next to it.

"Beware?" TJ says, scratching the back of his head. "Don't sound like a good idea to me. . . ."

"But it leads to the swamp. Look." She follows a black line that looks like a tunnel with her finger. "It's right where we need to go, and we'd make it in half the time if we go this way. And we'd be out of reach of the Elite."

"But what do you think the 'beware' means, though?" I ask.

"On our tamer maps, we usually write 'beware' if we've encountered bandits around. But we can handle normal bandits," Jada says, and we all look at TJ.

"We're going," Jada and I say.

"If we get eaten down there, don't come crying to me," he mutters, but we need to hurry. Plus, we have three umbra now, and we're trained in martial arts. *We got this.*

With a swift tug, the door lifts, revealing a deep, dark hole with a ladder leading down into it. We all gather around it, staring into the abyss, and I grab a rock and drop it down. A loud thud echoes after a few seconds.

"It doesn't sound like a big drop. I will look," Ruby says. She

transforms into her baby version and swoops in. She's soon back.

"There are definitely signs that humans have passed through here, as the map suggests, but it appears empty. The ladder will give you safe passage down. It is safe," she says, and we all look at each other again, waiting for someone to volunteer themselves.

"So . . . who's going down first, then?" TJ asks, and he jerks his head back when we all look at him. "Nope, not gonna happen. I vote Jada."

"Don't you think it's about time that you tried to be brave for once and take the lead?" she says, rolling her eyes.

"Nah, I'm good, thanks. Mia, you're a tamer now. Send one of your buddies down," TJ says, jerking his chin to Lux and Nox.

"No way!"

"You've got two, though!"

Lux growls and snaps his teeth at TJ, who quickly grins, raising his hands for forgiveness.

"You have to be nice to the horsey-foxes," Lucas says, wagging his finger at TJ.

"Our names are Lux and Nox, baby human. Our appearance just happens to resemble what you people call deer and foxes," Lux corrects him.

"I'm not a baby. I'm a boy!"

"You're all clowns. I'll do it." I stand up, grabbing a lunar torch from the bag and switching it on. I take a deep breath and climb down before I can change my mind. Everyone's shocked faces are the last thing I see, before I skip the last few rungs, as they don't fully reach the bottom, and jump, landing with a small thud below. I take the torch from my mouth and sigh in relief.

I look around, shining my torch into the tunnel ahead. The light doesn't even hit the back of it, like it's endless.

Wet drip-drops echo around me, and the smell of damp and mud floods my nose. I look up at the night sky, suddenly feeling very, very alone.

"Mimi. Are you okay?"

"You alive, superstar?"

I cup my hands around my mouth and yell. "Yeah! All good down here."

Two more thuds sound, and Lux and Nox are by my side, having jumped down. Their golden eyes glow bright in the darkness, and Lux's fur is like a white lamp, while Nox blends in with the tunnel, truly becoming a shadow. So cool. I grin, chuffed that they quickly came after me. I stroke their heads, enjoying the soft feel of their fur as their shadow matter tickles my fingertips.

"It's all right to come down," I call.

Above, I hear Jada trying to convince Lucas to let her lower him first. His voice is hesitant, because he's scared to climb down by himself, but he finally agrees.

"Mia, I'm lowering the little man down!"

"Cool, I got him!" I yell back.

Small feet appear from the hole as he nervously clings to the ladder for support when she lowers him down as much as she can, and I stretch my arms up as high.

"No, no, wait!" Lucas cries out. His body shakes and he clings to the rungs, not listening to any of us as he changes his mind, and I frown.

"It's okay. I'm right here!" I call up, and he relaxes a bit when he sees me. He steps slowly down the ladder one foot at a time, with me helping him down the last few rungs, and he smiles.

"I did it, Mimi!"

"Good job!"

We high-five as TJ, Jada, and Ruby come down next, and Lucas clings to my leg. I try to push his head away, but he's stuck to me.

"Yo, this place is so booky." TJ makes a face, touching something wet on the wall and sniffing it. He catches me watching him and gives me a nervous chuckle before wiping his fingers on his clothes. *Gross.*

"I've taken lots of different kinds of shortcuts on the plains on tamer patrols, but never one like this," Jada says.

We all look ahead down the endless tunnel. The path ahead is so narrow and cramped, we'll have to go single file.

Jada decides to take the lead this time. She walks forward with one of the flashlights from the rucksack in hand, and we follow close behind. We're careful not to touch the icky wet walls, damp with a strange water that turns from brown to blue under the light.

I slip through with Lucas holding my hand behind me, TJ ahead and Lux and Nox following straight after. The tunnel eventually opens up and gets bigger, allowing us to walk two across. The *drip, drop* of water echoes in the cave, and then the path opens up with more space and splits in two directions further down.

"Where now? The map only shows us the entrance," TJ says.

I flash my torch forward, and a shadowy shape quickly shifts out of sight.

"Hey!" I yell, giving chase a little further down the tunnel. Whatever it is seems to know where it's going, but it keeps just out of sight, dodging each time I shine my torch on it, and stops at the two forking paths.

"How are you gonna be breaking your own rules? Wait up!" TJ yells.

The others run after me as I race after the little shadow, never taking my eyes off it. It runs us around in circles, then suddenly stops, and we get a good look at it.

"Yo, it's an umbra!" TJ exclaims.

Right enough, a small catlike umbra crouches before us. The wings on its back stand up and it growls, baring little fangs.

"It's so cute!" Lucas chuckles, running up to it. "Hello."

He reaches out. The umbra hisses, then sniffs him, and we're all surprised when it bumps its head against Lucas's hand. He pets it gently.

I walk over too and it dashes forward, taking the path on the right.

"Great, your face scared it away." TJ laughs.

"Nah, it was your smell, you sewer-swimmer. . . ."

"He wants us to follow," Lucas says.

"Might as well. Maybe the umbra knows the way out," I say.

We walk down further through the tunnel, which still drips but grows hotter the deeper we get. Soon a wider opening appears up ahead. When we reach it, we come to a stop, all of us speechless.

The tunnel opens up into a giant cavern, and it's packed with umbra of all shapes and sizes. Umbra in the shape of mini elephants are cuddled with umbra who look like kitty cats, like our little friend from earlier. A tall umbra, with the long neck of an alpaca and the body of a kangaroo, with tusks and two big horns, stares at us.

In the center of the cave is a small unlit firepit made from sticks and stones. *Umbra don't make fires.* . . . Beside it is some sort of straw bed, and my heart swells at the sight of a little brown raggedy doll sitting on it. I wonder who it belongs to.

"This is nuts. . . . What are they all doing here?" TJ mutters.

"They've chosen life underground," Nox says.

"More like chosen to hide like cowards."

I shoot Lux a look, but he ignores me, his eyes uncaring as he scans the area.

"Looks like a kid or someone lived down here too . . . ," I whisper.

All the umbra are looking at us now. If they're speaking, it isn't to us, but I notice Ruby squint her eyes slightly, along with Lux and Nox, whose fur bristles.

"Well, they seem peaceful enough," Jada interjects. She doesn't seem nearly as amazed as I am at seeing all these shadow creatures together. "We'll rest here for an hour and then be on our way."

"NO!"

I almost leap out of my skin as a loud male voice booms in my head. It's not Lux or Nox. Jada jumps too. I look at my umbra, but they are staring at the owner of the voice—the tall alpaca-kangaroo creature. His tusks and horns glint in the torchlight, and his long tail is swishing, as if he's angry.

"You humans enslave us, like he did. Like that thing that calls himself a king. We will not be turned against our will," he yells, and my head jerks back.

"What are you talking about?" Jada asks.

"You people. You take advantage of the connection we have to you. Rather than ask for our help, you trap us!"

"No we don't. We . . ." TJ trails off.

I barely feel Lucas leave my side as I glance at Lux and Nox. I have no idea what this umbra is talking about, but he makes me uneasy.

"What do you mean, 'ask'?" TJ tries again, but the umbra doesn't reply.

Lucas is in front of the umbra now. He raises his little hands. "It's okay, Mr. Umbra-roo. We'll help you out of the cave."

"Lucas, NO!" I yell.

Jada, TJ, and I race forward as the umbra swings his tail. It smacks against Lucas, sending him flying across the cave toward us. Jada catches him, crashing to the floor, and I yank out my bo staff.

"Whoa, hey, calm down! He's a little kid!" TJ yells. "Listen—we don't mean any harm. You're talking about those Elite red-cloak thugs who took over our city. They're the ones doing bad things, not us."

"Liars! You humans are all the same!"

"No, they are not," Nox protests. *"Their thoughts do not*

control our own. They do not wield shadow powers like those other humans either. We have free will."

His voice is calm, but I clench my staff tighter, barely holding the anger in. Lucas is crying as Jada comforts him.

"Even if what you say is true, how do we know they won't turn like the others? Leave now, or more of you will be hurt!"

My jaw clenches. This is so wrong. We aren't the enemy! How can he lump us all together? Do they really think tamers force them to stay against their will? Do Mum, Dad, and everyone else even know about this? Is taming umbra actually *wrong*?

"We just need a place to rest for an hour, and then you'll never see us again," I yell. "Please!"

Lucas grips his head with one hand and squeezes my hand with the other. "My head . . . It hurts."

"You do not wish to listen, so prepare yourself! I will make *you leave!"*

"No! Wait!" TJ yells as the umbra charges toward us.

Lucas cries out again, and all the anger inside me explodes.

"Please listen to us!" I scream.

Energy bursts from my body with the scream. A bright light blinds us. Dust and dirt fly up into the air, swirling like a hurricane around us, making the whole cave rattle and rumble. Rubble tumbles from the ceiling, and the whole place is lit.

"MIA!"

The dust erupts in an explosion, filling the whole cave.

Boulders smash to pieces. Then everything suddenly stops. When it settles down, I blink in confusion.

Lux and Nox are standing with me, and Lucas is clinging to my side, but the others are pressed against the walls of the cave, thirty feet away. Ruby is shielding Jada with her wings, while TJ crouches behind them. The wild umbra are clustered together in a group on the other side. All of them have one common look on their faces: complete horror.

What have I done?

CHAPTER TWELVE

I wish I could hide. The air in the cave still feels electric, and everyone's eyes are on me.

"Mimi, you have magic powers . . . ," Lucas says.

I look down at my hands, then back at Lux and Nox.

What happened?

"I don't know . . . I'm not even sure if it was you," Nox says.

"How did you do that?" Jada asks, emerging from behind Ruby. "How? You're not supposed to be able to do that yet. Only Queen Katiya . . ."

"I don't know what happened . . . I . . ." I try to think back, but it was all so quick, my brain's a blur. I didn't even feel anything.

"Wait," I add. "What did you just say?"

"What is she?" a voice in my head interrupts.

"She's dangerous."

"Make her leave."

"We're not safe."

"She has powers like him . . . the king . . ."

What? I clutch my head, trying to push the voices out, but there are so many.

"Enough," Ruby says, raising her wings in an attempt to calm the other umbra.

Jada walks toward them, her eyes softer than usual. I'm still trying to get my thoughts together. What did she mean before? I look up at the wild umbra, each with fearful, untrusting eyes. Did they really think I would hurt them?

"I'm s-sorry," I stutter, but they all continue to huddle away from me.

The umbra with the ferocious tusks steps forward.

"What's your name?" Jada asks, and I watch him carefully.

"I chose not to give myself a name, nor do I wish to be named by someone else," the umbra says, and I raise an eyebrow at Lux and Nox.

"Some are just weird like that," Lux mutters.

"Many umbra prefer to be seen as a collective rather than as individuals. So they do not name themselves. Instead they are all known simply as umbra," Nox explains, but I'm not sure I get it.

"We're sorry for intruding. If you could tell us which direction leads out to the swamp, we'll go," Jada says, looking back at us.

I nod, hoisting Lucas up on Lux. TJ walks ahead with Nox and I look back at the cave, my heart heavy at seeing the destruction I caused.

"Down that tunnel and you will arrive at the swamp," the umbra says, nodding to the right.

"Someone used to live here . . . didn't they?" I can't help asking before we leave down the tunnel, and the main umbra turns to me, his golden eyes falling on the tiny bed. "Who was it?"

He's silent for a moment, as if deciding whether or not to reply. Finally he says, *"She was a human child, such as yourselves, but she was different. We took care of her . . . until she was taken by another human with a cloak as red as the blood you humans bleed."*

"We're saving our parents from the same people. If we see her, we'll help her. I promise," I say solemnly. "And I'm sorry about before."

All the umbra go quiet, seeming to have a silent conversation between themselves. My eyes fall back on the raggedy doll, and Miles appears in my thoughts.

We'll save them all, I tell myself.

"If your words are true, then we thank you. Her name is

Layla," the umbra says. *"I apologize to you and your friends as well, especially to the little one. However, do not ever return here. If you do, you will not leave so easily."*

We bid them all goodbye and take the tunnel that, according to the umbra, will lead us out of the cave.

Our footsteps echo as we venture on. A thousand thoughts are tapping away in my mind. Nothing makes sense.

"Hey, Jada, what did you mean before?" I ask. "You said something about me not being able to do that yet. Only the queen."

She wrinkles her nose, but I'm not letting it go; I'm almost scared that I already know the answer. She sighs heavily.

"When we get to Stella, I'll tell you everything. I promise. Just wait a little longer, okay?" She pats Ruby and they hasten ahead. I growl, frustrated.

"Mouse." I glance down at Lux, who looks over his shoulder at me. *"Whatever she is hiding will be revealed soon, but I don't believe there is anything wrong with you."*

I sigh, patting his neck. *Thanks, Lux . . .*

I hope he's right, but I can't help the sick feeling in my gut that says otherwise. That what happened in the cave was the final confirmation of what I've been nervous about all this time. I don't want to be different. Then my thoughts turn to what the umbra in the cave said, and I think about Spike and Bolt, Lux, Nox, and Ruby. Not once did I consider that they were trapped, bound to us against their will. The Spirit Calling is about finding a connection, not forcing one. Is it actually wrong to bond with an umbra? I never thought to ask Bolt and Spike. Maybe they aren't as happy as they always seemed to be.

"Lux?"

"What is it, little mouse?"

"Do you feel forced to stay with me?"

His chuckle tickles my mind. *"You couldn't force me to do anything. I'm staying because I think things will be much more interesting from here on out."*

"We accepted you as our tamer, just as you have accepted us," Nox chimes in, moving closer to us, and I smile at that. *"We've waited decades to meet you."*

I've read every book about umbra, and yet there's so much I don't know. Maybe umbra aren't the monsters I thought they were, but I still don't know what to feel about the fact that there are some who hate the idea of being tamed. Who hate humans. It's terrifying.

"Hey, I see starlight!" Jada yells. "We're nearly at the end of the cave!"

We hurry forward, and the ground turns into an upward slope as we head for the exit. I beat Jada and Ruby to it and burst through the opening.

And then I freeze, my heart skipping a beat as I stare straight down the barrel of a rope gun.

"Get out of there."

I slowly climb out of the cave, raising my hands.

Waiting for us on the grassy plains are eight of the Elite with their red-eyed umbra.

I glare at the owner of the voice. The leader's purple crown shines in the moonlight, and his umbra snarls as the others emerge behind me.

"Is that all of you?" the leader asks.

I nod.

"Go check," he tells two of his people. A man and a woman brush past me, but thank the kingdom they don't go far enough to discover the wild umbra. When they return, they stay firmly behind us, blocking any escape. TJ steps closer to me, and Lucas is safe on top of Lux. If worst comes to worst, I'll tell Lux and Nox to run with him. Without looking at them, I know they heard my plan. *Good.*

A smile plays on the leader's lips.

"I wasn't expecting you to unlock your powers so early," he says, eyeing me. "But you led us right to you."

Wait, what?

"Has anyone ever told you that you talk too much? I don't even know what you're talking about, mate," I retort. So there's no denying it. . . . It was me who did that in the cave, but how did they even know about what happened?

The man laughs. "You're just like your father."

My temper flares. How dare he mention Dad. "Thanks. I'll take that as a compliment."

His smile falters. *There's still something so familiar about him. Why can't I remember?* Eyes still on us, he gestures to his people to come closer, and I rack my brain for ideas of how we can all get out of this together.

"Enough play. It's time for you all to return to Nubis."

"You know, random thought, but all of this reminds me of our training earlier," Jada says with a chuckle. "You guys should have seen it. The prize was sick too. The best, actually."

I stop myself from looking at Jada as everyone else looks at her, confused. But I get her message, and I inch a hand toward my pocket.

"Shut your mouth, girl," one of the women says.

"Grab them," the leader says, pulling out those strange blue collars from his pocket. The same sort I saw around Spike's and Bolt's necks.

The Elite move in, and I grab the smoke ball.

Throwing it down, I yell, "Run!"

The whole area erupts in smoke, engulfing us all.

"We'll find you!" the man yells.

I dodge as someone tries to grab me.

Lux! Nox!

I race through the smoke, hoping it's the right direction, when someone grabs the back of my shirt.

"I've got you!"

I scream as I'm thrown into the air, and I land on something soft. Amid the smoke, I can barely make out Nox's back, but I'm so relieved.

Thanks, Nox!

We break out of the smoke with the Elite still lost within it.

"Where are the others?" I ask.

"Ahead. I can faintly make out their scent, but it is masked by the swamp. I always know where Lux is, though, and he told me he is with them."

Good. At least we've escaped the Elite.

"We must still be careful, and quick. They won't be scrambling for long."

The ground turns from grass to purple sludge. The trees are no longer crooked wooden witches, but willows weeping, sad and slumped to the side, their silver leaves lacking life. The air gets thicker, making it hard to see ahead as a mist forms from the swamp. We continue running in a straight line, scared that with one slight turn we'll accidentally be running back on ourselves, straight to the enemy.

Ahead, Lux, with Lucas on his back, stands with TJ, Jada, and Ruby. *Thank Lunis.*

"Mia, that was sick!" TJ yells. We bump fists, and before I can speak, Lucas hugs me.

"Good job, Mia," Jada says, patting my back, and Ruby

bows her head. "Now, let's go. Quick, quiet, and on foot. Keep a low profile for now and stick together."

I take Lucas's hand and we hurry through low bushes, doing our best to stay out of sight in the mist. We're slowing down by a huge willow tree for a quick break when Lucas gasps. I snap my head to him as he groans, yanking his feet out of the sludge. His cheeks puff out upset as he jiggles his foot.

"Mimi, my shoes are sticky," he complains.

"You're fine, Lu-Lu. You're fine."

A little mud isn't going to kill him, but he sniffs, crying quietly as he looks at his shoes. "Mama got me these. . . ."

I roll my eyes, then jump up and tear some leaves from under the willow trees. I quickly crouch down and wipe off his shoes the best I can before chucking the leaves away.

"Better?" I ask, and he nods.

"Thank you, Mimi," he whispers, taking my hand and kissing my cheek. I find myself smiling back at him, ruffling his hair.

"Anytime, Lu-Lu."

"Ruby, go scout ahead," Jada says, resting against the tree. The shadow bird disappears through the mist, and I try to catch my breath.

"But how will she find us?" I ask.

"Umbra can always find their tamers. It's like a homing signal," Nox explains.

TJ sighs.

"I still can't believe we got away," he says.

"For now," Jada adds.

"Yeah, low-key we got lucky," I say. I know there aren't any more smoke balls left.

A loud roar rattles the air, and Ruby flies back.

"We have a problem," she says, ushering us to follow. We hasten our march through the sludge until we reach a small opening within the dense swamp, where a lake runs through the swamp. The water bubbles, and we hide behind some tall purple reeds that surround the lake as something emerges from it.

A humongous, shadowy crocodile with a spiked back and legs like a crab skitters back and forth through the sludge of the swamp. The foul stench of Medusa vomiting plants mixed with the devil's breath of the croco-umbra burns my nose. TJ gags and I push my fist against my mouth, trying not to throw up.

"She can sense when someone disturbs her waters," Ruby says. *"If we can get past, the Elite are unlikely to follow—we'd gain much time."*

Just how, though?

I open and close my fist. I still can't feel anything. No power, no spark. Nothing.

"I'd rather *not* be eaten," TJ says. He looks at Ruby, Lux, and Nox. "Can't you guys talk to it or something? Distract it? Anything?"

The croco-umbra grumbles and growls, still oblivious to u̇
in the thick fog.

"We don't usually make 'friends' with others of our kind,"
states Ruby. *"We prefer to keep to ourselves, unless we wish for a
fight, and this one is too powerful for the likes of us."*

"You can tell how powerful an umbra is just by looking at
it?" I ask Ruby, and she nods.

Lucas claps his hand over his nose and mouth. "Mimi, I
don't like it. It's smelly."

*"How do you think we feel, kid? Our noses are infinitely more
sensitive than yours,"* Lux complains. *"But Ruby is right. We
would not be able to take her on. She's too strong."*

My eyes fall on a wooden bridge that's completely broken
and sunken in the middle—there's no way to pass over it. The
croco-umbra snaps her sharp teeth, and I lean my head back.
That thing could rip us apart.

"Jada, can't Ruby just fly me or something?" TJ asks.

*"I can carry only one at a time. It'd take too long with the Elite
still after us,"* Ruby says, and TJ blinks.

"Great . . ."

My legs start to cramp up from crouching too long, but I
don't dare move an inch to ease the pain. *There has to be something.* I spot a rotten fallen log farther down the lake and point
to it. If we can sneak past the croco-umbra without being
noticed, we can cross the lake and reach the other side safely.

If the log can hold out for us all to pass. Jada spots it too and clears her throat.

"That log is our best and only bet. We have to make it work. We'll go one by one. Lucas will ride on Ruby," Jada says.

"Yeah, yeah, I get that, but how are we gonna get across without big boy over there seeing us?" TJ asks.

Good question.

"And she's a girl," I correct him.

The croco-umbra lets out a giant yawn, stretching her spider-crab legs and crashing into the sludge. Half her body sinks into it, and it's our cue to go.

"If worst comes to worst, Ruby can distract her. Let's go," Jada says.

To make sure the log can hold our weight, Jada decides to go first. Ruby takes to the skies with Lucas, thankfully with no complaints from him, and I wait behind with TJ, Lux, and Nox, standing in their baby forms. Jada uses her arms to balance herself, taking one step at a time. She wobbles and my breath catches in my throat, but she gives us a thumbs-up and carries on across as Ruby flies ahead.

"How are you feeling?" TJ asks, keeping his eye on Jada. She's almost to the other side.

"Terrified," I reply.

He nods with a nervous smile. "Yeah . . . me too."

Jada stops and signals for us to join her on the log.

"She says that the log is very sturdy. So long as you take your time, it should hold you all as you cross," Ruby's voice echoes in my mind.

The croco-umbra rolls on her side in the mud, and when her eyes close, I make my move with TJ. Yanking my feet through the sludge, trying not to focus on the loud squelching of the mud under my shoes, I move as quickly as possible. I remain unnoticed, and Nox helps me up on the huge log. With my arms on either side, I begin to cross, Lux in front, TJ and Nox behind. TJ grabs me when I almost slip and keeps ahold of my hand as we sidestep and sneak across the murky waters. *Almost there.*

As soon as Jada's feet hit the sludge on the other side, a loud hum like a radio wave blasts my eardrums, and I clap my hands over my ears. I glance back and Nox shakes his head in pain. Still on the log, me and TJ struggle to keep our balance. I look up ahead again and my heart stops.

A group of men and women stand in the middle of the swamp on their umbra, their red cloaks blowing in the wind and sinister smiles spreading across their faces. The croco-umbra is nowhere in sight.

"Oh snap, it's them! Let's go, Mia!" TJ says. Lux makes it across ahead of us, but as he turns around, his eyes widen in fear.

"Guys, wait!" Jada yells.

"We're almost there—" TJ says.

The croco-umbra splashes up from the water with her jaws wide open, her eyes flashing red, and TJ pushes me to the other side.

"TJ!" I scream. He's thrown into the air before Nox can grab him, and the croco-umbra's mouth snaps shut, swallowing my best friend.

"NO!"

The monster crashes into the water with a splash and everything freezes. A thousand invisible knives pierce my heart. My brain tries to register that the spot where my best friend stood is now empty and I scream, my lungs on fire.

"One down. Capture the girl," I faintly hear one of the red-cloaked women say, but I can't move.

"Come on!" Jada yells, pulling me back as the croco-umbra turns to face us, her eyes flashing red again. This must have been what those cave umbra meant. The Elite weren't just taming umbra; they were controlling and using them as and when they wished. Or did that umbra know exactly what she was doing?

I stumble back as the Elite move through the lake toward us. The water splashes up as, trapped under the Elite's control, the croco-umbra charges.

"Mia, I'm so sorry, but we need to go! Now! They're coming! And we're so close to Stella."

My feet refuse to move. Jada continues to encourage me, but my mind completely blanks as I stare straight at the umbra. *They killed TJ. . . . Just like that, he's gone. No . . . NO!* Something inside me snaps. The umbra licks her fangs, and yanking my bo staff from my hip, I race toward her, forgetting the Elite, Jada, Lucas, everything.

"MIA, WAIT!"

Power surges through my arms straight to my hands, and my eyes zero in on the monster rushing through the water toward us.

"MIMI!"

My feet push off the ground as I leap higher than I ever have before, flying over the lake toward the umbra. Electric sparks rush across my body up to the back of my neck and behind my eyes. I raise the staff over my head and, screaming, swing it down as hard as I can, piercing the umbra's huge shadowy back. The staff snaps in two as light bursts from the croco-umbra. She roars, throwing her head side to side, bashing the Elite members back across the water with her tail.

My arms wobble, my feet almost slipping from under me as a loud rumble comes from the umbra beneath my feet. She lurches forward, heaving and then throwing up before crashing onto her stomach, tail thudding.

Jada and the others race over as the croco-umbra's body slowly rises and falls under my feet. Panic sets into my heart when I realize what I've done. The croco-umbra doesn't move, but Nox whispers gently to me.

"It's all right, young one. She is merely sleeping now," he says, and I look down at my shaking hands, feeling nothing but fear.

I actually have . . . powers. I can't deny it anymore.

"Mimi!" Lucas yells, and I slide off the side of the beast as Jada, Lucas, Lux, and Ruby stare at what must be croco-umbra vomit.

"What? What is it?" I call out, looking at the huge gloopy mess on the ground. It suddenly jiggles and we jump, screaming. I clap a hand over my mouth, barely swallowing down my own vomit, burning the back of my throat. The mess moves again and Lucas screams. Something lets out a disgruntled noise.

"Yo! What the . . . This isn't okay! I got eaten! Do you know what I saw in her stomach? I can't unsee it, okay? I'm traumatized."

"TJ?" His name tumbles out of my mouth as he emerges from the slop, wiping at his arms and legs. I stare at him in shock.

"No, it's your dad. Of course it's me, Mia! Look at me! I'm covered in this gross gooey stuff! My sneakers are never gonna be the same again! Look! They're green like a gutterslug! Someone grab me a towel or something, before I swallow any more of her stomach juices!"

I run over to him, tears streaming down my face as I jump and squeeze him tight, not caring about all the gloopy mess covering him. "I'm so glad you're okay! You clown!"

"Yeah, and TRAUMATIZED. What? No thank-you for saving you earlier?"

"You're the best." I grin, squeezing him again.

"We sometimes devour physical beings, consume their souls, and spit them out. Mia saved you before that process began. Count yourself lucky," Lux says.

"That's . . . disgusting, but I guess that makes us even," TJ says to me. He flicks his arms, and goo splatters into the marsh. I step away from the splashback and wipe my own clothes, and he scrunches his face with a slight smile.

"Thanks, Mia. I mean, I could have gotten out myself, but you were a big help, superstar," he says.

I look down and stare at my hands. *What's going on with me?*

"Mia, are you okay? How did you do that?" Jada asks, frowning.

"I don't even know what I did. I just moved," I say, looking at the broken bit of my staff in my hand. "What do you think?" I ask, eyeing her. There's only one conclusion that comes to mind, and I don't like it at all. We've all been probably thinking the same thing since I tamed Lux and Nox and saw them in that book.

"I think we need to have that talk, but not here," she says, diverting her attention to Lucas as he points to my hand.

"Mimi, your staff is broken. Did you get an ouchie?" asks Lucas.

"Nah, I'm okay. I can always get a new staff." I sigh with a smile, chucking the now-useless weapon.

Out of nowhere, the buzzing wave hits us again, and I clutch my ears. Lux catches Lucas before he falls, grabbing the back of his shirt with his teeth. He throws my brother up onto his back, and we all huddle together as my ears throb.

"What's going on? How are they doing that?!" I yell out above the vibrations.

"I don't know!" Jada says as the six people who were thrown into the sludge slowly begin to emerge. All of them staring right at us.

"It's time to come with us!" she yells. She clenches her fist, and it starts to glow. Weird red shadows swirl around, and I quickly back up, staying close to Lux.

The figures twitch, each of them with red shadows circling their fists. I feel Lux's and Nox's anxiety rise as they lower their heads, ready to attack.

"We can't fight them. Let's go!" Jada yells.

She jumps onto Ruby, but the Elite are ready for this. Each takes out a blue collar and throws it. The collars spin through the air, homing in on Ruby, Lux, and Nox and snapping onto their necks. With cries and growls, they drop to the ground, pinned down. I catch Lucas and hold him close.

Then it's our turn. Sprinting forward at lightning speed, the red cloaks flash-step closer to us, and someone grabs me before I can run. Lucas yells at the top of his lungs as he's snatched from me, and Jada thrashes her arms, but she's captured too. Somehow TJ has managed to break away, the sludge yanking at his ankles as he tries to escape.

"Keep going, TJ!" I cry out. He's fast, but one of the Elite flash-steps in front of him, grabbing his arms and lifting him above the ground like it's nothing.

The arms around me tighten, but I force myself around to face the figure that has me. When I see the face under the hood more clearly, I scream at the top of my lungs.

It's the man with the crown and the dark ruffled hair.

"Now the ritual can be complete."

As he speaks, his face morphs. I'm staring into a mouth full of shark teeth and eyes glowing red like the umbra.

I'm so scared I can't even think.

"It is time to take the Lightcaster to Nubis," the leader says.

Lightcaster!

Thoughts rush into my head, the confirmation leaving me reeling. Only royalty is supposed to have that gift, so how in Lunis do I have it? Did Mum know? Is that why she wanted me to run with Lucas? Did Jada know?

I don't want this. It's all too much.

"Nope! No way! It's not time for anything, you gutterslug. You better not hurt her!" TJ shouts, trying to break free.

Jada silently struggles, digging her shoes into the sludge, but the woman lifts her up higher and brings her over, closing the group.

"You see, children, we always knew where you were. I don't know how you hid your powers to begin with—it was good, I'll give you that, but not good enough. We just had to wait for Mia here to use her powers," the man says, the purple eagle pin glowing on his cloak. He passes me to one of the others and shifts the ridiculous crown on his head.

Just like Miles said . . . The one they were looking for was me. . . .

"It's time to go. Teleport."

We begin to glow. Red balls of light float around us, coming up from the ground. I squeeze my eyes shut.

This is it. We've failed.

As I'm despairing, I hear something burst out of the watery sludge behind TJ, and my eyes flip open. Mud flies everywhere, and a roar sounds.

The croco-umbra lands with a heavy thud, chomping down on the man who holds me, freeing me. She throws her head back, gold eyes glowing, and swallows the man whole.

I collapse into the sludge as the umbra turns toward Jada. The croco-umbra swings her tail at Jada's captor, throwing the red-cloaked woman off her feet. I see Jada break free as I turn to look for Lucas.

The man holding him is ready to run, but my feet move before my mind can think. I clench my fist tight and flip in the air, kicking straight down into his arm with all my strength. He grunts but still clings to my brother.

"Let him go!" I swing my foot around to kick the man's legs from under him, but he jumps back.

The croco-umbra moves on to free TJ, and I hear heavy paws racing toward me. The crowned man rides on his lion-tiger-wolf umbra, and a loud screech blasts from behind. The energy pushes me forward and I flinch, but there's no pain. The man drops Lucas, clutching his head, and the crowned man is thrown off his umbra. The collars on Ruby, Lux, and Nox crack off, falling to the ground. I turn to see Lux and Nox and grin at them. Lucas runs over to me as quick as his legs can take him. I catch him, lifting him up and hugging him hard. I turn to the croco-umbra as she stares at us.

"You are safe now. Leave these two to me."

It takes a moment before I can find my voice. "Why did you help us?" I ask.

"I was trapped under a spell, until you freed me with that staff of yours. Thank you."

I'm stunned, but I can't ask any more questions, because

the croco-umbra turns with another roar and charges at the leader of the Elite.

"Mia, we need to go," Nox says.

But what about the Elite? I ask. If they get away, they'll just be after us again.

"Worry about that later, Mouse. Let's go."

You better stop calling me Mouse, Lux.

"Never."

Jada takes to the skies on Ruby, while Lucas, TJ, and I pelt away from the swamp on Lux and Nox.

That croco-umbra actually helped us. Who knows what could have happened if she hadn't been there? Maybe that other umbra in the cave was right—all we have to do is ask for help—but is it really that simple? It was so wrong for the Elite to force that umbra against her will. I wonder what Mum would have thought about all of this, and then my heart feels heavy thinking about her.

"We'll save them." Nox's gentle voice speaks, and I glance across at him. *"You have the best partners, after all."*

I blink away tears, and the smile returns to my face.

Still . . . The Elite mentioned Lightcasters, and my power. Am I really one of them? A Lightcaster? It did and didn't make any sense all at the same time. Why would I only be finding out about this now? And where did this energy inside me come from? I look down at Lucas, playing with Lux's shadows. If it is me, then . . . did Mum and Dad already know? That this is the power inside me Mum was talking about? I shake the thoughts away. It's too much pressure, but I need answers.

"Jada!" I call out, and she flies down with Ruby.

"What's up?"

"What do you really think is going on with me?"

"What do you mean?"

I make a face. "About what happened in the cave, and then the croco-umbra and the Elite. Do you think that book is right? Do you think I could actually be a Lightcaster?"

Jada pauses for a moment. *Just say it already. . . .*

"Okay, fine. Let's talk." She stays flying beside me and Lux, but her eyes narrow, like she's still debating whether or not to speak.

"Please," I urge.

Her eyes still seem conflicted, but she takes a breath, and when she looks back at me, there's a new strong resolve. "Yes . . . I think you're a Lightcaster."

My lips part in shock. Hearing her actually say it hits completely different. Worse. "But didn't you say—"

"I know what I said, and I was telling the truth. We did think Lightcasters were only born in the royal line, but when you were born, your mum and dad wondered if that wasn't actually the case."

"Why?" TJ calls out, running closer with Nox. He looks just as confused as me. What would make Mum and Dad think that?

"I don't know," Jada says. "You'd have to ask them, but when they thought you might have the powers of light, they tried to decipher that book again. The one you found in your dad's office."

"So they think Mia's one of the kids in the book?" TJ asks. We dip in and out of a group of silver trees before racing out into the open again, coming back together.

"Maybe," Jada says. "They weren't sure whether those pictures were of the past or the future, but just in case, they kept it all a secret for fear that the Reaper King and his minions would come after Mia. Their fears were confirmed when the Elite came and invaded the city."

"So you lied," I argue, but she shakes her head, a slightly offended look on her face.

"I didn't lie. I didn't know for sure. Neither did your parents. Everything your parents did was a precaution, *just in case* they were right, and from the looks of it, they were. That's why they only told me, so that if anything went wrong, I'd be your protector. I trust them and the tamers with everything, Mia, and they were right."

"Well, I don't want these powers. Can't I give them away? Get rid of them or something?"

"What? And let the Elite win and do who knows what with that ritual? That's not an option, Mia, and you know it. Give your powers to me if you don't want them," TJ says, and I shoot him a look. If it wasn't for Lucas sleeping against me, I would've reached out and kicked him. I don't want all this pressure. I don't want to be a Lightcaster.

"I don't think it works like that," Jada sighs.

I don't want these powers.

"Why are you acting like this is a bad thing? You have magic powers. That's sick!" TJ says.

"Because I don't know how to control them! And if I didn't have these powers, Mum, Dad, and everyone wouldn't be in danger! Those people attacked Nubis, and are chasing us, because of *me*. I'm putting you all at risk just by being with you." The reality of it is setting in, and I can barely breathe. All of this is happening because of me.

"Hey, when we get to Stella, we'll work everything out. I promise, but we're sticking together. One step at a time, remember?" Jada says.

I nod at Jada's words, but they don't make me feel any better.

"That's right. Besides, your mum said your grandparents know what to do, and we'll get help from the queen. You may not even need to use your powers," TJ adds, which is true, I guess.

Still . . . they're all at risk of being caught because of me. What help are these powers if I can't use them when I want to protect people? I could have freed Mum, Dad, and everyone in Nubis, but I ran, not even knowing I had powers. *I'm such a coward. . . .*

"*You are far from that, young one,*" Nox whispers.

"*Now stop being so hard on yourself, or else, Mouse,*" Lux says. "*We do not have a weak tamer. We would have eaten your soul by now if that was the case.*"

I shake my head at him but manage to smile. *You know you can still be really scary, right?*

"*Yes, so keep on your toes, Mouse.*"

"Hey . . . there's another lake up ahead. Let's wash off and make a straight beeline for Stella!" Jada says, flying up with Ruby after quickly washing off.

The rest of us wash off all the mud and grime. The water gliding across my skin feels amazing, and I splash TJ and Lucas, trying my best to laugh and fight with them, but the worry won't go away. Jada and Ruby circle the skies above, and for the first time in a long time, we just have fun.

Lucas squeals as TJ dunks him in the water. Lux and Nox tackle me, crashing us back into the lake with a huge splash, laughing. At least for a moment, I can forget everything.

The good mood shatters when we hear a distressed cry from Ruby. I look up and see that something's pierced her wing, and Jada clings on with all her might as Ruby loses control in the air and cries out again.

We all scramble out of the lake.

"What was that?!" TJ shouts, and I scan the landscape frantically. Across the field between two silver trees, I spot the red-cloaked leader, battered, bruised, and raging. He survived!

"Over there!" I yell, pointing. He's lining up another arrow, and his lion-tiger-wolf umbra is charging toward us with his scorpion tail up, aimed and ready to strike.

I throw Lucas on Lux and hop on after him. We make a break for it, with TJ on Nox and the red-eyed umbra giving chase. Bright lights flash behind us, and I look over my shoulder and see that the red-eyed umbra has disappeared, and black shadows, white-striped in the same pattern as his umbra, blaze around the man's body. They encase him like armor. His long scorpion-like tail points at us.

"Faster!" I call out, and the man now transformed with his umbra gives chase, closing the gap between us.

"Oh snap! He's pacing! The gutterslug's coming!" TJ yells.

Another bright light beams behind us, and the ground quakes as something crashes down. We spin around, and my jaw drops. Ruby and Jada stand together in the third phase of transformation too—the ultimate human-umbra being. As one.

Shadow-armored and winged, golden eyes glinting, Jada stands strong, blocking the man's path. She faces him, aiming her own bow and arrow. "I'll hold him off. Keep going."

"No, Jada, wait!" I yell. I turn Lux toward her.

"Just go!" she orders. Her eyes are pinned on the man. "We don't have time. I'll be right behind you!"

I freeze. The worry that wells up in my chest is the exact same as when I left Mum. I didn't want to do it.

A sinister smile spreads across the man's face, his old bow and arrow thumping to the ground. Black smoke swirls around his hands, and a new weapon forms. A huge sword swings in his hand, and I feel the tension rife in the air. Jada rolls her shoulders back, her own arrow at the ready. Her shadowy wings stand strong, she and Ruby united.

"All right! We'll meet you there!" I yell back.

"We can't just leave her! There's only one of him. He's outnumbered," TJ shouts in disbelief.

"We have to trust her," I say. I don't want to go, but what choice do we have? The memory of Mum and Dad trapped in that cage rushes into my mind again. Just the thought of it makes me sick, but this time I'm listening, and now that I know the truth, I'm putting my faith in her, and my parents, to stay alive.

"Lux, Nox, can you keep going?"

"Of course," they say together.

"All right, let's go!"

Turning around, we make our last sprint to Stella, the City of Light.

A Report by Lila McKenna
(Confidential)
The Reapers and the Elite UPDATED

The Elite are a collective who seek to revive the Reaper King and are enemies of the tamers. They were originally residents and tamers of Nubis, until it was discovered that they were experimenting with new, dangerous ways of taming umbra. They are believed to be the reapers-in-training, and the reasons for this vary, but one purpose stands out among the rest: to destroy the monarchy within Stella and to be the new rulers of the world.

While the Elite may first appear human, their exposure to the Reaper King has granted them shadow powers that almost rival the abilities of Lightcasters. However, unlike the Lightcasters, these shadow powers eat away at their humanity, turning them into skeleton-like beings and ensuring that they become full servants to the king himself. When they are fully under the Reaper King's control, they are called "reapers."

It is unknown exactly what the Reaper King promised them, or what life is like under his command.

CHAPTER THIRTEEN

We don't stop running until the plains around us go deathly silent, all of us bruised but not broken. The forever moon lights our way, and the silver line in the sky attaches to each and every star for the last time before we reach Stella. We manage to find another abandoned hut and get a few hours' sleep with Lux and Nox keeping watch before making a last sprint to Stella. The number two in the sky changes to a one. One day left. I hope Jada is not far behind, but there's been no sign of her or Ruby and I grip my necklace. *Please, be safe.*

A yawn slips from my lips, and then something bright emerges from the horizon ahead. I shield my eyes, squinting as a fireball I've only ever heard about appears above: the *sun* lights the sky yellow, white, and blue, melting the darkness. It burns my eyes, and I blink twice, quickly patting Lucas awake.

"Lu-Lu, look! It's actual daylight! We're here!"

We get closer, and golden beams of light warm my face and cheeks. I reach up my hand, bathing my arm in the heat.

Lucas rubs his eyes and gasps. "Wow."

Enjoying the warmth, I look over at TJ, who is completely entranced and punches his fist skyward.

"We made it! I told you guys! We're awesome!" he yells. Lucas giggles, throwing his arms up in the air.

"It's nice to feel the sunlight again. Isn't that right, brother?" Nox says.

A wave of joy rushes through me, but it's not just my own. Lux's and Nox's emotions overwhelm me. Their excitement as wild as mine.

I never minded living in the night, but this is something I've never ever felt before, and I don't want it to ever end.

The ground changes from grass to a yellow cobblestone path lined with little pockets of red and green roses. Birds chirp, soaring through the bright blue sky, and huge gold statues of the queen and the many royals that came before her stand tall like a gateway along the path, greeting us.

It's everything I imagined, triggering the old memory that I had from visiting Nan and Grandad once so many years ago. Still buzzing with the excitement, we near a set of giant golden gates that tower over us.

TJ hops off Nox, and I dismount from Lux, leaving Lucas safely on him. We walk along the path until we reach two individual black concrete squares on the ground in front of the gates. One depicts the moon and the other the sun.

"That's random," TJ mutters, looking down at the symbols.

Clicks sound from above. Looking up, I see six people standing on a platform above the walls of the gates, their crossbows aimed, ready to fire.

"Put your hands up," I whisper to Lucas. He gulps but does what I say. Next to me, TJ does the same, just as nervous.

A woman's voice booms down.

"State your intent!"

"What's she on about?" TJ whispers.

"I said, state your intent!" the woman demands again.

"She means why are we here, you clown," I whisper, trying to stop my knees from buckling. I clear my throat. "We're from Nubis. Our city needs help. And my grandparents live here."

I sneak a glance behind us. We may have a chance to run if things go wrong. That's *if* these guards aren't as good as shooting as they look, but what will we do then?

"Nubis?" one of the guards gasps, but they're quickly hushed. I squint my eyes and see that one is muttering into a holo-phone.

"What are your grandparents' names?" the woman asks.

"Katherine and Nelson Greene. My nan goes by Kay, though."

The guards fall silent, and I breathe steadily in through my nose and out through my mouth to calm myself. I check on Lucas, then glance at TJ, trying to catch his eye. The woman calls out again.

"What of those umbra? Are they tamed? How did you travel all this way?" she asks.

"Yes, they're with me, and they helped us get here," I say.

The guards talk among themselves for a while, then make their decision.

"All right. You can come in," the woman says.

Two of them disappear, and we lower our hands and make our way through the gates.

TJ quickly walks up to me, tapping my shoulder, making me fall back a bit. "There's no way they don't know what's going on with the Elite. I know the holo-phones were down, but surely someone here must have known something was off? Look what happened to Ignis."

I look at him, sharing his confusion. The queen is supposed to have an eye on all the cities, so how can she not know anything? There are people here who must have had families in Nubis and Ignis. Or maybe because it's been a few days no one is concerned yet, but that doesn't explain how a whole other city could fall to the Darkness without anyone knowing a thing. . . .

Despite the sunshine, I feel a chill, but shake it off.

The gates open with a screech, and we walk through, Nox and Lux sticking close to my side. I help Lucas down and keep hold of his hand. Two guards, a man and a woman, are there to meet us. I'm wary as I watch them eye up Lux and Nox.

Lux's fur bristles and he grumbles, holding in a growl.

It's okay, Lux. I won't let them hurt you. I can't blame these people, though. I feared umbra too. I still do sometimes. For years, I thought they were all monsters, until Lux and Nox came along. They changed me a lot.

For once, Lux doesn't argue back. The guards shift their attention to us. We all clasp our hands and bow in greeting, and I take the moment to look at the armor they're wearing. It glistens, but despite the polish, there are cuts, scrapes, and a few dents. They're no strangers to fighting their own wars, animals, and maybe even reapers and the Elite then.

"What is going on? We've been trying to communicate with Nubis for days," the man says. So they do know. . . .

"It was the bad guys!" Lucas says.

"Our city's been taken over by a bunch of red-cloaked soldiers called the Elite," I say. "My mum and dad have been taken prisoner, along with everyone else. The holo-phones weren't working when we left, and Ignis has fallen. We think it all has to do with the Elite."

We see a ripple of shock and recognition go through the two guards, and I decide against mentioning Lightcasters.

"So you've heard of them?" TJ asks.

"Rumors," the woman says. "The queen always spoke about the rise of a new potential enemy, but we haven't seen them in the flesh as of yet." *Your armor suggests otherwise, though. . . .*

"Well, now we need help to take back our city," I say.

"We will report this to the queen. Follow us," the man says.

I catch the two guards sharing a look. I keep Lucas close and follow behind them. They walk along the wall away from the city center. Something doesn't feel right.

"Where are we going?" I ask.

"Just somewhere safe where you can wait. As you can probably guess, people around here aren't used to seeing umbra, except for the queen's," the woman says.

We walk down an alley, and the farther we go, the quieter the city gets. A strange place to go just to wait for the queen. TJ stays close, and the guards let us through some high-security gates, eventually stopping in front of a small black building in a walled-off area. TJ nudges me and I nod. Something is definitely off.

The blackened windows make it hard to see inside, and the doors appear to be made of iron. A bit much for a bunch of kids waiting for the queen. The woman guard swipes the key card that hangs securely from her belt, and the doors slowly slide open.

The lights flicker on and we cautiously step inside. The room is completely empty, except for four uncomfortable-looking chairs in the corners of the room and one in the middle. Nothing welcoming at all.

"Ow!" TJ trips and falls on the floor as he steps in, and the woman helps him up. He thanks her, brushing off his clothes, and I walk over to one of the seats. My hand brushes against it, but it doesn't move, being solidly fixed to the floor.

"Take a seat. We'll be back soon," the male guard says.

"But—" I turn around and the iron doors slam shut. The guards are gone.

"Watch them," I could have sworn I heard the woman say before the doors closed.

"We're not really going to stay here, are we?" TJ whispers, looking around. "What even is this place?"

Looking up, I see that the few high windows are barred from the inside.

"Looks like an interrogation room," I mutter. It's similar to the one in Nubis that Dad showed me once. The place where tamers would question bandits back in the day before taking them to the Hold. It's rarely ever used in Nubis now, but still . . . "We need to get out of here."

"Young one," Lux calls, and by the door, Lucas reaches up, pulling at the handle.

"Mimi, the door is stuck," Lucas whines, and I spot the key card panel. One way in and one way out.

"Great . . . ," I murmur.

"I mean . . . It's a good thing I stole this key card, then."

"What?" I spin around to see TJ waving the key card in his hand. "You genius! How?"

"I know, I know. I'm the best. I jacked it from the woman when I pretended to trip. I almost didn't get it. She had it pinned under her armor. Now let's get out of here before they come back," TJ says. The brilliant guy!

"I think there's a guard outside the door, though," I warn, trying to look through the windows, but it's impossible. Like the interrogation room back home, this room was probably designed as both a temporary holding cell and a place for questioning. If I'm right, I bet no sound from the inside can be heard from the outside, and no sound outside can be heard from inside. Beneath the floor around the middle chair, where suspects would sit, are likely hidden chains, ready to be used against them. The chairs in the corners of the room are for the interrogators, who question the suspect before taking them to the prison hold in Stella, if they're found guilty.

"They don't have umbra. Nox and I can take them. The human won't be able to move for hours," Lux says.

"Yeah, but they're not ordinary guards. The queen would've made sure they could fight against umbra," I say. "Besides, we don't know how many of them are out there."

"There is only one," Nox confirms. "We can sense them. Those guards are obviously careless. So long as they have hearing, that's all Lux and I need for our powers to work."

"So, are we doing this?" TJ asks, and I feel my nerves bundle up. We don't have any choice. We can't stay here.

"Lu-Lu, are you ready?" I ask him. He smiles, rubbing his eyes, probably still tired, and I face Lux and Nox. "Let's go."

TJ waits by the door with three fingers up. Me and Lucas sit on Lux, standing front and center with Nox, ready to attack. I signal to TJ and he counts down. Three, two, one. *Click.*

The doors slide open and the guard gasps. He turns around, crossbow up, but it's too late. Lux and Nox unleash a deafening scream that affects only their target, and the guard clutches his ears, falling to his knees.

TJ vaults onto Nox's back, and we all burst through the entrance and gallop far away from the guard. With little effort, Lux and Nox jump over the high wall and race off.

"We did it!" I whisper-shout. TJ lets out a loud roar of a cheer, but I quickly hush him, not wanting to draw any attention to ourselves. Lucas giggles as we speed past an alley, staying far away from the gates and heading straight into the city center. When we're close to the loud hum of people, we dismount, and Lux and Nox transform into their smaller size.

"Are you okay, Lu-Lu?" I ask, taking hold of his hand.

He nods and smiles with determination in his eyes. "Yes, Mimi. Let's find Nanny and Grandad."

I gesture for Lux and Nox to follow me. We don't have time to waste. Now we have to find Nan and Grandad. According to Mum, they would help me with "the next steps," whatever that means. Despite everything that has happened, hope flares up in me. We made it to Stella. We have a chance at saving Nubis.

We follow the road, out of the darkness of the area those guards took us to, and my heart is fluttering as I take it all in. I'm not used to all the light, and it makes my eyes water. There's so much to see! Little pockets of memories from my past visit here years ago flash before my eyes.

The city bursts with color. The houses, twice the size of ours at home, are red, brown, blue, or green, each with a gold door. I see every single crack in the road and the pavement we walk on, every little pebble, worm, and bit of rubbish. Larger buildings made completely from glass shine like diamonds in the light of the sun. At some point Lucas lets go of my hand and looks around, utterly entranced.

Then we see the citadel, home of the queen. Towers made from glass stand tall, while small travel pods fly around, in and out of the silvery bubble that protects the castle, a spell cast decades ago as a final defense against the Reaper King, something no other city has. Her castle sits in the center, with walls made from solar panels and the kingdom's strongest metals.

Unlike Nubis, this city has thousands of people. Crowds brush past us without a care in the world. No one seems to care that the Blood Moon is tomorrow. Maybe it's just another day for them.

I shove some people back, and more than once I check my pockets and rucksack to make sure everything's in there. Soon the novelty of being here wears off as my eyes adjust to the light and I take hold of Lucas's hand again. While everything is amazing, the more I look, the colder the place becomes, despite the warm rays of the sun. No one on the streets seems to talk to each other like they do in Nubis. It's as if they're all strangers. All in a hurry to reach wherever they're going.

We carry on and spot alleyways among the big sparkly buildings, with small huts draped with ribbon lights and decorations. The people there seem more friendly. None are dressed flashily, but they look happier than many of the people in formal wear roaming the main streets. But they still stare at us, and some hurry away when we approach.

Stay close to me, guys.

"*We will,*" Lux and Nox say together, and I smile at them. I squeeze Lucas's hand and make a point of keeping my eyes on everyone we pass. I don't trust them, either. Any random person could be an Elite in disguise, or a gate guard ready to capture us again.

"Do you remember where your grandparents live?" TJ asks.

"It's been years, but I'm sure it's this way. We have the address compass in the backpack. We'll be able to find the house. I remember there being this giant glass umbra statue that looked like a fox with eight tails. Oh, and it's at a dead end."

"Okay, umbra statue and a dead end, shouldn't be hard. This city is only humongous. No big deal."

I roll my eyes, taking the bag from him and pulling out the address compass, flashing it right in his face. "Let's skedaddle!"

I set the address compass for Nan and Grandad's house, and we follow the small arrow on the device.

Every road and path looks identical to the next, and after what feels like hours of walking, we stop in front of a large shop. It's nothing like Ms. Dawn's cute little flower shop—no wind chimes made from moon dust and crystals to ward off evil spirits from the Spirit Plain and negative vibes.

Despite all the glitz and glamour, the funky colors and blinding sun, all the shops here seem kinda dead. I frown at the red spheres hanging everywhere, almost in mockery of the Blood Moon festival, and I actually start to miss the dark.

"What if they're not home? How will we find Nanny and Grandad?" Lucas pipes up.

Good point.

"I guess we can ask around," I tell him. "Someone around here must know them."

I suddenly stop, lowering the compass.

"Wait . . . I think I remember that park up ahead. Their house should be this way!"

I jog forward, passing the glimmering park with kids swinging on the metal climbing frames and jumping on the bounce pads.

"Hey! Wait up!" TJ yells, running after me with Lucas.

I round the corner and slow down. On either side of the road, houses are sandwiched together side by side, just like I remember. Each home is narrow, but four stories high to make up for it. Nan said it was so they could build as many homes as possible for all the new people from Lunavale, Astaroth, and the few who left Nubis, seeking refuge in the city from the Darkness. Not everyone wanted to learn how to live in the dark like we did. Even Nan and Grandad didn't want us to at first, and I think they still don't.

We carry on, analyzing the houses. The ones at the end are bigger than the others, with their curved front gardens making it a dead end like I remember. Completing the cul-de-sac, and in the middle of the semicircle, is a tall glass statue of an eight-tailed foxlike creature shimmering in black crystal. It must be a sculpture of Queen Katiya's umbra. I can't help but wonder why everyone here is scared of umbra when the queen herself has one.

"There it is!" I say, pointing ahead. "The second house at the back on the left."

Finally!

I ring the bell and knock on the door, yelling, "Nan! Grandad! It's Mia! We need your help!"

I step back, waiting to hear the hum of the scanner and the click of the door, but there's nothing. I ring the bell again.

"Maybe their scanner's broken?" TJ says, and I look up. He's right. There's no small red light in the camera.

"They should still have heard me yelling, though. Let me try knocking on the windows." I bang on the glass, calling out again. Lucas shouts too, but it's still quiet inside, and my heart sinks.

"Are Nanny and Grandad not home?" Lucas asks, and I take another step back, craning my neck to see if maybe they are upstairs. There's not even a twitch of a curtain. They would have answered by now. . . .

"How are we gonna find them now? We're running out of time," TJ says.

I chew my lip. They could be anywhere in the city.

"We do not sense or smell anyone similar to you nearby, young one," Nox adds.

"Maybe we can ask for help," Lucas suggests.

"Let's head back to the city center and ask around," TJ agrees. I hum, frustrated. We're so close I can almost taste it.

"We have to find them," I mutter.

I march forward, away from Nan and Grandad's house and back to the crowds. I ask the first person I get close to, a man with a backpack slung over his shoulders.

"Hi," I say, jogging up to him. "I'm looking for my nan and grandad. Their names are—"

The man brushes past me and continues walking. *What the flip?* I approach another person, but they ignore me too. I growl, looking at the others. We don't have time for this!

"Shall I get their attention?" Lux asks, but the smirk in his voice is enough for me to say no.

"My turn, then." TJ pats my back and runs off with a cheeky grin on his face.

"Where is this fool going now?" Lux says, exasperated as we jog after him.

He slows down by a clothes stall, and a woman yells at him as he climbs up on one of the tables, waving his hands.

"All right, ladies and gents! Gather around! Gather around!" TJ yells, with charm in his voice but at the top of his lungs. A few people turn around to glance at him, and some actually fully stop to listen. I can't believe my eyes.

"He's certainly not shy," Nox says, completely amused by it all.

TJ grins at the gathering crowd. "My friends and I have

traveled all the way from Nu—I mean, a faraway city, and we're looking for an old woman—"

"Elderly lady!" I shout at him, and he nods, whispering a *sorry* before continuing.

"We're looking for an elderly lady called KAY GREENE! Anyone know a Kay Greene?"

Lucas and I look around hopefully.

"Mia?" I turn around as someone calls my name. My smile drops when I see not my nan, but a different woman. Her graying hair is braided up into a knot, with small pretty beads. Her eyes wrinkle at the corners as she smiles kindly. I step back, pulling Lucas with me. "You probably don't recognize me, dear. I'm a friend of your grandparents. I live next door to them. My name's Stephanie."

"Do you know where they are? We need to see them. It's urgent," I say. Her eyes sadden and she looks down. Her hesitation to speak makes me nervous, and I glance at TJ.

"Dear . . . did no one call your parents?" she asks, and I shake my head, confused. "They're both in the medi-center."

What . . . ?

I freeze up, not knowing what to do.

"The holo-phones are all down in Nubis," TJ says.

"Why are they in the medi-center? What happened?" I ask, trying to wrap my head around what I just heard. I try to think back to the last time Mum called them. It was only a few days ago, and they were well, nothing was wrong. My chest feels tight, like it's about to burst, and it's suddenly hard to breathe. What is happening right now? She has to be lying.

"*Mouse, try and keep calm,*" Lux says, but his words are a blur. I need answers.

"I'm sorry, I don't know all the details," the woman says. "The last time I spoke to them, they said they were going to visit you in Nubis, but—"

"Please, just tell me what happened," I urge, unable to control the strain in my own voice. My heart is beating so fast I can't even think.

The elderly woman puts her bags down, narrowing her eyes, not even trying to hide the worry anymore. "Yesterday they were found outside the walls, not far from the gates of Stella with their pod turned upside down. They were both unconscious."

"No way . . . ," TJ mutters.

"Where's the medi-center?" I ask.

"Dear—"

"Where is it?" I repeat with a harshness I can't take back.

She slowly points behind us. "Follow back down the road, until you reach the water fountain. Then take a left."

I'm running before anyone can stop me.

"*Get on, young one.*" Nox catches up to me and runs slightly in front so I can vault onto his back. Lux hangs back to get

Lucas and TJ. Anxiety creeps all over my body like a thousand little ants. *Nan . . . Grandad . . .*

"Focus on getting to the medi-center," Nox says, interrupting my thoughts, but I can't stop my eyes from burning with tears. Maybe she's wrong. Maybe Nan and Grandad are fine and they've woken up. Maybe they're getting ready to leave the medi-center right now.

The winds push against us as we pass the water fountain with speed, take a left, and arrive at a huge, glossy white building. People rush in and out the sliding entrance doors. Flashing lights of emergency pods pull up on both sides of the medi-center, bringing even more injured people. It's nothing like Nubis. There are so many more people in need of help, and suddenly my own city feels so small.

Nox grunts and I quickly let go of his shadow fur; I didn't realize how hard I must have been pulling it.

"Sorry . . ."

"It's okay, young one. Are you ready?"

"No . . ." I don't know how I feel, but ready is far from it.

Lux joins us with Lucas and TJ on his back, but I find myself frozen, sitting on top of Nox. *What if they're really hurt?*

"Mia . . . Maybe it's best if Lux and Nox wait outside," TJ says, and I look at him, confused, before the meaning clicks in my fuzzy mind.

"Yeah . . . sure," I say.

I don't know when Nox lets me down, but I feel a small hand slip into my own and look down to see Lucas squeezing it.

"Let's go find Nanny and Grandad, Mimi."

I wonder if he even understands what's going on. Still, I'm grateful for his hand holding mine. Together, we step inside and TJ walks ahead to the counter. Lucas and I stand in the waiting area for him, but I feel numb.

The lights are too bright and the stench of cleaner burns my nose, almost making me throw up. I twist my sleeves. Was it the Elite that got to them, or a simple accident? What if Nan and Grandad aren't okay? What do we do then?

I jump, feeling a hand on my shoulder, and TJ smiles softly at me, not saying a word, but within his comforting eyes, his own anxiety mimics mine. He nods to the receptionist desk, and Lucas and I walk up to it with him. The man points down the hall.

"They're on the seventh floor, room 714," he says with that sickly sweet and sympathetic smile he must give every worried person here when he tells them their loved ones are upstairs, hurt or dying. I shouldn't be here.

My feet feel like weights walking to the elevator pads. We walk through the doors into the glass capsule; the padded floor sinks against our weight when we step on it. TJ presses the seventh-floor button, and the pad beneath our feet shoots us up.

Floor after floor, we see different parts of the medi-center.

There are people being pushed in wheelchairs and walking with crutches. Some family members sob in waiting areas and others simply sit. When we pass the emergency floor, we see surgeons, doctors, and nurses rushing up and down the corridors with patients on stretchers, some of them crying in pain. I picture Nan and Grandad on those stretchers and squeeze my eyes shut, wishing the image away. *They're fine. . . .*

The bell dings, announcing the arrival at our floor. We step out, and it's eerily quiet. All I can do is breathe and walk, focusing on each door number that we pass: 710, 711, 712.

I try to imagine Nan and Grandad well and smiling, waiting for me to see them. I imagine them telling me that they just had an accident, but they are fine and we can leave the medi-center together to save Mum and Dad. That they can explain these powers and what they mean.

713 . . . 714.

I stop. TJ and Lucas slow down behind me. It's completely silent on the other side of the door. Maybe they've already left, or maybe they're sleeping. I slowly push open the door, and my knees buckle at the sight.

Across the room, my grandparents are lying in two beds next to each other. They are completely still. If it weren't for the slight rise and fall of their chests, I would have thought . . .

"Mia?" I push away TJ's hand and force myself forward.

The smell of disinfectant is overpowering. *No . . . Why . . . ? Why them?*

Each *beep*, *beep*, *beep* of the health machine feels like a sharp jab in my chest. I reach Nan's bed, and the railing shakes under my grip.

"Nan?" My voice is barely above a whisper, but her eyes don't even flutter. "Grandad?"

"Mimi, why won't Nanny and Grandad wake up?" Lucas asks. I feel him gently holding on to my leg, but I can't take my eyes away from them.

"I don't know . . . ," I mutter. The words tumble from my lips, and I can't control the tears anymore.

"What are we meant to do now . . . ?" TJ asks quietly, but I have no idea. The whole plan was to get here so they could tell us what to do. They were supposed to help us save Nubis. Everything was supposed to be different.

First Mum and Dad. Now Nan and Grandad, too. When will this all end? I can't . . . I can't take it anymore.

Something sparks inside me, and the lights in the room flicker. The doors behind us rattle as the anger in me builds.

TJ places a hand on my arm. "Mia, I know this is bad, but we'll figure something out. We can still talk to the—"

I shove his hand off. He just doesn't get it. It's over. It's all over now.

"The Elite's taken EVERYONE from me!" I yell.

My arms and legs shake, and something bubbling in my core spreads like wildfire across my body, growing bigger and bigger.

"I just want it all to stop!" I scream. A bright light explodes from my body, shattering the lightbulbs. The beds rattle and TJ pulls Lucas back, shielding his eyes. An emergency bell rings, and the light from the windows is the only thing keeping the room lit.

"M-Mia, your eyes . . . ," TJ gasps. I blink, running into the connecting bathroom. Bright gold eyes flash back at me in the mirror.

"Mimi . . ."

I race out of the bathroom and burst through the main room door into the hallway. My body pulses, and I struggle to hold in another surge of power. Someone grabs me and I throw my arm back, an invisible force pushing them down the hall until they crash into a wall. I rush out down the stairs and don't stop until I'm through the medi-center exit doors.

What's wrong with me?

I stumble outside, gasping for air. Everyone's going to die. If only we'd made it to Stella sooner, if I had just known about my own stinkin' powers! None of this would have happened.

I shake my head and dash off, barging past people on the street. I close my eyes for a moment, ignoring Lux's and Nox's calls after me, blocking out their voices.

At the city gates the guards race down from their posts, but an invisible force throws them back when they try and grab me. And a sudden bright light flashes from my hands, bursting the gates open, and I run into the Nightmare Plains.

I run until my knees give out. The taste of blood fills my mouth from pushing my body too hard, and I crash to the ground.

"I can't do it!" I yell, banging my fists against the dirt. "I'm sorry!"

I can't stop the tears as I pound at the ground over and over again. Everything hurts. I can't be brave. I'm a gutterslug coward.

My fists are red with blood from where the pebbled ground has cracked open the skin. I fall back onto my bottom and hug my knees. Why couldn't TJ or Jada have these powers? Why me?

The tears don't stop, and I lose track of time. Eventually, gasping for breath, I'm distracted by a *clink-clank* noise nearby. I rub my eyes, blinking, as a little robotic bird flaps toward me. I look around, but I'm still alone. I think it's a messenger bot. I remember Mum mentioning something like it once, but no one has them in Nubis. Too expensive. Its blue eyes scan me and turn green, confirming I'm the receiver.

"Mia McKenna," it says with a loud crackly voice. "Do you accept this call from: Miles Tanaka?"

My head jerks back. *Huh?*

I look around, but there's no one else here. What does he want to talk to me for? For a second, I consider saying no, but . . . curiosity wins.

"Yeah . . . I accept," I whisper, drawing my knees closer. A light shoots out of the bird's beak, and I find my old best friend looking back at me in hologram form.

"Hey . . . ," I say.

"Hey . . . ," he replies.

He keeps his distance, staying seated far across from me, his hologram almost as clear as the clouds in the sky.

"Where are the others?" he asks, looking around, but when his eyes fall back to me, he pauses, his face softening. "What happened?"

"Like you care," I mutter, rubbing my eyes again. It doesn't matter anyway. I deserve to be alone. Because I can't save them, Mum and Dad are going to be gone forever.

He tilts his head to the side, but I look down in my lap.

"I'm glad the messenger bot found you. I didn't think you'd accept my call. . . ."

"I was gonna say no." I probably should have.

"But you didn't."

Something flickers in my vision, and I look back up to see his face right in front of mine, his finger ready to flick my cheek, but his hologram-hand goes right through me.

"So, I guess you know what you are now, huh?" he says, and I nod, not knowing what to say. Every time I think about it, I want to be sick.

I'm this *thing*, and no one told me.

"You really didn't know?" he asks.

I have to clear my throat before I can speak again. "No idea . . . ," I say, and he sits beside me.

"I missed you when I left that day, you know. And every day after," he says, looking ahead. There's a ghost of a smile on his face and I join him in the memories, thinking back to our childhoods. Back to when people with the power of light were just bedtime stories . . . when my family was together. Including Miles.

"I missed you, too," I say. *So much* . . . No one got me like he did.

His faraway gaze shifts to me, and I manage a smile back at him. Even if it's just for a moment, it feels like everything is okay, like for the first time since seeing him in that alley, the old Miles is here. I find myself looking down, picking at the grass.

"I still have the little Luna Bear charm you made me. You gave it to me at the Moon Festival, remember?" he says, and my eyes snap back to him.

"No way! You really kept that thing? That was like five years ago, when we were, like, seven," I say, and he nods.

"Yep, and actually, *I* was eight. *You* were seven, mate,"

he laughs. "I never threw it away. It's been my lucky charm. Whenever Mum and Dad put me through training, I had it with me." He digs in his pocket and pulls it out. The little bear looks tattered and discolored in the moonlight, but the little crystal moon on its head shines bright.

"I can't believe it," I say, and I can't help but wonder what kind of training he had to go through.

"I know, right? I still think Luna Bear is creepy, though. I hated when the adults would dress up as her during the festivals. No kid liked her."

"So why did you keep it, then?" I ask.

"Because you gave it to me." He puts the bear back in his pocket with a half smile. "I remember it was also the day I found out I had to move back in with my parents when they came back from that four-day mission."

"Oh yeah, I remember. . . ." He cried the day he had to go back home, so I made him the charm and gave it to him at the festival. Knowing what I do now, I'm sick over the thought of what his parents could have been doing on that mission.

"It was creepy, but cute," Miles adds.

"Well, I don't find her creepy. She's the cutest Moon Festival mascot ever."

We both laugh, but Miles falls silent first. It almost feels like the weight of everything is on his shoulders too. He seems far away in his thoughts again. Whatever he's going through, it's bothering him. Badly. I try and work out where he's talking to me from, but it's impossible to see from his hologram.

I want to believe that he didn't mean to do any of this. That he was being forced to. I know I can save him. The old Miles is still in there.

"It wasn't meant to be like this, Supernova. I swear. If I'd known it was you—"

"What?" I ask, cutting him off. "What would you have done? Stopped the attack? And if it wasn't me, then what? You would have done to another kid what you and those red-cloak thugs did to me and the others?"

"No one was meant to get hurt," Miles says. "He said that once we found the Lightcaster, he would be free and the world would be right."

"He?"

"The Reaper King," he says, leaning back on his hands. "He said we'd all be safe . . . that *you* would be safe."

Yeah, right . . .

"Then how do you explain what happened to my nan and grandad?"

"Wait, what?" His face is full of confusion.

"Don't give me that. Nan and Grandad were found unconscious outside Stella with their pod upside down. You're telling me that wasn't the Elite?"

"It wasn't, I swear. I'd know if it was us. Why would we attack your grandparents?" he asks.

"Quit lying."

"I'm not." He stares me dead in the eyes, and for some reason I feel like he's telling the truth.

I let it go for now. "Look. You don't have to do any of this, Miles. Just stop chasing us," I say, but he shakes his head.

"Mia, I don't have a choice. I have to do this."

"Why?" It just doesn't make any sense. "If you help me save everyone, then maybe we can fix this. If someone's forcing you, just let me help you. Is it your parents?"

This time he narrows his eyes. I struck a nerve. "Mum and Dad say that freeing him will free us all. I believe it too. We won't be stuck under the rule of the queen anymore. All the cities will be connected again. Life will be so much better—"

"What are you talking about?" I throw up my hands. That's ridiculous! "I don't like the queen, but she's a hundred times better than that monster you're trying to release. Do you know how many people he's killed? Hundreds! You didn't see what we saw in Ignis."

He falls silent, and I think I see pain and a little sympathy in his eyes. I see the old, kind Miles.

There's no way he's buying what his parents are saying. The trouble behind his eyes is clear, even from the hologram.

"Are you honestly okay with what's happened to our city?" I ask.

"It's not my city anymore."

"Miles."

He presses his lips together and sighs. "It's complicated, Mia. You don't understand. I'm doing this for you, too."

"Well, don't," I say, jumping to my feet. "I don't need saving. My mum and dad do because of *your* Reaper King. *You* don't get it, Miles. You're the one who needs saving, and once I free my parents, I'm gonna save you, too. I promise."

He frowns. "I don't need saving."

"Yeah, ya do."

He goes to argue again, but stops and places a hand on his earpiece.

"Okay," he says after a moment, but it isn't to me. He sighs and slowly stands up.

"What?" I ask. "What is it?"

Miles closes his eyes, and when he opens them again, his eyes are hard. "They've found you. They detected your powers. We're going to be moving in on the capital city now."

What?

My head jerks in the direction of Stella.

Electric sparks tingle across my body.

"Mia, wait—"

I stamp on the message bot, crushing it under my foot. The hologram cuts off, and I spin around and dash off as fast as I can, the sparks tingling stronger and boosting my legs.

I have to make it back to the city before the Elite. I won't let them hurt my friends. They won't touch Lucas. We need to talk to the queen. Fast. She's our last hope.

"Young one!"

I gasp with relief as Lux and Nox dash toward me from the trees.

Guys! What are you doing here?

"We can always find our tamer," Lux says.

"We never left you," Nox adds, and I can't help but smile at that. I hop onto Nox's back, and we gallop back to Stella.

I still don't know if I can control these powers. . . .

"You can," Nox says. *"You are more powerful than you think. You won't know until you try, and you are not alone."*

But what if I fail?

"It's better to try and to fail than to fail without trying at all," Lux says. *"Besides, we'd never have a weak tamer, remember?"*

"We will be by your side," Nox adds.

"Forever," we all say together.

"Now calm your mind. Deep breaths. We're almost there. Do this, not for others, but for yourself. Trust your instincts," Lux says.

I do just that and inhale deeply.

We slow down in front of the gates and I gasp, spotting Lucas and TJ arguing with the guards.

"Mimi!" Lucas races over, and I smile in relief, squeezing him tight.

"How did you guys know I left the city?" I ask.

"Lux and Nox," TJ says. "When we got to the gates, some of the guards were about to go looking for you, and we wanted to come."

I shoot the guards a suspicious look. After Miles's betrayal and how these guards tried to lock us up, I don't know how to fully trust anyone new anymore.

"Mia!"

I look over past him, and my jaw drops as I see Jada standing there with Ruby, a small smile on her face. Without a second thought, I run over and hug her. Thank Lunis!

"But how? When did you get to the city? I didn't see you," I ask.

"It must have been just before you left. Those guards said that you guys had run off somewhere, so I literally searched the whole place until I heard the commotion you made. I followed the noise and found TJ and Lucas by the medi-center," she explains. "What happened?"

"We don't have much time. The Elite are coming. They know I'm here," I say, pulling away from Jada.

"Wait, how do you know that?" TJ interrupts.

"I spoke to Miles. Now come on. We need to talk to the queen." Before he can say anything else, the guards block our path, and the ones who were sent after me return, fuming.

"You're coming with us, and if you try to escape again, I'll tie you up myself," one of the women says, her crossbow strong in her grip.

"You all deserve worse after what you did to Luther," one of the other guards mutters.

"You don't understand. The Elite are coming. We have to—"

"We're taking you to the queen. Follow, and be quick," the woman says, cutting me off. One of the guards ushers us forward to follow her with more force than necessary, but my heart skips a beat. As much as I don't trust them, I have no choice but to play nice, for now. There's still hope left. The powers old Queen Lucina had to seal away the Reaper King in the first place were those of a Lightcaster, and for some reason I've got them too. If I can master them with the queen's help, then we can really stop the Reaper King from coming back. We can defeat the Elite and save everyone in Nubis.

Whether I like it or not, I have to accept it, at least for now.

I am a Lightcaster.

Reaper King vs. the Old Queen
An Analysis of the Mural by Lila McKenna

While at first glance the mural on the wall of Nubis could be mistaken simply for beautiful engraved images, I have deduced that it depicts actual events that took place long before our lifetimes.

I believe it tells the story of the great battle between Queen Lucina and the Reaper King. While it's common knowledge that magical powers run in the blood of royalty, no one seems to know who the Reaper King is or the extent of his powers, which seem to still have a grip on this world.

However, there is evidence to suggest a link between him, the royal light powers, and the crystal fragments we found on the Nightmare Plains.

Could it have been our taking of the fragments that caused him to stir in the Spirit Plain? We still need evidence of that. But it is known that the crystals and the powers of the queen are linked. This is why she is so protective of the one she has in her keep.

The Reaper King sought to destroy every Lightcaster in existence and take over every city. The reasons for this are still unknown. But

Queen Lucina had enough and decided to fight against him.

As a result of the battle, the Reaper King was sealed away in the Spirit Plain and the umbra were created, but echoes of his power still haunt the lands, and his minions continue his work.

CHAPTER FOURTEEN

People stare as we arrive closer to the citadel, and another gate blocks us from going inside the bubble that leads to Queen Katiya's castle. Two men stand on guard with swords in their hands and shields on their arms, their faces covered by black helmets that show only their eyes.

"Step aside, Roe, Yan. I need to take these children to see Queen Katiya. Be on guard: there are suspected enemies on the way," the woman with us says, and the other male guards who were with us stay behind.

The guards, Yan and Roe, allow us through the gate and the

vibes change instantly. There's no one walking around inside the bubble, apart from soldiers.

A vehicle pulls up in front of us. It's a large black pod with the queen's gold insignia on the side, far bigger and fancier than any other travel pod I've seen. The driver gets out and opens the door for us.

"I shall take you to the castle. Please ensure that you buckle up, and that your umbra stay in their . . . smaller versions," he says, pushing his glasses up his nose. He brings his hands together and bows to us as we all get in.

"Don't worry, the queen is expecting you. You'll be going the rest of the way alone. I need to go back to my post," the woman says, stepping back from the royal vehicle. She clasps her hands and bows with a frown.

And then we're off.

From here, the castle looks as if it's made completely of ice. Every piece is created with perfection, square and even. The tall walls, made of the strongest crystal, were crafted over many years, built to protect one family and now one person alone. Queen Katiya. She was the only child of the king and queen before her, and since they passed away several years ago, it's just been her. As we draw closer, we see that the smaller towers around the main castle have watchers, stationed with crossbows ready to fire.

Queen Katiya's family reigned here for years, free of the

Reaper King after Lucina sealed him away in the Spirit Plain. They oversaw the land as saviors who protected the light in the kingdom, but for some reason, despite being sealed away, the Reaper King's Darkness seeped through into the kingdom again and he took the first city, Astaroth. No one knows why, or what sparked his rage, but something tells me the answers are in Dad's book.

Then there's Miles and the Elite. Why do they even need me for their ritual? They must know I won't help them bring back the Reaper King.

The royal pod comes to a stop, and we step out to a grand set of stairs covered with a long purple carpet, leading up to the castle doors. We reach the top and two men open the doors to us, revealing the inside. *It's beautiful.* . . .

Decorative pillars rise up, painted a brilliant white with gold edges. The floor is completely marble, so shiny that even my sneakers feel like they're slipping a bit when I take a step. Paintings of centuries-old royal ancestors in gold frames decorate the walls, their beady eyes watching our every move. Sculptures of lions perch on pedestals on either side of a water fountain in the middle of the hall, but the ceiling is by far the best part. Clouds and stars themselves are shining above, looking so real—like the actual night sky. It's the perfect painting of twilight over our heads, with even the Capricornus constellation included, and it warms my heart, reminding me of home.

"This way for the queen," a man in a long black tailcoat says, leading us down a hall. His voice is sickly sweet and proper. When we finally stop at the doors, I hear TJ gulp.

We can do this. We may be about to meet the queen, but she's just a person. Nothing to be nervous about. I look over to TJ, whose hands are firmly jammed in his pockets. He looks like he's about to pee himself.

Jada stands with her arms crossed, but I see her fingers scratching at her sides. She must be nervous too. Lux and Nox look on, unfazed, and I mimic their emotion and push open the doors.

The moment we walk in and see Queen Katiya, my senses are on high alert. Six guards stand beside her, three on either side. They are wearing royal-blue jackets, unzipped, with the queen's insignia embroidered on the right side. Their hands are protected by short, sleek blue gloves, except for one on the end who has longer ones. She must be an archer.

Underneath their jackets, they all wear steel-gray shirts that to the untrained eye look completely normal, but I know different. Mum told me that those shirts are claw- and arrow-proof, and it would take one mighty sword to cut them. On their feet they wear buckled boots in the same blue as their jackets. These people are undoubtedly the Queen's Guard.

TJ's eyes immediately widen in adoration as he stares at them, like he's completely forgotten those gate guards tried to lock us up. The Queen's Guard are probably worse. He looks like he wants to ask a billion questions, but he holds his tongue, focusing on the queen.

She's sitting on a throne with a big star-shaped back, one of her arms casually resting on the arm of her royal chair and another on a sword sheathed in the ground next to her. Her nails are perfectly manicured and painted blue, the same shade as her royal guards' uniform.

Her dress is a darker blue, like the midnight sky I've lived under my whole life. The close-fitting satin bodice flares out from the waist into a long, elegant skirt, and it's trimmed with gold that glitters just like the jewels around her neck. Beside her throne, a long crystallized staff hovers with stars on either end, exactly like the one Queen Lucina has in the mural in Nubis. It floats in the air somehow, and I clock a small ring of crystals on the floor and on the ceiling that must suspend it.

Upon the queen's head sits the royal crown, made with stones crafted from forever crystals, stardust, and the energy of the galaxy itself. It shimmers like a rainbow. There's not a hint of softness in her eyes, and nothing about her is inviting. Her famous foxlike umbra fans its eight tails, sitting at her feet like a giant house cat, with a long nose and strange white stripes on its shadowy black body. Its golden eyes stare us down.

"Come forward." Queen Katiya beckons us. Her voice soft, yet regal and powerful.

TJ clears his throat and steps forward.

"Hi, Your Highness . . . Your Majesty . . . Queen . . . err . . . all of the above." He gives a nervous chuckle, fumbling over his words. "My name's TJ."

I roll my eyes and walk up beside the goofball.

"My name is Mia. This is my brother, Lucas, and my friend Jada. We need your help, Your Highness. We're from the city of Nubis, which has been invaded and captured by the Elite. We have less than a day to save everyone, and apparently I'm a Lightcaster. Please unlock my powers or something so we can go." I do a quick curtsy for good measure. When TJ gives me a look, I shrug. What did he want, a speech?

The queen freezes. It's just for a split second, but I catch her shock before she can hide it. She leans toward one of her guards, never breaking eye contact with us as she quietly says something to him. What's going on . . . ?

"First, I wish to apologize for the misunderstanding you had with some of my guards. I assure you, there was no ill intent." *Yeah, right . . .* "Now explain it to me again. Why . . ." She trails off. Something glints in her eyes, and she presses her lips together. She leans back like she's come to a realization of sorts. "I cannot do it. I can't help you stop the Reaper King. I can't unlock your powers."

My jaw drops. Is she serious? Anger starts to bubble up from the pit of my stomach.

"What do you mean, you can't do it?" I knew the queen would be a waste of time, but no one would listen.

"But we came all this way, Your Majesty. There has to be something you can do!" Jada chimes in. "Mia is a Lightcaster, like you. She can help stop the Reaper King from coming back . . . but she can't control her powers yet. Only you can help her."

"I . . . am not my mother or my ancestors. I don't have the same strength Lucina did," says the queen.

"So you're useless?" I say, earning a sharp elbow jab from Jada.

Katiya gives me a look, her eyebrow raised, with a slight mocking smile that rubs me up the wrong way. She leans forward, her eyes fully focused on me like I'm some sort of creature she's never seen before. Her unwavering stare and strong demeanor has my guard up, and I find it hard to believe that this woman is powerful at all.

"What my friend here means is that we need your help to stop the Reaper King from being summoned again in our city," Jada says, but that's not what I mean at all.

I meant what I said. Coming here was a waste of time. We should be saving Mum and Dad right now!

I'm getting angrier, but at least this time my powers stay dormant. "All this time our city has been doing *your* job, protecting the people of Lunis! When cities were taken by the

Darkness, our parents were the ones saving people, not you! Now everyone in Nubis needs help, and you're saying no?"

"I told you, it's not that I don't want to, it's that I *can't*," sighs the queen. "My powers started diminishing years ago. It's why we have not been able to do anything about the Elite or the Darkness." She pauses, and her eyes turn softer, older, weaker. The hand that rests on her sword falls down to her side. "Are they doing the summoning during the Blood Moon tomorrow? How much can you do with the powers you already have?"

"I'm guessing it'll be at Sky Connect," Jada says. "But so far we've only seen outbursts of Mia's powers. She doesn't know how to control them yet."

Queen Katiya leans back in her throne, drumming her fingers against its arms. Her umbra flicks its tails. "That means they haven't started the summoning yet. You still have time to stop them from bringing back the Reaper King."

The queen moves her eyes back to me. "Mia." I look at her, disgusted, and she regards me with another strange glint in her eye. Then she reaches over to her tall floating staff and it glows at her touch, the stars at either end pulsing brightly. For some reason, my bracelet begins to glow too as she stands and walks over to me. "I'll give you my staff."

What in this galaxy is she doing? I gaze upon the mighty weapon. I feel the metal of my necklace against my chest, each star cold against my skin, reminding me why I'm here.

"The legend says the Children of Light will have to seek help from a queen much like themselves. Bestowed upon one child is the power of the moon and stars, and the other child is light itself." Her eyes flick to Lucas, or maybe TJ. "One protects the other, but only together can they defeat the king once and for all. Everyone thought I was a Child of Light, but I'm not at my full capacity. . . . And besides, the prophecy mentioned two, not one. I may not be able to unlock your powers, but with the help of this staff, I believe you will be able to do it yourself. It previously belonged to my mother and grandmother. With this, you might be able to stop the Reaper King."

TJ and I glance at each other, and Lucas tugs my hand.

"But I don't want these powers," I say, earning a look from TJ. "I don't want them," I say again. "You can have them, if it means you can save everyone."

I just want everything back to how it was before. I don't want to be responsible for everyone getting hurt. I don't want to be the reason Mum and Dad are killed. I don't want to fail!

The queen looks at me with an extra edge of softness again. It's sympathetic and . . . sorry. It makes my stomach twist.

"Forgive me, children. I can only imagine how hard your journey has been, but you cannot give away your powers. They're a born gift. The staff will help you. It has been passed down through my family for generations, starting with the founder of Stella, one of the first-ever Lightcasters. And this . . ."

Her umbra stands, and Katiya takes the small garnet crystal from the collar around its neck. "When the time comes, throw this into the summoning spot, which should be drawn as a crescent moon. The crystal is strongest when thrown by a Child of Light, but regardless, it should be able to stop the Reaper King from coming into this world if you're quick enough. It is my most prized possession, from my mother, and holds power from the Spirit Plain, dating back to the founders of this kingdom."

"It 'should'?" I question. What if none of this works? What then?

"The Reaper King needs souls to keep his strength up. The more strength he has, the higher the chance of him escaping the Spirit Plain. That's why the Elite need you, Mia. It's to feed him your soul, so he will be strong enough to return to our world permanently. Your powers will give him the strength he needs to take over the kingdom and rebuild himself as a fully physical being in this world. Without you, even if he does have the strength to come into our world, it wouldn't be for long. So throw this crystal into the summoning spot the moment the portal opens."

To my surprise, she hands the crystal to Lucas with a smile, and my brother's eyes widen. I clutch the staff. Why can't she just come with us?

"The crystal should work. It's the most important part of stopping the ritual, and if you make it on time, you won't even need to use your powers other than to fight the Elite. I—"

I clutch my ears, hearing a high-pitched scream, and the queen looks startled. "Can't you guys hear that?" I say.

Everyone looks around confused.

"What are you talking about, Mia? I don't hear anything," Jada says. The queen suddenly frowns, but the door bursts open and the scream stops.

"Your Highness!" A man runs into the room, almost stumbling to the floor. "A group of rebels have just invaded the city!"

"They're here . . . ," Jada mutters. How did no one else hear that scream?

"They have red cloaks on their backs and a young boy with them. It has to be the Elite," the man says in a panic.

My heart leaps. *Miles!* TJ's and Jada's eyes fall on me, and I take Lucas's hand.

"Guys, we gotta go. Now," Jada says, ushering us to the door, and the queen rises from her throne.

"So they're finally here," she says, and I look back at Lux and Nox.

"Your Highness, we should be on the move. They're after the girl, but that doesn't mean they won't come for your powers, too," one of her royal guard states.

"We will not bow to these beasts," she responds, and turns to us. "'Go back to Nubis, and make sure that crystal is thrown into the drawing of the moon. I will send some of my guards with you. Stop the summoning. You will know what to do with the staff. It will help you to unlock your powers."

She yanks at her gown, and a sword slides from within the fabric by her leg.

"Take the secret passage. It will lead right out to the street," Katiya says. She ushers us toward a passage hidden behind a bookcase that stands beside a moving portrait of herself.

Four of her guards join us, but there's no time to be amazed or protest as she closes the bookcase in front of us, sealing us in. In seconds, our eyes adjust to the dark, and the guards lead the way through the dimly lit corridor. We're quick on our feet, with Lucas holding my hand and keeping up. Lux and Nox keep close, and in my mind, I never lose track of where they are.

One of the guards speaks. "My name is Adrian. The other three are Castello, Hayes, and Arto. Hayes will be staying behind to protect the city. When we get out the other side, we will head into one of the royal pods and go straight to Nubis. It'll take a few hours to get there."

Another reminder of the advanced technology within Stella and travel pods compared to the umbra-pulled ones we have in Nubis.

"Okay, but if we bump into the Elite, we're finished. Their umbra are strong," says Jada. "And no offense, but you guys don't have any umbra."

"Yeah. Those umbra are no joke," TJ adds.

At the front, Arto looks back at us with a slight smirk. "You don't have to worry about us, kid. We don't need umbra. We know how to fight."

TJ's eyes are wide with delight as he watches the men leading us out to safety. He's probably picturing himself in the same role.

"I can't believe we came all this way for a crystal that might not work, and your powers aren't even fully unlocked," Jada mutters. "I just hope we make it back in time to stop the summoning without having to test either of them."

I tune her out and stay focused. Adrenaline pumps through my veins, pushing me on. I have to be brave.

Mum, Dad, we're coming.

CHAPTER FIFTEEN

We reach the streets of Stella and screams hit me straightaway, triggering memories of Nubis. My pulse races. The cries for help, the children being taken . . . Mum and Dad behind bars . . . confronting Miles . . . It all comes rushing back, and I grip my head.

Something tries to break through the memories, voices calling my name, but my brain pushes out every attempt until something nudges me forward and I gasp back to reality.

"Mia, focus!" I stare at Lux and Nox, coming back to my senses as the guards look over at us.

"Are you all right?" Castello asks, and Lucas's cries break

me completely out of my trance. I run over to him, and he grips his hair tight in a panic.

"Breathe, Lu-Lu," I tell him as his chest rises and falls. I gently touch his back. "We're going to save them, right now," I whisper, and he jumps at my words, snapping out of it. He nods, a new look of determination crossing his face instead. The royal pod is already waiting by the curb.

"Quickly, we must go," Adrian says, opening the door. I watch everyone get in, then throw in my rucksack and grab TJ's hand to stop him. He turns back to me, and I do my best to smile, even though my stomach churns with nerves. Only he would understand. I take a moment, looking down at the ground before meeting his brown eyes, my decision made. No more running away.

"TJ, I'm trusting you with my brother," I tell him.

"Mia, what are you—"

"The Elite are only after me. I can distract them. You guys have the crystal to stop the summoning. Remember what the queen said. Throw it in the middle of the crescent moon drawing just when the portal opens. Until then, hide."

"But, Mia—"

"I've got Lux and Nox. Plus the staff now," I jump in. "I'll be fine. Promise. Just please look after Lucas. I'll be right behind you guys."

"How, though? It took us ages to get to Stella, and you won't be driving back like we are. We should go together."

"I can't explain it. Ever since I touched that staff, I feel . . . It's like I can feel my power for the first time. If we go together and get captured, it's over. At least if I get captured, you guys have the crystal."

TJ stares at me square in the eyes and takes my hand, squeezing it.

"All right, fine. You got this, superstar, but be careful, and you better make it on time. We're counting on you."

If I can do one thing, I can make sure they get to Nubis with the Queen's Guard to stop the summoning. The crystal is the only thing that matters now. Even if I can't save Mum and Dad myself, I know the others can. TJ's smart. Jada and Ruby are the bravest, and Lucas . . . Even if something happens to me, he'll be safe with them.

"What's taking you two so long? We have to go," Arto says.

Lucas climbs out before Jada can stop him. "Come on, Mimi," he says, and my eyes sting as I look at him. It's time for me to be a good big sister. I can at least keep that promise.

"I'm not coming," I tell Arto, and he arches his eyebrow, but I quickly crouch to Lucas, not having time to explain.

"What do you mean? We have to go save Mummy and Daddy," he says, grabbing my arm, trying to pull me to the travel pod, but I don't budge. I place my hand gently on his head, running my fingers through his curls, fighting the burning sensation at the backs of my eyes.

"If you're not going, then I'm coming with you," he says, but I shake my head. I see the tears welling up in his eyes, and his grip tightens on me.

"You're breaking one of the family promises!"

I press my lips together. Every part of me screams out not to leave the others, but I have to. *I have to . . .* Looking into Lucas's eyes fuels my resolve even more. We can't risk Miles and the Elite chasing after them. They're after me, so if I can distract them for even a second, it'll be a second more for the others to reach Nubis.

"Do you have your whistle?"

He nods slowly, showing me. I smile, doing my best to keep back my own tears.

"Good, because I need you to go with TJ and the others to save Mum and Dad. I'm trusting you with this, Lu-Lu. Think you can handle it?"

He sniffs, rubbing his eyes, hiccuping. "Yes, Mimi. I'll save Mummy and Daddy," he says, and I believe every word.

"I'll catch up to you guys later. I love you, Lucas."

"I love you too, Mimi. To the stars and back." I rise up to my feet. It's time. I jump on Nox's back as TJ takes Lucas to the pod.

"The Elite will have come in through the main gates. We'll use the queen's private gate to escape. Good luck!" Adrian yells, and I nod.

Lux, Nox, let's go.

"*Yes,*" they say, and we're off like lightning, dashing out of the giant bubble of the castle and straight toward the main gates. My body feels electric and I draw the queen's staff, ready to fight, not looking back. This is it.

Energy flows through my arms and legs, and I hold on to it, feeling one with my umbra. I follow the energy building up inside and swing the staff up. A purple light bursts from it, and like sparks, images flash in my mind. At first, I see the car with everyone driving across the plains at high speed, and then I see the faint gold-highlighted images of Nan and Grandad all the way back in the medi-center. From the main gates ahead, I see the Elite illuminated in red, racing toward our direction, the opposite way from the others escaping, and I sigh in relief.

It worked.

"*Look closer,*" Nox says, and I squint my eyes, focusing on the mental image of the men and women. One person in particular rides in the middle on a hellhound umbra. Miles.

We need to split them up. We can't take all of them at once.

"Everyone get inside!" I yell to the people on the streets, as men and women scramble off to safety with their kids. We dodge carts, travel pods, and market stalls. We jerk left, barely missing a rope net. They're gaining on us. If they can somehow track me every time my powers spark, let's see if this plan will work.

I look to Lux and chuck the glowing staff over to him.

You know what to do.

He nods, catching the staff in his mouth and parting from us, as Nox and I carry on ahead through the city.

We keep track of the Elite behind us, and some suddenly turn in Lux's direction, with Miles and a few others still after us.

"Yes!" I punch my fist in the air with a grin. *Slow down a bit, Nox. I'm ready to take them.*

"Get back here!" one of the Elite yells, coming back into sight behind us.

I swing my arm back and light shoots out, throwing one of them off their umbra.

The downed Elite trips up a few of the others, and my eyes connect with Miles. He smirks, but there's something off about his eyes. *I'm still saving him, too.* Nox jerks left, dodging another rope net, and I kick at one of them who gets too close. *We need to lead Miles to the plains.*

We take a sharp right, and I gasp as an umbra bashes into us, knocking me off Nox. I crash to the ground and pain shoots up my back. I hiss and the red-eyed umbra snarls, stalking closer. I push my hands out, but nothing happens—the energy that swirled around them has vanished, and my vision snaps back to normal. No, no, no! *What's going on?* I thrust my hands out again and again, but nothing happens, and the umbra pounces. I scream, and something crashes into it.

"Nox!" I yell, seeing my umbra run and bite the red-eyed

one, kicking a red-cloaked woman away with his hind legs. Lux rejoins us, having lost the Elite that was after him. He chucks me the staff and throws his head back, letting out an ear-piercing scream that stops Miles and Shade in their tracks. He scoops me up on his back and we're off again.

"My powers aren't working!"

"You lost focus, Mouse. Don't worry about it for now. Let's go," Lux says, with Nox following straight behind.

"Mia!" I hear Miles yell, but if he wants to get me, then he'll just have to keep following.

We make a break for the main gates.

"Get out of the way!" I yell at the guards, racing through and out into the Nightmare Plains. We keep running farther and farther away from Stella, and the sun from the city fades to the darkness that I've known all my life.

"Did it work?" I ask.

"Yes, the Elite brat is still following," Lux says.

We slow to a stop by a giant hollow tree forest and I hop off Nox, feeling the nerves building. It's now or never, I guess. One last chance to get through to him.

A loud laugh echoes among the hollow trees. I jump, and my umbra snap their heads behind us. He's here.

"Found you." The trees carry his voice around us, and my guard shoots straight up as Lux and Nox stand on either side of me, horns at the ready. From one of the trees, Miles sidesteps into view, and my breath hitches in my throat. Just like when he first returned to Nubis with the Elite, he stands before me, the moonlight hitting him. No hologram this time, but a sickening smirk on his face. The old Miles I saw earlier is a distant memory, but he's still in there. I know it.

"I just want to talk. I can help you," I say, my fingers drumming against my new staff. Behind him his umbra, Shade, lingers in the shadows of the hollow trees. Ferocious like the first time I saw her, with those bloodred eyes and sharp canine teeth.

"I told you. I don't need help."

Miles strolls over to me, seemingly without a care in the world, until he stops, this time keeping a careful distance. He never used to be this cold. A sword is attached to his hip, and his eyes acknowledge my umbra, and it's my turn to smirk. He laughs again, and I hate how it still sickens my stomach.

"Which one's yours?" He runs a hand through his hair, keeping his composure. I look at him, smug.

"Both." He loses his cool for just a second. But I catch it, and my smirk widens.

"Supernova strikes again. Guess I shouldn't be surprised." He steps forward and his umbra does the same.

"So, that was a cute trick you pulled, getting your umbra to distract us," he says, but his words just bounce off me, and a new sense of calm takes over. By now, the others should be more than halfway back home. Holding the staff sparks the energy in me again.

"It took you guys long enough to find us in the city. I told you not to chase us."

He chuckles. "Looks like someone's gotten a bit overconfident."

"Looks like someone's gotten a bit dumber," I retort, and his eyes change again. Just for a split second, but I see it. Anger.

Nox, Lux, get ready.

"Of course," they say together.

"All right, enough games," Miles spits at me. "Where are the others? I need you all to come with me. If you don't, you're gonna end up like your parents and everyone else."

The threat to my parents fuels my purpose. I taunt him back. " You can't be clown enough to believe the Reaper King won't turn on you. What happened to you, Miles? Like, really?"

He smirks as he shakes his head. "Mia, he gave us powers, and we believe in his vision. Didn't you wonder why we were always on your tail? Your powers led us to you. How'd you think we caught your parents and the other tamers so easily?"

Something in me almost snaps, but I hold on by a thread, my hands clenching and unclenching. The power sparks once again.

"Relax, they're most likely still alive," Lux says, and my heart leaps. The others could still save them.

"Any more nosy questions?" Miles asks.

Tons.

I focus on his eyes—softer, just like when we spoke through the hologram. The old Miles is still in there. That earpiece in his ear is the problem. A glaring reminder that he still needs saving too.

"Why didn't you holo-call or message me during all this time? You just left and never said a word!" I say, stepping forward.

"I would have if I could have," he says with a strange smile, but his eyes flicker with a different emotion. "Did you think it was on purpose that I didn't message you?"

Yeah, I did. He raises an eyebrow, but I hold my nerve.

"You missed me that much, huh?" Miles asks with half a smile.

I sigh. "It just would have been nice to know where you went."

His smirk widens, as though he doesn't believe a word of it. Then he narrows his eyes, rubbing the back of his neck. "A lot has happened these past three years, Supernova."

"Did you want to leave that day?"

He raises an eyebrow, shocked. "What kind of question is that?"

"Just answer it. Did you want to leave the city that day with your parents?"

He scratches his chin. He's gonna lie. "I wasn't against it."

"Liar."

For once, the smirk is wiped completely off his face. He huffs, looking anywhere but at me. "I just didn't want to see you sad before I left. That's why I didn't tell you we were leaving. It was fun living with you and your family, Mia, but my parents needed me, and your parents wouldn't have wanted me to stay with you. Not after what mine did, and I . . . didn't want to say goodbye in person," he answers, but it isn't enough. I want to know *more*. I want to know what in this galaxy happened to him during those years. I know Mum and Dad would have let him stay with us if he wanted to, and if his parents allowed it. There's more to this than he's letting on. He was himself during that hologram call. I felt it and saw it.

"If I go with you . . . what happens next?" I ask. If I can drag this out as long as possible, maybe, just maybe I can break through to him.

"You help us with the ritual, of course. Dad says your powers can unlock the seal forever." He smiles. "Then you meet the Reaper King."

Chills tickle my back. So it *was* his parents at the other end of that earpiece. It had to be. Alarm bells ring in my head. He's only on the Reaper King's side because of his parents. *Beware of the Reaper Creeper, creeping in the night. When innocent children meet the tragic ends of their short little lives.*

"I heard you experienced some of our power already in some tunnel or something. Did it scare you?"

"Calm down, young one." I fight the urge to look at Nox, tangling my fingers in my sleeves. I tell myself over and over again that the others will make it, and with the queen's crystal they'll be able to stop the summoning if I don't make it back. I focus on my breath, breathing in and out slowly. Lux and Nox are right. They'll stop the Reaper King from coming, and I can do this. My fingers slowly release their grip on my sleeves.

Miles raises his hand, and for a second his eyes flicker red and his grin is filled with shark teeth. I jump back as a red shadow mass floats around his hand, just like the Elite who captured us.

"Our powers increase when we're in the presence of a Lightcaster. We can *sense* you like a shark smelling blood. We will be the new reapers."

The energy sparks in my body again, surging in my hands as I look down at them with a sudden urge that tugs me to Miles, almost telling me something.

"You're one of my best friends. I don't wanna fight you. Please. I'll go with you if you free my parents," I say, reaching my hand out to him.

He tilts his head to the side, and for a split second a light enters his eyes, making them shine brighter than I've ever seen. My stomach flutters as I lean forward. Nox's and Lux's eyes are on me, but I focus on Miles. *Please.*

"You mean it? You'll come?" he asks, looking at my hand in surprise.

I smile, giving him my "word," and he reaches out for my hand but suddenly freezes. He touches his ear, and that's when I see the earpiece again. His face twists to anger as a low, muffled voice speaks to him and I gulp, getting a bad feeling. His eyes snap to me.

"You liar . . . I can't believe you actually lied to me! You were stalling!"

I raise my hands. "Wait, what? No! I want to help you!"

"Liar! There's a travel pod heading to Nubis," he says, tapping the earpiece. "Whatever your plan is, it isn't going to work. They're gonna be captured as soon as they get there."

His eyes are a mix of shock and . . . hurt, but before he can do anything, I hop on Nox, and we dash toward Miles.

Now!

A flash blinds us all. Black-and-white shadows spread across my body like armor. My heart races as Lux spins, transforming into a shield that falls into my hand. I feel two horns grow from the top of my head. A chill slithers up my spine, and my stomach wrenches with nerves as I become one with my shadow beasts. The very thing I feared. A monster. Nox seems to smirk beneath me as his and Lux's shadows wrap around me, our bodies blended together. Our third and final form complete. And I'm not afraid.

I race forward, blocking Miles's first attack with my shield. He growls in frustration, the black shadows around him flaring. He jumps onto his rabbit-eared hellhound before I can stop him, yanking out his sword as we collide. The ground rumbles, the force of our attack blowing the trees back. My shadow armor pulses.

"Listen to me! Whatever this Elite group is, I'll get you out! Just let me help you!" I yell.

I slash my shield at him and we separate, then clash once again. My staff presses against Miles's sword as Nox's horn pushes his umbra back, making him stumble, but Miles and Shade hold their ground, and my teeth clench as Miles's whole weight pushes against me.

"His shadow powers are increasing. We're not strong enough yet to overpower him!" Nox's voice hums through my mind.

Sparks of energy bubble up between our weapons. Sonic booms rattle the plains with each connected hit.

"I told you, I don't need your help!" Miles yells, and we clash again, the energy building once more like a pressure cooker. This is just a glimpse of the Reaper King's powers, and yet we're struggling.

The winds whip furiously around us. His shadows push against mine, both of us refusing to give up and break apart. My staff shakes and so does his sword. Our eyes widen as the energy explodes, blowing us both back across the field. My body smacks against the dirt, and pain shoots through my back again. I hiss and roll onto my stomach, seeing my staff far away beside Nox.

"N-Nox . . . ," I breathe, clawing against the grass, and I feel his and Lux's shadows zap from my body, leaving behind a sharp emptiness. A loud growl forces me to turn around, and my heart skips a beat. Shade stares me down, licking her lips, with Miles barely holding on to her back. His eyes are furious.

"Enough now, Mia. You're coming with us."

I fall back on my butt, trying to scramble away as the red-eyed umbra pounces. Suddenly Lux, having changed back from a shield to his normal form, smacks into the hellhound beast from the left, knocking Miles off. Before I can even blink, the shadowy savage canine slashes her claws and sinks her teeth into Lux in retaliation. His scream pierces the air, and my heart almost stops. Nox and I dash after Lux but something smacks into me, knocking me off my feet, and my body bashes against the ground, which scrapes my arms and legs. Miles stands back on his feet from diving at me and Nox skids to a stop, hesitating, but I scream out to him.

Go help Lux!

He obeys and aims straight for Shade, kicking her off Lux and attacking with his horn.

I hiss, pain shooting through my body. The leftover shadows from being in the third form clump and rush to my pain spots like cool compresses. My eyes sting with tears, but I refuse to cry.

"I don't need your help. I know what I'm doing!" Miles yells.

I force myself to my feet, my knees wobbling, but I'm very much determined. If there's ever a time to save him, it's now.

Miles pants, wiping blood from his mouth and looking at it with a sharky smile of disbelief. "You're pretty strong, Supernova," he chuckles darkly. "But you gotta pay for that."

It's my turn to laugh as I roll my shoulders back.

"Yeah, you're pretty strong too, but I'm not so little anymore," I say, lifting my staff and pointing it straight at him. "And that's the last hit you're getting on me, mate."

The staff glows as a smirk of my own appears on my face. Energy shoots up my arm, spreading across my body like wildfire, boosting me. This time, I'm the first to move. Our weapons clash, and his teeth clench this time, with bangs and crashes going on around us as our umbra fight. The ground rattles; the wind is razor-sharp. Neither of us give in.

"Tell me what the flip happened to you!"

"No!" Miles shouts back angrily. "What part of that don't you get?"

My staff and his sword clash again and our eyes connect. The boy who's been my best friend since I was born is refusing to see sense. We've always been together, but whatever happened over these past years can't have changed him forever. I refuse to believe that.

We jump away from each other and dash forward again.

"You're really turning your back on all of us? My parents did everything for you when your parents were away! We were like family!"

I dodge his strike and smack him in the back of the knees, making him crumple to the ground. He hisses as I jump him, pinning his arms above his head. "Don't move!" I snap as a high whistle pierces through the air, straight to my ears. A single sound meant for me.

I let Miles go. It sounds again, and I'm off running. *Lucas.*

"MIA!"

Quick as my feet can take me, I race through the trees, Miles's yells fading.

"Mia, we're here."

I jump, almost tripping over my feet as Lux and Nox run beside me, leaving Shade behind. For the first time I see Lux properly and I almost trip again, feeling my heart tear as I notice black flicks of shadows dripping from his body like blood.

"Lux?"

"Don't worry, it'll heal. We need to get to Lucas. Get on."

Nox speeds slightly ahead, and I vault up onto his back. I pull out the staff, and it quickly extends. Lux and Nox's trots turn to full-speed gallops, and a bright light engulfs us. Energy rushes through me, forcing my hair up in the air.

"This is so cool!" I yell.

"*This power!*" Nox mutters. His whole body feels like it's vibrating with energy, and it shoots to Lux, too, as his eyes widen. The three of us snap our heads in the direction of Nubis, and suddenly we speed off, quick as lightning across the plains, as one once again, transforming into one ultimate being. There's nothing else on my mind but that whistle and what could have possibly happened.

"*It definitely sounded like it came from Nubis,*" Nox says as I grip onto him and the wind thrashes at us. I nod, worried. Did something stop them from making it? Did they get ambushed? Were they with Mum and Dad already? Anxiety zaps through my body. *I need to get home.*

We race through the purple flakes of grass, stomping on the snapping carno plants that once bit at our ankles. We tackle the swamps, and I wave at the croco-umbra as we pass it, promising to get revenge for her, too. We break back out into the field, passing the underground umbra cave, and I focus ahead.

The sweet scent of rosy-dill flowers fills the air, and we breathe it in, not stopping, weaving in and out of the bare-boned trees, which no longer look like faceless scare-crows but beacons of encouragement that push us on. The sun is a distant memory as our moon sits high and proud in the sky. Then we see it and skid to a stop. Standing tall as the day we left, the giant gate of Nubis is before us, wide open. We pause as the world around us turns slowly red, and the once-bright white moon turns to blood.

"Are you guys ready?"

"Of course."

It's time to finish this.

Umbra Tales:
Legends of the Lightcasters
Author: Unknown

The Founders of Lunis

This book will be an official and personal record of the history of Lunis, a kingdom founded by Ria, Rehan, Kikyo, Aurora, Blaze, and me.

I will be as objective and factual as possible. May this book always help my family to know where they are from and what may await them in the future. Let me start from the beginning.

This is the story of the founders of Lunis.

Once there were six individuals who sought to create a new home in a new far land, free from war and poverty.

There was the one who led, one who was brave, one who was afraid, one who was smart, and two who were siblings, both the same. Together, the six traveled far and wide, across lands of snow and ice, up mountains filled with smoke and soot, and along rivers of raging fire.

After much tiring travel, the six finally found a land that was dark and quiet. In this land were crooked silver trees, shiny purple grass, wild animals, and plants that could eat you alive if you took one misstep. It was a wild land they had not seen before, but with much potential.

The group came across one particular tree—taller than the rest, but with the same silver color. Its long branches jutted out in all directions, but tucked away in the trunk of it was a crystal brighter than any star. A crystal that would change their lives forever.

CHAPTER SIXTEEN

I race through the gates of Nubis, screaming Lucas's name. The whole city is bathed in red from the hue of the moon.

The whistle sounds again, and we run through town. In the outdoor market, stalls are broken and scattered over the road. Windows of houses and shops are shattered, their doors busted, abandoned. We gallop past Ms. Mabel's old stall in the market. The sweet cinnamon smell no longer greets me; instead soot and dust fill my nose. The pretty fairy lights that once hung from it and her big sign are broken into pieces.

We leave the market, and even the trees are no longer silvery bright; they're almost unrecognizable—bare, broken, and collapsed, and not a single glow bug in sight. I look upon the walls of Mum's great lab, all smoking and damaged, making my heart ache at the very core. I slow to a stop, feeling numb as I look at the world around me. My beautiful town is in ruins.

"Over there!" Lux says.

We reach the town center. The black-and-white shadows disperse from my body, and the horns I feel on my head crumble away. I stare ahead in shock. Everyone is here—Mum, Dad, and all the tamers, and the umbra still captured and trapped. Ruby silently calls out to me, and I spot her, Lucas, Jada, and TJ, hiding behind a bin in the alley—the very same one TJ and I were behind when everyone was first taken. The Elite haven't started the summoning yet. TJ, Jada, and Lucas look at me with fear in their eyes, and I almost choke on my breath when I realize why. Twenty Elite stand in a line with their red hoods up, looking far from the humans they once were. Their bony fingers point at our kneeling captured family and residents of Nubis no longer in cages. Others are gathered around a giant symbol of the crescent moon, which is drawn on the ground in front of them, just like the queen described. Some of them mumble a strange chant under their breath, the shadows from their hands pouring into the drawing, but there's no portal yet.

Dad spots me and his eyes widen. He mouths for me to hide, but it's too late. I'm not running anymore. A familiar pale man with shaggy black hair, a purple crown on his head, and an eagle badge pinned to his cloak stands in front of the prisoners, next to a pale woman with long brown hair and blue eyes. They look at me, and that's when it hits me. I know exactly who they are.

"You're Miles's mum and dad. . . ." The words tumble from my lips, and the man claps his hands together patronizingly. It sends a shiver down my spine.

"Glad you could finally join us, Mia." He smiles and walks over to me. His entire presence weighs down on me, almost suffocating. I try to step back, but fear burrows inside me, pinning me to the spot. *Is this how Miles felt?*

"If you touch one hair on her head, I'll kill you!" Mum yells, trying to get up, but black shadows wrap around her body, stopping her. One of the Elite stands in the distance, his hands oozing the stuff. Then, as I look closely at all the other Elite, realization strikes. Yasmin Lucia, Robert Michaels, Gabbie Rose, Chenai Evans, Lamron Jones . . .

People who went missing during the previous Blood Moons.

Did the Reaper King force them to join the Elite, or were they hypnotized? My eyes stop on one woman in particular. Amber Halliwell, Jada's mum. There's no mistaking those same eyes. She and Jada are the spitting image of each other. I snap my head to Jada, but I can't read her face.

Castello and the other guards are all bruised and bloodied, and my stomach lurches.

Magnus . . . that was his name, I remember now, and his wife—Miles's mum—Maria. I remember all the times Miles came to my house crying because his parents were forcing him to read these weird, scary books, every day. I didn't know what books he was talking about back then, but I can guess now. They were always so tough on him, but that's because they were converting him, especially his mum. The happiest I ever saw him was when he stayed with us, when his parents went on missions outside the walls.

I scowl at the woman as she smirks, swishing her wavy brown hair, and steps forward. Her heels click against the concrete, her blue eyes connecting with my brown ones. "The Reaper King needs powerful minds, and for the powers of the Lightcasters to fully come back to life in this world. Everyone in Nubis with an umbra has proven their worth. You will all be sacrificed and given to the king. And you, Mia, are the one to seal the deal."

"With his power we will take over the kingdom and plunge it all into Darkness. We will be the rulers of a new Lunis!" Magnus yells. His tone is erratic. There is lunacy in his eyes that makes my teeth clench.

"We knew you kids were up to something the moment we saw that travel pod and Miles told me he was chasing you. Why do you think we waited to start the summoning?" Maria laughs, and I struggle to control my rage. The gutterslug.

"Where are the others, by the way? I bet they're watching us right now."

"Mia, look out!" Dad yells, and I scream as I'm grabbed from behind. Collars click around Lux's and Nox's necks before they can fight.

"Let her go!" Somehow pushing through the hold of the shadows and forcing themselves to their feet, Mum and Dad run over to me, pushing through the shadows that try and hold them back. They're intercepted by four red cloaks.

"Mimi!" I snap my head left, but before I can scream at Lucas to run, one of the Elite grabs him from TJ. I scream out, trying to muster up and push out my light energy like before, but nothing happens and I yell out in anger. *These stupid powers!*

I feel the staff attached to my thigh. If only I could reach it!

"Leave them alone!" Jada yells, running out with Ruby and attacking one of the Elite.

"No! NO!" Lucas screams, thrashing about.

"Lucas! Look at me. Look at Mama," Mum calls out, yanking against the shadows again. Magnus laughs as Lucas's cries get louder. The wind roils around us.

"Son, it'll be okay. We're here." But Dad's voice doesn't reach my brother. The man who has Lucas struggles to hold him as he shakes violently.

"No . . . No . . . ," he yells, the ground rumbling, and the man holding him stumbles. "LEAVE US ALONE!"

A huge blast sends us all flying. Just like what happened in the umbra cave, I crash back into the man who holds me, falling to the ground. I scramble to my feet and kick him where the moon doesn't shine. I backflip away and look ahead to where the blast came from. My pulse races. Mum and Dad free themselves, each knocking out their captors single-handedly. All the Elite have been thrown back onto the ground, freeing everyone, the shadows dissipating into nothing.

They all follow my gaze, shock written on their faces. Standing alone in the midst of the chaos, my little brother cries, rubbing his eyes with his fists.

"H-how?" I mutter.

The winds whip up again loudly, and a blue light spins around Lucas like a hurricane. "I want the bad guys to go away!"

My mind is all messed up as Mum and Dad run over to him, but the light pushes them back.

"Lucas!" they yell, shielding their eyes from the harsh winds. I push forward past them, covering my eyes with one arm and reaching out with the other toward the light. Lucas grips his hair, sobbing. The light around him flares out like angry flames.

"My head hurts!" he sobs.

"The power's too much! His body can't take it!" Mum calls out.

"Lucas, it's me!" I yell, pushing closer. The light spins around him with no mercy, shoving me back each step I take. "Lu-Lu, I'm coming!"

I reach forward, gritting my teeth as the light pushes against my body with all its might and Lucas cries out.

"My head hurts!" he cries again, pain filling his voice.

Some of the red-cloaked men and women get back on their feet, only to be knocked down again in the rage of Lucas's powers, forced to the ground with the others.

I'm coming, Lu-Lu! I close my eyes and focus on my core, searching for my light, remembering every moment of anger, every sad and happy emotion, channeling them. I remember the day Lucas was born, the day I first met Miles, and the day he left. . . . I remember hanging out with TJ for the first time and the first day Dad taught me martial arts. . . . I remember the looks on my parents' faces when I told them I wanted to be a tamer. The light in me sparks. I remember when they were captured . . . the scared look in Mum's eyes, the pain and worry in Dad's as he distracted the guards for us. . . . I remember it all!

The energy zaps through my body, bursting through my hands. A purple light tangles with Lucas's and I break through the hurricane barrier, holding him close to me.

"I'm here, Lu-Lu. . . . It's okay, you did it. You helped save everyone."

"Mimi . . . ," he hiccups, sobbing into my shirt. The winds slowly calm down and the light around us fades as Mum and Dad run over. The aftermath of Lucas's powers is still sparking the air.

Jada and the other adults and tamers immediately set to work tying up the Elite. The collars around all the umbra snap off their necks, and they growl and roar, chasing after the Elite's umbra. Booms and bangs clap behind us from the clashing shadow beasts, but I focus on Lucas, almost nervous to hold him. All this time, it was him, too. He has the powers the Elite want. He's a Lightcaster. My tears burn hot and angry. He's now in danger too, but they aren't gonna hurt him. Not while I'm alive to stop them.

I let go of Lucas and Mum picks him up, frantically checking him over to make sure he's okay. I feel numb when Dad does the same to me, and my eyes don't leave Lucas. Why didn't they tell us we had powers?

"He'll be okay, baby-girl," Dad says, following my gaze. "You both did so well, but the mission isn't over until we lock up every member of the Elite in the Hold."

I shift my attention to Dad and nod. He's right, but when this is over, I have a lot of questions to ask.

TJ rises to his feet with both of his mums. He's in complete shock too. He looks at me with a mix of confusion and relief, but he and his parents keep watch over Magnus and Maria.

"No way . . . it was him, too!" Jada says, walking over and looking kind of dazed. "Lucas was the one who did the blast in the umbra cave. I thought it was just your powers that were unlocked."

Lux and Nox were right. It wasn't me who done it. I look back at my umbra, and they nod at me with hints of smiles on their faces. Jada slowly walks over to her mum. It's hard to read her expression.

"My head still hurts a little . . . ," Lucas whispers, and Dad strokes his head and kisses his cheek.

"You did it, Lucas," I tell him again with a smile, but I can't help feeling nervous. He doesn't need to have this burden on him, too. "You saved us, Lu. Just like you promised."

"You can't stop the Darkness; it's too late!" Magnus suddenly yells from the ropes that TJ and his mums have tied him up with. "He will get the souls he needs and rise! It's not over!"

Dad's eyes harden, focusing on the rugged man with a dangerous look.

One of the Elite suddenly breaks free, his body erupting into shadows as he runs to the crescent moon summoning spot.

"Stop him!" Dad yells, running after him, but the man reaches the huge symbol before us, screaming as his shadows seem to devour his entire being and flow into the moon.

"We just had to stall you all long enough for him to come! A sacrifice from one of us was all that was needed to kick it off! Once he appears and consumes the Lightcaster, he can't be stopped!" Magnus laughs.

"What?" someone yells out, and it's Miles who stands. He looks shocked, and Shade is by his side, growling with wild eyes.

"You said that you just needed Mia to open the portal! Not that he would kill her!" he yells, but his dad shakes his head.

"Remember why we are doing this, son."

Nox suddenly whines and cries, shaking his head from side to side, and Lux starts to do the same. One by one all the umbra, including Spike and Bolt, do the same.

"What's wrong?" I ask, and look at Maria. She smirks, jerking her chin at the giant symbol of the moon as it glows red.

The concrete beneath it begins to crumble away, and red shadows burst from the drawing. My breath hitches in my throat and I stumble back. It's unlike anything I've ever seen. An invisible pressure forces me to my knees. Lux and Nox whine as they're forced down too, and I wrap my arms around their necks, keeping them close. All around me, everyone is forced down by an invisible power. Then . . . a creature slowly rises out of the crescent moon.

A crown made of bone is the first thing visible, resembling the very thing I saw in my dream, the first night we slept on the plains. Twice the size of any crown fit for a person. Red shadows whip around it, beginning to form a face. Someone screams, and complete fear pins me to the spot.

"The king is coming!" Maria yells, snapping me out of it.

"Lucas, the crystal!" I yell.

Held protectively by Mum and Dad, Lucas scrambles in his pocket and pulls out the shiny crystal. He looks at me, worried, but I give him the best smile I can muster up. "You can do it!"

Red eyes appear on the king's shadow-face as his body rises out of the circle. His shadows burst out from him, floating around everyone, keeping them pinned. Lucas yells, trying to fight them off, but the shadows pin him to the ground with Mum and Dad. I panic, yanking the staff from my thigh. It glows at my touch, and the king's shadows crash against an invisible barrier a few feet from my face.

His sharp eyes fix on me, but I squeeze mine shut, focusing on the flow of energy through my body. Like a bright lilac light, it travels along my legs, arms, and fingertips. My mind goes back to the croco-umbra and the feeling I had when I ran from the medi-center, building on that power. Something roars, but the sound doesn't touch me. I keep my eyes shut and my mind calm, pushing all the energy to my hands, gripping the staff. *I can do this.*

My eyes burst open and my feet are no longer touching the

ground. A purple light glows around me. I smile as I swing the staff up.

"Go kick rocks, you gutterslug king!" I snap the staff down like I did before, and all the energy bursts from it straight to the circle, shoving all the red shadows back to him, freeing everyone. He screams in rage.

Lucas sucks in a deep breath, and pulling his hand back, he throws the crystal forward as hard as he can. My breath traps in my throat. The tiny magic stone flies through the air toward the circle as the king scrambles to escape.

Miles jumps up, catching the crystal before it reaches the circle, and my heart skips a beat as the shadows start to push back against my power, fighting me off to reach the others again. The staff shakes in my grip, and I try my best to keep them at bay.

"Miles!" I yell. "Throw it in the circle!"

"Destroy it, son! You know what to do," Magnus interrupts. *The gutterslug!* The red shadows pin me down as Miles looks at me and then my parents. The crystal clutched in his hand, he turns around to face the king. Shadowy clawed hands and arms form, and the shadows push back stronger.

"Please, Miles!" Mum calls out as the shadows rage, slowly draining my energy, and my knees buckle. *I can't hold it!* I hear Lux and Nox call for me, but I can't focus enough to respond.

"We'll help you," Dad says. Miles turns back to us, hesitating. His dad seems to mutter something, but I can't hear; my power is dwindling, the monster shadows are eating away at my energy. My legs shake as someone else grips the staff with me. I look down in shock to see Lucas standing beside me.

"I'll protect you, Mimi!" he yells, and the energy from the staff blasts out doubly stronger, shooting the red shadows right back, creating a shock wave as the purple energy wraps around the king like a rope. He roars as the crystal flies through the air, landing right under him in the center of the circle. His roars turn into screams as he thrashes about, but it's too late. A bright light shoots up, engulfing him.

The Elite yell with anger, and all the weight lifts off everyone, their energy zapping back like an electric jolt. I sprint to Mum and Dad with Lucas. I hug my family tightly, my heart filling up with happiness and nothing else. Everyone's okay. Lux and Nox stand, and I wiggle out of Mum's arms to hug their necks and bring their heads close to mine. Their shadows kiss my cheeks, and my eyes well up. The thought of losing them is indescribable. I can't, not ever. This is what having umbra partners is about. I finally understand.

"I'm so glad you guys are all right," I say, managing a smile, but I'm completely exhausted. I hear Lux snort, and he nudges his head against me.

"You do have the best umbra partners, you know. Don't disrespect us with that doubt of yours, Mouse."

I chuckle, squeezing them closer, before it hits me.

"Miles?" I let go of the umbra and run over to him. He's still on the ground, half his body on Shade. Unmoving. I shake him, my pulse racing with panic, but he doesn't move. "Miles! Wake up! Come on!"

My eyes fill with tears, and my heart's ready to explode.

Suddenly he bursts into laughter, peeking through one eye.

"You're really loud, you know that?" he says, and I smack his arm as hard as I can. The jerk. He hisses in pain as he slowly sits up.

"Thanks for the save, Shade. Thought I was a goner against the Reaper King," he says to the umbra, and when he looks back at me, he knows exactly what I'm about to ask, and sighs.

"I don't know why I did it," he says wearily, a weird look in his eyes, like he's still thinking about whether he did the right thing, but after so long, he did. Maybe the old Miles is back. I give him a big hug as someone yells out.

"You brat! You ruined everything! We were doing all of this for you!" Magnus shouts across the street, and Miles winces as his parents look at him with such rage, even I flinch. They're taken away by Castello and Adrian. They'll be going to prison in the Hold for all they've done, and it's what they deserve.

"Are you okay?" I ask Miles, watching him carefully. His eyes don't leave his parents.

"I'm fine," he mutters, but it's obvious he's not. Seeing how Magnus and Maria were acting . . . It showed just how much he must have gone through. He should have stayed with us, and they wouldn't have been able to mess him up like this. He's finally safe too, but . . . part of me still can't trust him. Not yet.

Dad walks over to us, and his worried look softens as he sees Miles, but for some reason, Mum doesn't share the same joy. She and Dad glance at each other, having one of those silent conversations they always have. I look for TJ and Jada and smile when I see them safe. We made it. . . .

"Mia, we need to talk." At my mum's words, my gaze flicks to Lux and Nox, both of them nodding for me to go on. Miles quietly steps away and gives us space. We all have a lot to talk about.

"We did what we thought was best for you. There's still so much we don't know about Lightcasters," Mum begins, her eyes never leaving mine, and I listen to every word. "We suspected everyone in Nubis was being watched."

"And we couldn't risk you knowing about your abilities and somehow unlocking them too early," Dad adds.

"And have Miles's parents finding out," I breathe, and they nod. I mull it all over. If I had known I was a Lightcaster, would anything have changed? Would I have stayed in the city and tried to fight, or would I have still left?

"It wasn't just them," Mum says, bringing my attention back as Lux and Nox walk over. "Everyone who left Nubis that day several years ago was a traitor. They followed the Reaper King. We found out by chance and forced them out the city, and with you and Miles being so close, we couldn't risk Maria and Magnus getting any hint you might be a Lightcaster."

"And I get that now," I say, looking at my hands. "But . . . just tell me the next time there's something big. I'm stronger than you think. I'm not afraid anymore." After all that's happened these past few days. I know I'm not weak, and it's not because of these stinkin' powers. *I'm* strong, my umbra are strong, and my friends are strong. We saved Nubis together, Lightcaster or not, and if I have no choice but to have this silly "gift," then so be it. I'm done with running away.

"We've always known you were strong, baby-girl," Dad says, a big smile spreading across his face.

"You're a McKenna," Mum adds. She squeezes me in a hug, and I wrap my arms around her.

"And a Lightcaster! Like me, right? Right?" Lucas chimes in, jumping up and down. I smile, but my stomach sinks. A part of me wishes that he didn't have it, this power that whirls inside us . . . can we really control it? I would give it away if I could . . . Lucas's powers too. I want us to be normal, but nothing is ever going to be the same again. I guess it could be worse; at least I'm not in this alone now.

"Something happened to Nan and Grandad too," I say. Mum's eyes widen. "They're in the medi-center in Stella. Their travel pod was found upside down in the Nightmare Plains. I don't know what happened to them."

"We'll talk about this at home," Mum says. "We need to arrange for them to be transferred to the medi-center here instead."

Her voice is shaky, and I see the worry in her eyes. Dad hugs her.

"What about Miles, too?" I ask, watching him from afar as he pets Shade. His eyes don't leave her, but there's a loneliness there. Dad follows my gaze and sighs.

"We have to keep strict watch over him. We'll talk with the other tamers, but for now, he still can't be trusted," he says, his voice faltering. What choice do we have?

As if sensing our conversation, Miles glances at us and then down, a pained look in his eyes. Why would he want to go back to his parents? They're evil. But then . . . they are his parents. I wonder what his dad said to him. What would I do if it were my parents?

"Okay. Can I talk to him?" I ask, and Dad nods, completely understanding.

I walk over to my old best friend. Crouched with his umbra, he strokes her head with care, but even he can't hide the sadness in his eyes.

"Hey . . . ," I say, crouching beside him.

"I'm gonna go away for a bit. . . ." His attention stays on Shade, and he seems reluctant to look at me as he brushes the umbra's shadowy back. I look at her too, the monster that once haunted my dreams. Her eyes are still bloodred, but with a softness I haven't seen before. She doesn't say a word, sensing the slight caution that still fills my heart, and I sigh.

"Why?" I ask him, touching his arm, and he looks at me. Maybe it's because we've been through a lot already that despite the hurt that boils in the pit of my stomach, I don't yell for him to stay. The last thing I want is for him to go away forever, though. Not again. We've missed so much time.

"It's okay." His hand thumps on my shoulders, and he smiles a lopsided smile. "I'll be back this time. I mean it." For a moment, he stares at me, and I see the quiet promise in his eyes. The old Miles, who was kind, honest, and trusting. The boy who would give me piggyback rides and stay out late to watch the stars with me. I give him a toothy grin and flick his forehead.

"You better, or I'm coming to find you." *That's a promise.*

He hisses, rubbing his forehead, but smiles brighter and winks. "Don't I know it."

We stand up, and I gasp as he pulls me into the tightest hug. My arms squeeze him right back, and for a single moment, I have my best friend again. No red cloaks, no Reaper King, no Lightcasters. Just two friends saying a temporary goodbye until we see each other again.

"See you later, Supernova," he whispers, gentle as the wind. Then the warmth of his hug disappears and he's gone, jumping on his umbra and disappearing into the night. Still, I find myself smiling, hoping that he figures out what he needs to figure out and clears his head, so he comes back the old Miles.

"Hey, was that Miles? Did he just leave?" Jada asks, running over with TJ, and I nod. *He'll be back.*

"Good," TJ says, staring straight back at me when I glare at him and gently punch his arm. That was so uncalled for. Lux and Nox walk over, and I stroke their snouts, dodging TJ's attempt to get me back.

"He's not gone forever. He's coming back," I say, but TJ shrugs. One thing is for sure: Miles will have a lot of making up to do when he does come back. I'm sure he and TJ will actually become good friends one day. The two are alike and so different at the same time.

"I don't think I'll ever trust that guy. Just look around. It's gonna take a lot for us to fix our home again," TJ says.

I look back around at our city. It's still completely in ruins, and it's time to rebuild, but it's true: How are things ever going to be the same again?

CHAPTER SEVENTEEN

It took three months of nonstop grinding to really start rebuilding our city, but there's still a long way to go. Everyone in Nubis pitched in, and the queen actually sent over hundreds of people to help us too. All the houses were redesigned and rebuilt, with many houses having that cool panel system to open the doors by themselves, just like ours had. Mr. Davies's bakery is now up and running again, good as new. The marketplace is thriving again. Our training field is reinforced with steel gates, and half the grass has been replaced with a cool spongy surface. Mum also arranged for Nan and Grandad to be transferred to the medi-center in Nubis. We visit them every other day, but they still haven't woken up yet.

At home, I tell Mum and Dad about what had happened in the umbra cave with Lucas. At first they're surprised, but then they smile, and I decide to finally ask the two questions I've been meaning to for a long time. First, "How did you even know I was a Lightcaster in the first place?"

"We found out about your powers when you were born. You had gold eyes at first, just like it said in the legends. The book you found in your dad's office has been in my family for many generations, but we couldn't understand the language," Mum says. "For years, I've been trying to decipher it, but from what I gather so far, the legends speak of two children. Your father and I assumed Lucas had powers to be unlocked as well, but when he didn't have gold eyes like you did when he was born or show any sign, even when he got older, we thought maybe we were wrong."

"That's why whenever we left the city, we asked you to look after him, and there'd always be one tamer with you," Dad says.

Jada . . .

Second question. "But why not tell me?" I ask, and Mum sighs, tenderly brushing my cheek with her hand.

"We thought about it for a long time," she admits. "But in the end, how could we put all that pressure on you when you're so young, Mia? If you knew about your powers when the kingdoms fell, you wouldn't have run away. You would have endangered yourself trying to protect everyone." I make a face.

"We were scared for you, baby-girl," Dad says. The words sound almost too painful for him to say. "We tried our best to keep you safe."

"We kept your existence as a Lightcaster a secret from everyone except Jada—we hoped Magnus and the Elite wouldn't ever work it out, but we had a backup plan just in case, and thank Lunis it worked. You did it," Mum says.

"We just wish you never had to go through all that," Dad says with a sigh. "We should have been there to protect you and your brother, and we failed. We're sorry."

There isn't anything to be sorry about. . . . I hug them close and chuckle as Lux, Nox, Bolt, and Spike tumble into the room, play-fighting.

"Hey! What did we say about fighting in the house?" Mum calls out, and the umbra break apart, quickly apologizing.

Thankfully, Lux and Nox get on with Spike and Bolt. Most of the time my umbra stay with me, but they always explore the city when I have classes.

Sometimes the cave umbra's words echo in the back of my mind. That rather than just asking them for help, we trap them with the spirit calling. Lux and Nox say they want to be with me, and the same with Spike, Bolt, and Ruby. They all say they're happy being with their tamers, but . . . What if one day they want to leave? I never imagined almost half a year ago that I'd ever want a pair of umbra with me. Now I can't imagine my life without them, but is it wrong for them to be stuck with me forever? In Nubis, no one is judged, whether you have an umbra as a tamer or not, but I guess time will tell if it truly is the right thing to do. At least for now the Elite are locked up and the stinkin' Reaper King is gone.

With Lightcasters back, no one knows what will happen now, but Mum and Dad believe that it still isn't the end of the Elite and that there may be other Lightcasters out there. If Miles was telling the truth about them wanting the royal line gone to "free" everyone in the kingdom, then they'll strike again somehow, but next time we'll be ready. I have no choice but to try and harness my powers. Maybe if I do that, then Lucas won't have to. I can protect him from all of this.

At the end of the fourth month since the incident, Queen Katiya invites me, Lucas, Jada, TJ, our parents, and our umbra to her castle in Stella. We all stand in the grand hallway together, and this time, she is in a beautiful purple-and-blue dress, with her six royal guards, including Castello and Adrian, in matching colors. Mum squeezes my shoulders as the queen addresses us.

"I'd like to invite all the children, with your parents' permission, to train directly under me, with the intention of becoming part of my future Queen's Guard."

Jada coughs loudly, and my eyes widen. Katiya looks at me first with a kind smile on her face, waiting for my answer, but I already have it.

"Thanks, but no thanks."

I hear gasps all around me, but Mum and Dad are completely calm, already knowing what I'd say. Honestly, something still doesn't sit right with me about her. If she really had the power of the Lightcasters but they were diminishing, how was she keeping the Darkness away from Stella and Nexus for so long? Or had it been only a matter of time before they were taken? The queen steps back, a subtle look of disbelief in her eyes. Her mouth opens and closes, with the want to say something, but she decides against it.

I was giving up an amazing opportunity. A chance to live in the City of Light, full of luxury, where the sun rises and falls over the land every day and every night. But it's not home. It's not what I want to be. I was born in darkness. It's what I know and what I love. The dark is warmer than the cold light of Stella. I just never appreciated it until now.

TJ looks at me with nothing but surprise in his eyes. But it's his dream, not mine. I want to be the best tamer and teacher in the world, teaching kids when I get older how to defend themselves and others with their umbra. That's the goal.

"Well," Queen Katiya says, twisting one of the many rings on her hands. "If that's your decision, I can't stop you."

"I'll keep the cool staff, though," I say with a proud smile, and she smiles too. I kinda want to paint it lilac like my old one, but I keep that to myself. Her eyes shift to the others. "What about the rest of you?"

TJ looks torn as he takes a moment to answer. Jada, on the other hand, has made her decision.

"I'm staying in Nubis too. I like my job as it is, and I've still got a class to train," she says, and Lucas grabs my hand, swinging backward and forward.

"I'm staying with Mimi," he says, and I notice that the queen's eyes stay on him a little longer than usual.

Her eyes go back to TJ, who still seems torn. He looks at me for some reason, and I hear Lucas giggle. What is he waiting for? Why doesn't he just say yes already?

I nod for him to speak, but his brown cheeks redden and he clears his throat. He rubs the back of his neck and addresses the queen.

"Yeah, erm . . . I'm gonna stay in Nubis."

My jaw drops as this clown rejects the offer, and I snap my hand up.

"Group meeting!" I yell before the queen can speak, and I grab the boy over to the side with Jada and Lucas.

"What in the Star Nebula are you doing? This is a one-way ticket to your dream. Why are you throwing it away?" I whisper-shout, and he gulps, looking away with a nervous smile. I smack his arm and he chokes on a laugh, grabbing his arm in shock.

"What was that for?"

"For being an idiot. Say yes!"

"No!"

"Why?"

"Oh boy . . ." Jada sighs, rolling her eyes, and my attention snaps to her.

"What are you guys not telling me? Come on, spit it out," I say, and I catch TJ pressing a finger against his lips to silence Jada, and she smirks.

"Just tell her the reason already," she says, and TJ presses his lips together. He fidgets with his fingers as he tries to find whatever words he's looking for. Then, rubbing the back of his neck again, he sighs, finally looking at me. I arch my eyebrow and his face reddens. Maybe he's sick. *Why else would he . . . oh, snap . . .*

My stomach fills with a thousand butterflies as he opens his mouth to speak, but I clamp my hands over his mouth.

"Don't let me be the reason you don't follow your dreams, you clown," I say. He mumbles something against my hands, but when he tries to remove them, I push them harder against his face. "I'll make sure to visit you, and you better visit me, too, okay? I can't have my greatest rival slacking. The next time we meet, you better have an umbra. Got it?"

He mumbles against my hands again, and Jada covers her mouth with a fist, almost bursting with laughter.

"Nod if you got it," I say, and the moment he nods, I release his mouth and he gasps for breath.

"Jeez, you're as bossy as ever," he says, wiping his mouth, and we grin at each other. Both of our cheeks are red, and with that agreement, we finish the group meeting and walk back to Queen Katiya. She has an extra-amused smile on her face, and something tells me she heard everything we just said.

"So, are you coming?" she asks TJ, and I give him the thumbs-up.

"Yes, Your Highness. If my mums are okay with it," he says, and Lucas jumps up and down happily.

"Amazing. I will set you up with accommodations for you and your family. As for the rest of you, may the light bless you and the city of Nubis."

Then, for the first time ever, the queen bows her head. Her royal guards follow, and I quickly bow back with the biggest grin on my face, along with the others.

"You children are certainly something," she says, raising her head and looking at our parents. With that said, she leaves with her guards and I turn to Mum and Dad. They stand with

TJ's parents, their eyes shining brighter than any sun I've seen, and they share a look of pride that warms me up inside. Lucas gives me the thumbs-up too, and together with Jada we leave the city of Stella, with its shiny buildings and ball of fire. My heart's heavy leaving TJ. But I know he'll be amazing, and I hold on to the hope that we'll see each other soon. He's my best friend, after all, and this was where he was meant to be.

I return to Nubis, our city bathed in moonlight and shining with stars. We'll see each other again, and next time, we'll both have some pretty cool umbra.

Umbra Tales:
Legends of the Lightcasters
Author: Unknown

The Founders of Lunis (Continued)

Each of the six were intrigued, drawn toward the little crystal tucked away under the tree. Together they touched it and a bright light flashed, teleporting them to a place between life and death. A world meant for spirits: the Spirit Plain. It was just for a second, but they returned to the world of the living with new powers. They became the first Lightcasters. . . .

With their newborn powers, each of the six went to a different part of the new land they had found, each creating a city. The leader created the city of Stella. The one who was afraid made the city of Lunavale, the one who was smart made the city of Nexus, and the one who was brave made the city of Ignis. As for the siblings, one made the city of Astaroth, and his sister made the city of Nubis.

EPILOGUE

The grass has a slight spring to it, wet with dew from the rain yesterday. For the first time in years it's rained on the Nightmare Plains. The tree branches bounce, while the silver leaves dance to the breeze with me. Lux and Nox prance around me, and my heart swells as I breathe in the sweet smell of pine and rosy-dill. I listen to the clicking of the glow bugs as some scuttle by my feet. Others float by my head as they light the world around me, not a red-eyed umbra in sight. Not a shadow out of place.

"Mimi! Wait for me!" Straight out of the gates of our city, Lucas races after me, and I spin on my feet, perfectly landing a backflip ahead as my long legs carry me farther.

"Listen, pipsqueak. If you're gonna be a tamer too, training starts now. I'm gonna help you, so you're extra ready for your Becoming One with the Darkness, but you gotta keep up! We'll practice our powers a bit too."

He huffs, swinging his arms for extra momentum, and I can't help but laugh at how he looks doing it.

"I'm gonna get you!" He pulls out his boomerang and I stop, throwing my hands up, with the biggest grin as Lux sneaks behind him and steals it.

"Hey!"

"Better luck next time, tiny one."

The white umbra prances away from him and gives the boomerang to me, then joins Nox. I wave it back and forth. "First lesson: always be on guard. Now, come on. Try and take me down without it."

Nox tilts his head to the side as my little brother smiles, running at me. He punches and kicks, but I dodge, jump, and block every one, backflipping away. As my feet touch the ground, I gasp, seeing him dash and crash into me, laughing.

"All right, I'll give you that one," I say, tickling him, and he squeals, rolling all over the place.

"Lightcasters . . ."

We both pause, looking out to the plains. It's completely empty and no one's there, but the air suddenly turns chilly, and I stand up. Lux and Nox walk over, their shadow fur bristling. Lucas looks at me. I keep my eyes ahead, but nothing's there.

"All right. Come on, Lu-Lu, let's practice our powers," I say, pulling my staff from my thigh. "Remember, you have to concentrate really hard. Feel the energy, see what color it is in your head, and move it across your body."

We close our eyes and instantly, the lilac light that flows through me ignites in my heart, spreading all the way to my fingers and toes. I slowly open my eyes and grin, seeing my body glowing in the purple light. Lucas opens his eyes next and gasps as he manages to get his hands glowing with a yellow light.

"Mia . . ."

I freeze as the energy zaps out of me. Lux and Nox suddenly whine, shaking their heads side to side, and something shivers through me. I gulp, pulling at my sleeves.

In the distance, I can't help but notice tiny flowers crumbling away, and the sparkly purple grass fades to red. Lucas cuddles close to me as the smell of pine disappears and a faint voice is carried on the wind.

"I will return."

ACKNOWLEDGMENTS

There have been so many amazing people who've helped me on this long but brilliant journey to becoming an author. I'm grateful for every single one of you who helped me transform this story into a book.

First I want to thank my amazing mama for being my biggest support, raising me to be the woman and writer I am today. She's my rock, and she has been with me throughout this entire journey and has been my calm in what sometimes felt like a storm. I'm forever grateful for her. Without her support and her reading stories to me as a child, I may have never found my love for writing or believed I would ever get this far.

The same goes to my grandparents, especially to my nan, who is forever my guiding star. My nan and grandad always supported my dreams of being an author without question.

Huge thanks to Ricky, for being the best big brother in the world and always supporting me on my author journey. My whole family have been so supportive.

Robert, one of my best friends in the world. He's always been there for me, one of my biggest cheerleaders behind the scenes, supporting me through both the ups and downs all the time while we game together, haha!

Special thanks to Saira and Brian from Stepping Stones for giving me spiritual encouragement to keep going with my writing journey and personal growth.

And to my literary family. Thank you so much to my amazing agent, Rachel Mann. The first person in the literary world to believe in me and my vision for *The Lightcasters*. She's a warrior who could take on the Reaper King herself, and I can't think of anyone better to champion me and my stories.

Thank you so much as well to Charlotte Colwill, who was my cover agent and helped me with the final bits of putting this book together!

It was truly a team effort to make this book perfect, and I would like to thank the ultimate umbra tamers, my editors and publishing teams at Faber Children's and Aladdin. Thank you so much, Leah, Stella, and Jessi for all the effort, patience, trust, and love put into every edit of this book. You all changed my life forever and helped make this book the best it can be.

On the amazing Aladdin team, I'd also like to thank Chelsea, Sara, Heather, and the entire design team, as well as the S&S sales and marketing team. Together you all made *The Lightcasters* a beautiful masterpiece for our readers.

I'd like to thank Valerie and Jen for copyediting and proofreading *The Lightcasters* and perfecting it for me with your excellent eyes.

To Jeffrey Oyem, my brilliant cover artist for the US edition of this book. With a single cover, he encompassed *The Lightcasters* story in the most badass way, and I couldn't be happier. Just look at Mia with her bo staff—it's so cool! Thank you so much, Jeffrey.

Many writers and friends have also helped me on my *Lightcasters* journey.

I have to give shout-outs to my writer friends, who all played a role in this book in the early days, before I even had an agent or a book deal. First has to be Louie Stowell. My first author friend, Louie is the definition of kindness. For years she has been there for any questions I have had, and she helped me refine my pitch, my cover letter, and bits of my manuscript in the early days before I had an agent. Not only that but she is an extremely talented author and illustrator as well.

Rachel Greenway helped me refine my cover letter in the early days too and always cheered me on.

Amanda Woody, for her fantastic help and tips with my original query letter, which would later help me get an agent. I can't thank Amanda enough for that.

J. Elle, another talented author who took time out of her day to help me refine my manuscript before I had an agent.

George Jreije also helped me in the early days of *The Lightcasters*, reading the first few pages and being a wonderful voice of encouragement for me.

Claribel Ortega helped me so much when it came to refining my pitch for this book, which led to my pitch doing amazingly well in a contest that jump-started my career as an author. Whenever I had questions or needed advice, she was always there. I'm forever grateful.

To Yasmin (Yasminos), my soul sister. We met in sixth form, and you've been there for me, both in life and on this writing journey. You're truly the best, and I appreciate your support, girl.

Annie, although we don't get to see each other often, I'm so thankful for all the love and support you've given me over the years, especially when I was writing during our uni days together.

Finally, my gamer buddies, who I love and who have been a brilliant support system throughout the years on this journey to getting my book published: my little brother, Lamron; Josh; Kadz; DG; Deniz; Shem; Cheylakes; Bryan; and the Tan brothers, Lewis, Evan, and Sam.

I love you all—thank you so much for being a part of this journey to getting this book published. Words can't express how much I appreciate every single one of you. Thank you. x.

ABOUT THE AUTHOR

Janelle McCurdy is an author and fully fledged gamer. Having started writing and querying at only sixteen years old, she joined Jo Unwin Literary Agency in her early twenties. After graduating from Royal Holloway, University of London, with a criminology and sociology degree, Janelle moved back home to London and began writing middle-grade fantasy. In her free time, you can find her holed up in her room, gaming and watching anime, or attending numerous comic cons and gaming events. Follow her on Twitter @JanelleLMcCurdy or on Instagram @JanelleMcCurdyy.